RED CLOAK MOON

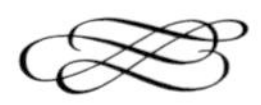

FIONA LAWLESS

Thank you to all the readers who have embraced Flawless Fairy Tales.
I could not do this without you!

CHAPTER 1

Once Upon A Time...

Thierry huddled beneath a thin blanket, listening to his parents argue. The farmhouse—a hovel, really—was never meant for a family of nine, so even hushed whispers carried to every ear. Other sounds carried too. You didn't create seven children without passion. Thierry was the middle child. He'd come between his alpha brothers, Jean and Julien, and beta sister, Esme—and the three omegas: twins, Ophelia and Olive, and baby Alice. He shared his bed with Julien and Jean, and since they'd shot up and filled out, he barely had three inches of the outermost sleeping space to cling to at night.

"He's unnatural." Pa's voice was low enough that it only carried when he raised it. Which was always. "This proves it."

"It is what it is, isn't it? People will forget all about it in time," said Ma.

"No one will forget. Every time I'm in town, someone starts yapping about our omega boy. It's not what they say to my face that bothers me. It's what they say behind my back. They think we're cursed."

"Cursed, bah. With seven healthy children from six pregnancies? I'd say we're Goddess blessed, may we be worthy."

"You're too soft, Amelie."

Thierry had heard all this before. The argument was a nightly ritual of sorts. If his parents weren't making children, they were fighting. More often than not, they fought about him.

"I won't listen to you call any of my children cursed." Ma shifted, probably turning her back on him.

"*I* never said he was cursed. It's what they think in town. What if they're right?"

"Titou is a bit different."

"Don't listen to 'em," Julien mumbled.

"He isn't a bit different. He's not right," said Pa.

"You're not right," Ma muttered.

"Come on. Who ever heard of an omega son? Thierry's thirteen. He should be growing into manhood, but he still looks like a child. He'll be useless as paint on a pig if he doesn't grow."

"People bloom when they bloom."

"I was shaving at his age. My voice had dropped. Thierry is neither nor, and people are taking notice."

"Well? What do you want me to do about it?" she asked.

"We should keep him home from now on."

"What about school? He's smart. His teachers always say so."

"I need him here on the farm. And we can't have him running about like he does. What if he ruins the girls' chances?"

Thierry sat up and drew on his shirt.

"Where are you going?" Jean caught him by the wrist.

"Outside."

"Don't listen to them. She always gets the upper hand. It'll blow over."

Until the next time. "I have to piss."

Jean shoved him. "Go then, cabbage. But don't be so sensitive."

"I'm no more sensitive than you." Thierry left the house quietly. The last thing he wanted was for his brother to think he was upset.

After he took care of business, he looked up. The night was clear, the cloudless sky black as pitch. A half-moon frosted the tops of the trees in the forest beyond their shabby farm. Stars glittered like gems—thousands upon thousands of diamonds—winking and twinkling and even streaking across the vastness as he watched. He was nothing compared to nature. He was less than a speck of dust.

Jean was right: why should he be so sensitive? His problems wouldn't matter in fifty or a hundred years. He'd be dead and long forgotten, but all of nature would still be there as wild and beautiful as ever.

A faint, out-of-place sound caught his attention—a mockingbird's song—the little warble a most welcome intrusion into his black mood. His friend Charles appeared a second later.

"I hoped I'd find you awake." Charles gave Thierry his dimpled, mischievous smile. "There's a star shower tonight. It's been going for an hour."

"I saw one!" Thierry followed him behind the barn where he watched the older boy pull out his pipe. The scratch of a match illuminated his familiar face: blue eyes, a slightly crooked nose, fair cheeks—once chubby but now hollowed with a recent growth spurt and featuring a spotty beard.

Charles's family were their closest neighbors, and they'd gone to the same one-room school. At least they had until Charles had found his magic and left to attend the local mage's academy.

Charles was a year older, and Thierry had always been a little in awe of him.

Wherever Charles was, mischief and excitement were sure to follow.

"How come you're out here? I thought I'd have to give our signal and wait for you to join me like always," Charles said.

"They were at it again." Thierry rolled his eyes.

"They're coupling?" Charles asked wickedly. "There'll be another bundle of joy for you to look after five moons from now."

"Nah, they're fighting. It's mostly what they do now."

"Oh, sorry." All the cheer fled Charles's features. "Are you all right?"

"I'm fine." Since he'd confided in Charles, Thierry shouldn't feel awkward about him knowing what his parents fought about, except that he did. Charles had been kind when Thierry's omega status became apparent; he'd shown real empathy. Charles was well favored, athletic, and skilled in rudimentary magic. His parents were proud of him. Thierry wished he knew what it felt like to have parents who only ever said good things about him.

They watched a few shooting stars curve across the sky in silence.

"We haven't heard much about male omegas," said Charles, "but that doesn't mean there aren't any others."

"I know."

"I mean, imagine if you were one of those farmers who go to sleep when the sun sets and wake when the sun rises. You'd miss all this, wouldn't you?" He motioned toward the sky. "If someone then told you stars blaze across the sky like fiery boulders launched from a trebuchet, you'd have trouble imagining it. That doesn't make it any less true."

"You think there are more omegas like me?" Thierry asked.

"Well, it stands to reason. You exist, and only a handful of people know about you. There's a whole huge world out there,

Titou! Why not imagine there are other male omegas, equally hidden and wondering about the same thing?"

Thierry's breath caught when their gazes met. By day, Charles's eyes were so blue they were like cornflowers. At night, in the moonlight, they appeared silver. Some emotion powered Charles's earnest expression, some excitement.

"But I don't believe there's anyone quite as perfect." Charles's gaze held his.

Heart beating faster, Thierry wasn't sure how to put a name to what he saw. Very deliberately, Charles knocked out his pipe and put it back in his pocket.

"I like you, Titou." Charles's throat worked. "You're unique, not weird."

"Thanks for that." Thierry knew Charles meant the words kindly.

"No, I mean I *like* you." Charles wrapped his hand around the back of Thierry's neck and pressed their lips together, shocking him and at the same time claiming a kiss that felt so utterly natural he wondered why they'd never done it before.

Thierry's body went all fluttery and hot.

This was the best thing to ever happen to him.

It was as if the stars they'd been watching fell on him, sank into his skin, and fizzled over his cock.

"Charles." He gasped and pulled away. Charles's eyes widened with horror.

"You didn't like that. Oh, blast. Oh, blast, *oh, blast*." Charles darted away, muttering the words over and over. "Blast, blast, *blast*!"

"Wait, Charles. *Wait*!" Thierry chased him down and pressed a kiss to Charles's cheek. He didn't need to see the fiery flush to know it was there. He felt the heat against his lips.

"It's all right. I liked it. You just surprised me."

"I never meant to—" Charles took a deep breath and let it out slowly. "You liked it?"

"Of course I liked it." Thierry let his hands slide down Charles's arm to clasp his wrist. "Let's do more."

"All right. I liked it too. I want to do it again. But—" Charles's eyes widened, and he tugged Thierry toward the trees. "That's not why I came. I have something to show you. You'll never believe—"

"Hey." Thierry resisted. "Slow down. My mind's in pieces right now."

"I'm glad to hear that." Charles gave a pleased grin.

"What does it mean? Why did you kiss me?"

"I told you. Because I like you."

"But—"

"Have you never heard of courting, Ti?" His eyes danced with mischief.

Thierry's mouth dropped open. "You're—"

"It'll be ages until I finish school, and until then I have to rely on my parents. But we've been best friends forever, and lately, I've realized"—he swallowed hard—"it's more than that for me."

"But I'm a boy," Thierry argued.

"You're a good person. You work hard. You'll be an omega fit for any alpha, and I'll be a mage. No one tells an alpha mage what to do."

"Your parents will murder—"

"Psht." Charles shrugged it off. "My parents want me to be happy. I'll be happiest with you, don't you think?"

"I don't know." Thierry had loved his kiss. "Maybe you should kiss me again so I can—"

Charles's mouth crashed into his, and the tip of his tongue ran over the seam of Thierry's lips seeking…what? Entrance? Hesitant and somehow eager for more at the same time, Thierry opened to him.

If that first kiss felt like star showers, this one was a bonfire. Thierry's whole body seemed to go up in flames. If he had any doubts about his manhood, Charles vanquished them. Sudden, helpless desire drove him to kiss Charles with primal urgency that was wholly new to him but old as the earth beneath his feet.

"Oh Goddess." Charles whimpered as they broke apart. "I thought we were going to have to practice a bit before we got good at things."

"You're a natural, I think." Thierry staggered into him.

"You too." Charles wrapped both arms around him and kissed his forehead.

"You wanted to show me something? I'm all yours."

"Goddess, you're going to kill me." Charles chuckled. "I do want to show you something, but not that."

"Oh, fiddle." That was disappointing.

"At least not while we're young and penniless, and we don't know whether you can have children or not."

"Wait. What?" Thierry shoved him away. "Shut up!"

"Oh, come on. Don't tell me you've never wondered whether a male omega can bear a child."

"I have never wondered about that." Thierry folded his arms. "Not once. Not ever."

Charles let out an exasperated sigh. "The world is made up of—"

"Charles, I have a *penis*. I'm familiar with where babies come from, and—"

"Ti, since you've matured, you smell like every other omega." Charles caught Thierry's hand before he could shove him again. "I'll bet you're even feeling slick now. You smell delicious like something ripe and tasty."

Thierry froze. He squirmed. Was that...Did he feel something? *Oh Goddess.* His head swam.

"I think I'm going to be sick." Thierry bent over, bracing his hands on his knees just in case.

"Oh, Titou. I'm sorry." Charles rubbed circles on his back. "I assumed you'd know."

"How would I?"

"You're only a year behind me. Haven't you ever"—Charles swallowed—"experimented a little?"

"Where? Our house is so small you can hear every fart. We sleep three to a bed."

"Well, now you know," Charles offered. "That's why we need to take things slow. I won't even graduate from the Academy until I'm eighteen, and we'll have to wait a year after that before you're of age. There is plenty of time for you to learn about your body."

Thierry almost felt betrayed. Charles had known this…this crucial thing about him, and he'd never considered mentioning it? Not once?

"Glad you finally let me in on things."

"Don't be like that, sweetling. You're only thirteen. With your status, I thought surely your mother might have told you." Charles slid his hands around Thierry's waist and kissed his nose, stilling him. "Can I call you sweetling?"

"Not where anyone can hear you."

"But you don't mind?" Charles asked gently. "Now that we're courting, I can call you my sweetling?"

"All right." Thierry felt naked beneath Charles's intense gaze. He lowered his eyes. Tilted his chin up. Realized he'd given Charles, an alpha, his submission.

Goddess, this is real.

I'm an omega, and Charles is an alpha, and…this is real.

When we grow up, we might be mates.

"Now will you come with me?" Charles wrapped an arm over Thierry's shoulder and drew him toward the woods. "I hope we haven't missed the show."

"What show? What are you talking about?"

"You'll see." Charles was now alive with excitement of a different kind. "Only, when we get there, you must stay behind me and be as quiet as you can."

Even on a clear night with a half-moon shining, parts of

Hemlock Forest made Thierry uneasy. It was dense with trees and thick undergrowth. Locals still hunted there, and woodcutters eked out a living, but in these times, only hermits, outlaws, and those made destitute by the king's high taxes attempted to make their homes within the forest.

As boys, Thierry and Charles had explored the forest together many times, but something about this night felt different.

Instead of entering the woods behind Thierry's farm like usual, Charles led him to the trader's road and into the village of Amivienne where they passed taverns and shops and fine houses.

"Where are we going?" whispered Thierry.

"To a place where Hemlock Forest is steeped in magical tradition." Charles's eyes sparked with deviltry as he lifted a tiny glass sphere, lit it with some kind of golden magic, and held it beneath his chin. "The shadows are deeper, and the unknown is more unknowable there."

"Right." Thierry gave an eyeroll.

Mages. They spoke in Old Rheilaise, wielded their intellect like fine steel, and loved nothing more than scaring the nonmagical. Thierry adored Charles the person, he truly did, but the older boy was going to be an unbearable mage. *He'll be harmless, though. Probably.*

When they reached the Temple of the Sisters of the Merciful Moon, Charles stepped off the rutted dirt road and into the virgin woods. The path they used was little more than a matted, brown battle of contention between the human feet that used it and the forest that wanted to reclaim it.

Did Charles know what he was doing?

The woods north of Amivienne could be extremely dangerous.

Thierry had never been there before. Except for the sisters, who were known to go about with lanterns at all hours to aid the sick and deliver babies, few stepped off the road used by merchants and travelers. If Charles had a reason for going farther into the trees, Thierry didn't know what it could be.

Charles had also kissed Thierry.

Charles had caressed him, given him a pet name, and practically planned out their whole future.

Until that moment, Thierry had been ignorant about… everything. Thierry would take his memories of this night and put them in an imaginary keepsake box—to take out and think about another time—because now it took all of Thierry's attention to move soundlessly over years' worth of rotting vegetation. They made their way as silently as hunters.

Suddenly, Charles flung his arm around Thierry's waist. The action sent a shockwave of pleasure racing through him, even as it stopped him from taking another step.

"Look there." Charles pointed ahead.

Some distance away, an unexpected light glowed over the treetops. It was cold and almost green so not a campfire. There was no hint of smoke, no aroma of roasting meat. Just odd light unlike anything Thierry had ever seen before.

He sought Charles's eyes, now just shadows in the outline of his face.

"What is it?" he whispered.

"Mage light," Charles answered. "From now on, be silent, and if we're discovered, run like a lion is chasing you. We'll split up and meet back at the road."

"That's not ominous at all."

"*Shh.*" White teeth flashed, and Thierry felt a kiss on his cheek. "Just do as I say, and we'll be fine. This is going to be amazing. You'll see."

They crept forward together, sticking close to the shadows. The going became more difficult as they got closer to the strange light.

When Thierry could finally see what Charles was looking

for, things made a little more sense. There was a man in the clearing, dressed in mage's robes. He was crafting circles and symbols using fat bags of colored chalk and lit candles. The green glow came from a series of orbs floating ten feet off the ground.

A lump in the center of the circles suddenly rose with a piteous yowl. Someone had chained a huge dog and drawn the circles around him. The animal was muscled—the kind used in blood sports like bearbaiting.

"Oh no," said Thierry. Nothing good ever came from being chained in a mage circle.

"What's he up to?" Charles mused aloud.

"Charles—"

"Hush. I want to see," Charles hissed.

Thierry didn't like to see animals hurt, but he swallowed his protests. Maybe this mage wasn't planning to harm the animal. Maybe he would be helping it somehow.

The mage added more symbols that Thierry couldn't make out.

"Look. See?" Charles pointed at the chalk drawing. "It's like a compass with the candles glowing at cardinal points. That's routine, but the symbols he's drawing now are ones I haven't seen." Thierry supposed any magic user would be interested. Magic required a whole lifetime of learning, and Charles had taken to his lessons like bread sopping up milk.

Uneducated, low-level magic users worked small charms in the marketplace, mostly love spells or illusions. Whatever this was, it went far beyond rudimentary. This mage must be one of Charles's older classmates—or even a teacher—working a spell in private for some reason of his own.

Secret magic practice was lost on a poor rustic like Thierry. He watched without much interest, noting Charles's obvious delight by the way his gaze followed the fellow's every move.

Charles had ambition.

Thierry did admire the graceful way the mage moved, the way he sprinkled his powdered chalks, the certainty with which he spoke his incantations. But there was a predatory fierceness to the man that frightened Thierry's omega. The mage was obviously alpha and more dominant than most Thierry had met. He was clearly a perfectionist. He seemed driven. Thierry couldn't help but wonder if he was up to no good.

"What's he want with that dog?" Thierry asked.

Charles didn't answer. Thierry assumed he hadn't heard, or maybe he was too mesmerized to reply. Thierry let it go. They didn't always share the same interests, but watching Charles enjoy himself could be rewarding enough on its own.

"I've never seen anything like this," Charles whispered after a few minutes. "I know those symbols, but he's drawn them oddly. I wonder if they teach the upperclassmen to deviate according to their instincts?"

"Maybe so," Thierry agreed, just to be polite. To him it was like trying to read answers from clouds.

Whatever the mage had planned, he'd set things up to his satisfaction. Dusting chalk off his hands, he stood back and surveyed his work. His brute of a dog whined. He lay with his massive paws out in front, cheeks puffing with each outgoing breath, and shrank back when the mage joined him in the innermost circle.

Thierry looked to Charles with some unease. Charles's gaze stayed riveted on the mage.

The mage pushed his sleeves to his elbows and raised his arms before beginning an incantation of some sort. Thierry tried to make out the words, but he didn't understand Old Rheilaise. It was almost like some kind of play until Thierry noticed fingers of oily mist creeping around his feet as if being drawn to the clearing by some central force.

He nudged Charles and pointed down. Charles's eyes widened with surprise and excitement, especially when the viscous black fog began boiling up from the earth clearing on all sides. Whatever it was, it must be heavier than air. It stayed low, billowing around the magic circle but not entering it.

"Goddess. It's working."

"What is it? It stinks."

"It's a *magnificent* display of power." Charles breathed the words with awe.

Thierry wished he had Charles's confidence. Instead, he had his mother's pragmatism. If something had to be done in the forest away from prying eyes, it probably wasn't something he should see. His shoulders felt the touch of strong, unfamiliar magic, and his instincts took over.

"I think we should go, Charles."

Charles gripped his hand tighter. "No."

Fear gripped Thierry. He knew he should leave. But Charles was the mage. He was older. Thierry didn't want to look like a coward.

He looked back toward the clearing. He stayed where he was.

CHAPTER 2

"This is amazing. Look at his power!" Charles's eyes held the same wonder as when they'd kissed.

"Why does it stink? You think it's bad magic?" Thierry knew it wasn't *good*.

"He's got my school's crest on his robe. They don't teach bad magic."

The mage had started shouting the incantation, and now, the mist on the ground began to rotate in the circle. A strong wind kicked up. The very air crackled. When Thierry looked up, the tops of the trees were bending inward as though a sudden whirlpool was dragging the forest itself to a single point. Windswept dirt and debris made it harder to see. Thierry held his arms up to shield his face.

The dog rose and paced uneasily on his short chain. He barked rapidly, finally frightened by the sudden tension in the air and the man standing over him. The man caught his collar, causing a choked whine.

Thierry's instincts were screaming that they shouldn't be there, shouldn't be watching this. His gut told him to run and never look back.

He took Charles's hand.

Just as he started to repeat that they should leave, the mage whipped a knife from his belt and drew it across the dog's throat. Gouts of blood spattered onto the ground at the mage's feet. Sickened, Thierry closed his eyes, but not before he saw the dog fall.

The two of them stood frozen—Thierry stunned, Charles...

What did Charles think of this?

Thierry glanced over and saw shock on Charles's face. Distaste.

But Charles still had that same breathless intensity, the same excitement that made his face glow, and Thierry suddenly knew something he'd only vaguely understood before.

Mages worshipped magic.

They weren't drawn by ancient mysteries. It was no scholarly pursuit.

Mages were drawn to magic's *power* like moths to flame.

It was hard to imagine how something like that would affect even someone you knew very well. Thierry had never been touched by magic, but if he could work spells, if he had promise —if he could afford school—would he be so excited to see this mage, whoever he was, kill a dog?

Or would he still be as revolted, as enraged as he felt right now?

He tried tugging on Charles's hand but couldn't budge him.

Wasn't it over? Thierry looked into the clearing again and saw the mage had removed the dead animal's restraints. He hoped they'd at least bury the poor thing, not just leave it out for animals to tear it into pieces. He was well over magic and ready to leave.

"There." Charles grabbed his arm. "Look! Oh my Goddess, he's—"

The blood-covered beast staggered to its feet.

There was a new kind of tension in the air. Thierry felt its thick, oily persistence and caught its charnel house smell and the feel of ghosts walking over his grave.

Thierry's skin crawled.

"*Necromancy.*" Charles barely breathed the word. "I never dreamed we'd see anything like this."

"I want to go now, Charles. Please." Tears stung his eyes. His throat burned. He'd never been so afraid in his life, but when Thierry tried to jerk his hand away, Charles wrapped his arms around him.

Evidence of Charles's arousal—magic was probably the cause—pressed at his back. Thierry had been right to worry. Charles lusted after magic. Yearned for it. His greed was turning him into someone Thierry no longer wanted to know.

Did Charles want to be the mage in the clearing, even after the man had committed a horrific act?

Thierry swallowed hard, so disappointed by the Charles he was seeing that tears stung his eyes. All the happiness he'd found only a half hour before died. He didn't know Charles at all. Not anymore. Not if he wanted more of something like this.

The green orbs gave the beast's blood-matted fur a fierce, luminescent sheen. His eyes glowed red, and great glops of foamy saliva dripped from his gaping maw. The mage laughed out loud, his delight so complete that he clapped his hands together like a child.

Charles let out a strange, shocked cry.

The mage and his beast suddenly turned in their direction.

Charles gasped, his mouth forming an *O* of frozen horror.

"Run!" Charles gripped him by the collar and yanked him backward. Thierry wasted no time. He turned and charged headlong through the dense trees. Charles's footsteps thudded a half step behind.

A high-pitched whistle seemed to deaden all sound.

Thierry's heart beat frantically.

"This way. Come on." Thierry looked back. Charles was

having trouble keeping up. He spent his time sitting in school. He lacked the wind to run.

Looking around, Thierry made the split-second decision to climb a tree. Charles couldn't run, but he could probably cast some illusion over them to make them harder to see, to scent. Thierry's choices were limited: hemlocks were hard to climb and hard to hide in, but playing with his brothers, he'd learned to shimmy up the trunk and stay pressed against the bark. With his dark clothes, he should melt into the tree itself.

"This way," he hissed. "Up here."

He got a grip on a sticky, resinous branch and swung himself up until he was able to get to the next and the next. Charles was right behind him. He wasn't as fast, but he was making all the right moves. Thierry held his hand out, and Charles grasped it.

Thierry felt a *zing* because it was Charles, even if his eyes were still wide with magical lust as he looked up into Thierry's face. For a single second, a smile ghosted across his lips, and then *crack*, the branch beneath Charles's foot broke.

Thierry wasn't ready to catch him. His hands were sticky, but he wasn't braced to lift Charles's weight. He no sooner closed his fingers around Charles's damp hand than it slipped through them.

Charles screamed all the way to the ground where he thudded and lay stunned, eyes wide with shock. Barely a second passed before the beast was on him. It grabbed him by the throat and shook him like a rag. Blood spurted from his wounds. His cries tore scars upon Thierry's heart.

It was over in a heartbeat.

Thierry couldn't think, couldn't move. He held his breath and waited for the mage to spot him.

Charles can't be dead. He can't.

Despite what he'd told himself in the clearing, there was nothing in Thierry that could accept a world without Charles in it. The mage joined the beast below him. Thierry pulled back into the shadows, frozen with dread.

He saw the mage's face clearly.

That, too, inscribed itself inside him.

At his master's sinister whistle, the corpse dog sat, obedient as any shepherd's working animal.

"Good boy." The mage's dulcet tenor slid silkily along Thierry's spine. It was as oily as his magic. Self-satisfied. Grotesque. "What a good dog."

Blood no longer pulsed from Charles's wounds. His vacant eyes had clouded. Even if Thierry leapt down, pulled the knife he wore concealed in his boot, and fought both of them, even if he died for his trouble, he could not bring Charles back.

Thierry didn't move. He didn't breathe.

The dog's body jerked. It made a terrible gurgling sound, and its muscles spasmed, its eyes rolled back in its massive head, and foam poured from its mouth.

The beast gave several great heaving jerks and then froze as stiff as if it had been dead for some time.

"Five minutes." The magician kicked the dog's corpse. "You didn't last very long."

Thierry lost time after that. He stared at Charles's body, replaying every single minute of the night, following different scenarios in his mind, thinking over all the decisions they'd made.

If he hadn't gone with Charles.

If he'd made Charles leave sooner.

If he'd run instead of climbing.

If he'd only been able to hold on...

If only.

Charles lay beside the beast that had killed him. Drops of dew clung to his eyelashes and the tip of his nose. Thierry didn't know how much time had passed before he climbed down in the blue of predawn. He wanted to be gone before the sun could rise and shine its light on his guilt.

He approached the fallen dog, even stuck his knife beneath its jaws and lifted its head to look into its horrible red eyes, only they weren't red anymore. They were a soft, milky brown. Just dog's eyes. He thought they looked lonely.

Without the oily dark magic that had animated it, the dog was just a dog. Big and brutal but no longer supernatural. Thierry wiped blood and flecks of fur from his knife and tucked it back into his boot.

If he'd stood his ground.

If he'd used his knife.

If he'd only sent Charles up the tree first and climbed up behind him…

Chilled to the bone, Thierry slunk back to the farm and fell into a stupor in his brother's small shed. Though it stank of the tanner's trade, there was no magic there.

His brother entered, hours later, to work.

"Titou, you idiot, did you sleep out here?"

Thierry seemed to hear Jean's words from far away.

"What's wrong?" Jean gave him a playful shove. "Have you been out here all night? You're freezing."

Thierry closed his eyes to control the nausea that had become part of his new life. Jean spoke again, but the words didn't mean anything. Or maybe they did, just not to him. He stared at nothing and replayed the whole awful night in his mind.

"Where's your head, brother? You're frightening me." Jean shook him. "If Pa sees you lying about, he'll make your day a misery."

As if his day wasn't already a misery.

Thierry heard laughter. Was that him?

Jean dragged him to his feet, and they staggered into the

sunlight together. Jean dunked his head into the trough and swirled him around for good measure.

Thierry wished he didn't have to breathe. He'd never have to talk again if he didn't have to breathe. Grim reality robbed him of focus, of speech. Horror stole his words and clouded his mind. Everything around him seemed unreal now.

Charles was dead. Killed by a monster.

A kiss. Footsteps. Decisions.

Thierry had nothing to say, even when Charles's body was discovered along with the beast that had killed him. They came to Thierry for answers, knowing that wherever Charles went, Thierry had probably gone along.

They added up the clues: a beast's slashed throat. Thierry's bloodied knife. When they laid Charles to rest, everyone lauded Thierry as some kind of hero. They got the order of events wrong. They believed he'd killed the animal who'd murdered his friend. There was even talk of a medal from Amivienne and its sheriff.

For the first time in Thierry's life, his pa was proud of him.

At least he was until the mages finished their study of the dead beast. Somehow, they could tell there had been dark magic at work. They said it didn't have the aura—whatever that was—of Charles's magic and determined there had been another mage present.

Charles's mother harangued him for answers. He had none to give her. His silence eventually drove everyone away, shaking their heads.

They'd called him addled ever since.

People still thought he'd killed the beast, so they gave him a wide berth. But when they were alone, his own father called him *curse tainted.* Father was only guessing. He couldn't know what Thierry had done, what he'd seen, how the night that Charles had died had changed him.

Silence was the only way to end his battles.

Why had Thierry never considered keeping his mouth shut before?

~

Charles's mother never believed Thierry's story. She'd begun a campaign of revenge that did what his father had not been able to do before that: forced his mother's hand.

Now, his mother hid him at home where he tended to every odious job on the farm. He couldn't go to town because the gentlefolk of Amivienne worried that he'd been tainted by evil. The few times he'd left the farm, he'd had to put up with insults and jeers. Twice, he'd suffered a beating.

Yet something strange happened after all the commotion died down, something even stranger than losing his words.

Charles's magic seemed to follow him around.

He *felt* Charles nearby. Sometimes, he could even hear his voice.

It was madness. He knew it couldn't be real, but that didn't stop Charles from talking, and once Charles realized Thierry could hear him, he talked all the time.

"By the Goddess, this isn't what I planned at all," Charles had said. "First, I was going to finish my studies, and then I was going to ask you to be my mate."

Thierry let his carefully neutral thoughts slip.

As if your family would have allowed that.

"Oh, so you do have words!" Charles's magic fizzed around him. "Only you think them instead of speaking them."

You heard that?

"Of course. Say something else."

You aren't real. I'm going mad. This is all a fever dream.

"Of course I'm real. Do you mean to say you can't see me?"

You are a figment of my imagination. How could I see you?

"I can see myself. Wait. I'll wave my hand." Thierry waited. "Do you see it now?"

No. He hadn't seen it, but he'd felt a vibration, a warmth maybe. A brush of energy that felt like air but tingled?

I can feel your magic!

"You can? You shouldn't be able to. You're an omega. What does it feel like?"

It feels clean. Pure. Not like the mage or his beast at all.

"This is amazing. Wait—" A bright, bubbly *something* surrounded him. "You sensed the necromancer's magic? What did it feel like?"

Thierry shivered. *Like the scum on top of a washtub after lots of people have been in it.*

"You should know since you only get the tub after your brothers have finished bathing. You've got magic, Titou! Oh no. This is not good."

What? Thierry didn't like Charles's sudden stillness.

"Did they ever test you for magic?"

Of course they didn't. I'm an omega. Flat as a pancake. What isn't good?

"You aren't flat at all, so I don't know how I missed it. Your magic is positively vivid from here. Perhaps your nature hides it."

What do you mean?

"In school, we're taught that alphas are essentially magical lightning rods. Betas who have talent can combine natural elements and use ritual to effect lower-level magic. They're witches, not mages. There are many very skilled beta witches, male and female. Omegas are said to be incapable of magic."

Perfect. Another thing about me that's all wrong.

"You are perfectly all right, Titou. How many times do I have to tell you? But now I wonder if other omegas carry magic. We need to take a look at your sisters. This could change everything!"

What good does having magic do? It ruined our lives.

"That was death magic. It's different. The necromancer's power was overwhelming. It was...seductive."

Not to me. I thought I'd be sick.

All the sparkle left the air around Thierry. "I'm not sorry you were there. At least I wasn't alone when—"

Well, I'm sorry. I wanted to save you. Instead, I just scampered up a tree—

"It's not your fault. I couldn't look away."

I should have stood beside you. Instead, I was a coward.

"The king's best men would flee a necromancer's beast. I'm glad you're alive. I love you."

I love you too, Charles. Face hot, Thierry glanced at his hands. *You should know—given what's happened—I'm not sure we were fated mates.*

"Obviously not." Charles's magic seemed to squeeze him. "You're the only male omega in who knows how long? Your destiny never included a minor mage like me. That doesn't mean I love you any less. Even if I was only meant to be there at the start of your journey, I'm glad."

Thierry's heart ached for him. *My curse strikes again.*

"You're alive, and now we know you've got magic. Maybe we can figure out what you're meant to do with it. One man's curse is another's blessing, after all."

It was no blessing to lose you, Charles. I miss you so much.

"I miss you too. And I'm not lost. This is fun, actually. You won't believe some of the things that go on."

Are you stuck here? How does this work?

"I'm...here. That's all I know."

This is going to take time to get used to.

Light laughter effervesced around him. "You have no idea."

CHAPTER 3

FIVE YEARS LATER

"Thierry!" Olivia barreled toward them along the path from the cottage, abreast with Ophelia. "Father—"

"Wants to see you in the house," Ophelia finished for her.

"I was going to say it." Olivia folded her arms

Ophelia glared. "No, I was. As usual, you—"

"I did *not* interrupt you." Olivia narrowed her eyes. "I was supposed to tell him."

"No, I was." Ophelia stamped her foot.

Thierry clapped his hands. They turned to face him. He lifted his brows as if to say *Tell me what?*

"Father wants you," said Ophelia.

"You're not going to like it. *Ow.*" Olivia jumped when her sister pinched her.

"Don't tell him that. Father said to just tell him to come."

"But Mother said—"

Thierry clapped his hands again. His sisters turned to him with wide, round eyes. He made a shooing motion. They ran back to the cottage as quick as their little bare feet could take them. Thierry frowned after them.

What's Pa want this time?

"Who can say?" Charles answered. "Whatever it is, you don't have to do it."

You don't understand.

Even thinking about his father brought on bone-deep exhaustion.

I know what my father is capable of. Jean and Julien can take care of themselves, but I can't allow Pa to take his anger out on Ma and the girls.

"He doesn't, though. He wouldn't. He's chosen you to be his whipping boy."

And Ma.

"Because she's trying to protect you."

Are you saying they'd be better off without me?

"Not exactly. But maybe."

Thierry put his scythe in the shed and trudged toward the house. When he got close, he could hear his parents arguing. He didn't catch their angry words until he entered.

"Don't you dare!" High color crested Ma's cheeks. She balled both hands into fists at her side. "If you ever intend to—"

"You're out of line, woman. You want this?" Pa held up his open hand.

"Pa," Jean's voice growled with warning.

"If you do this, Claude," she warned, "you'd better not come home."

"I'll do what I like. I'm the man here." He thumped his chest. "I'm the alpha. You'd best remember that, or you'll be the next to go."

With that, he grabbed his cap off a hook by the door and strode out.

"Ma—" Jean gave Thierry a look he couldn't name. Not anger or sadness. Resignation? "Maybe Pa's right. Maybe it's better this way."

"What's better?" asked Charles. "What are they talking about?"

"Titou," Ma said with a sigh. "Wash up and peel enough potatoes for a shepherd's pie."

No matter how hard he stared, she didn't tell him what Pa was on about, though he had the sense that all eyes were on him.

Something's going on.

"Obviously," Charles said. "What are you going to do?"

What can I do? I don't even know what's happening.

"Best prepare, then. I didn't like the look in your father's eyes."

Esme was in the kitchen when he got there. As usual, she wore a put-upon expression.

"Good, you're here." She shoved a basket of potatoes his way. "Get started on these."

He cleaned his hands and dried them, then picked up a knife. He and Esme ordinarily worked companionably together, but today, he could tell she carried an unusual amount of tension in her sturdy shoulders. As the only beta in the family, Esme's future options were worse than limited. She'd always resented it —resented her omega sisters and alpha brothers—but she'd never been openly hostile with him.

He understood her frustration. He was equally uncertain about his future, especially now. He was nearly eighteen but still unable to talk. His failure to return to normal had done little for his already sketchy self-esteem. In town, the few times that he'd gone, people had associated his lack of speech with a lack of brains. He'd spent most of his time with furious heat in his cheeks and unspoken angry words on his tongue.

"Look," Esme said quietly. "We don't always get on, but you should know that Pa's made some kind of arrangement for you."

He narrowed his eyes so she'd elaborate.

"He's found some spice merchant looking for boys to fetch and carry. I think he means to sell you."

All the blood in Thierry's head seemed to leave.

"Ma's dead set against it. That's what they were rowing about. She says that if he wants you gone, you'll be eighteen in a few days and free to do as you please, and of course, he can't legally sell you—"

"Esme," Jean interrupted them. "What did Ma and Pa say about you carrying tales?"

"He shouldn't be kept in the dark about this." Esme heaved a cast iron pot onto the stove to heat. "If Pa has his way—"

"He won't," Jean said darkly. "Ma won't allow it."

"Won't she?" Esme's flush wasn't only because the kitchen was hot. "No matter what an alpha does, no matter who they hurt, they get what they want. It's an alpha's world. The rest of us have to survive in it." She turned away to add vegetables to the pot. "You wouldn't know about that, would you?"

Thierry watched her, unsurprised by the bitterness in her voice. Of all the siblings, Esme had the fewest choices. As the only beta, she would naturally be required to stay at home and care for Ma and Pa as they aged. Perhaps she might go into service or, if she was lucky, work in a shop. But it was far more likely that she'd continue as free labor for as long as Ma and Pa lived.

He knew she resented it bitterly, but he'd never heard her speak of alphas in such terms. Neither had Jean, it seemed, because he was looking at her closely.

"Esme. Has something happened?" Jean's shrewd blue eyes narrowed. "Did an alpha hurt you? Why didn't you say something?"

"It's nothing." She didn't lift her gaze from her work.

Helplessly, Thierry looked to his brother for aid. If someone had hurt Esme, taken liberties, treated her unkindly, there would be hell to pay from her brothers, him included, omega or not.

"Esme—"

"I don't want to talk about it right now," Esme snapped. "It's none of your business anyway. Just know that as an alpha, you are at the top of a steep hill, and shit flows downward." She wiped her hands on her apron. "I need some fennel."

With that, she left the cabin.

Thierry and Jean exchanged speaking glances.

"I'll find out," Jean said. "In the meantime, she's right about Pa. Watch your back. Woe betide him if he tries anything without telling Ma, but I wouldn't put it past him."

Jean followed Esme. Thierry was left to finish dinner alone. Nothing more was said that afternoon and evening, and Thierry went to bed as usual, but eventually, sleeplessness and anxiety drove him outside to sit under the stars and think.

"Jean's right," Charles told him. "I've been watching your father. He's up to something, Titou."

It's because I'll be eighteen soon. If I'm free and I leave, there's no way for him to profit off me. He sees it as his right to recoup his investment, just as he will with the girls. They're pretty. They'll bring a good bride price.

"It's barbaric, selling one's children."

The law demands consent, but no one really cares whether the omega wants the union or not. No omega is going to gainsay her parents anyway. That's just the way it's done. Parents are supposed to know what's best.

"There's a huge flaw in that logic because most people believe that money buys happiness, and it unequivocally does not."

Thierry laughed. *Wish I knew a way to test your theory.*

"Me too. I would like a better view if I'm to remain stuck in this realm."

It's abysmal here, I know. I'm sorry.

Thierry was also sorry he couldn't *see* Charles. He missed his friend. Charles's eyes used to sparkle whenever they'd shared a private joke at school. Thierry could well remember the impish way he'd grinned when they were children.

How Thierry wished he could turn back time.

Even if it meant their situations ended up reversed with Charles the lone survivor of their terrible adventure, Thierry would go back and relive everything just to see Charles's smile again.

"Thierry, son of Claude and Amelie Guillard." As he did sometimes to tease, Charles put on a sepulchral voice to sound more ghostlike.

Very scary, Charles. I'm shaking with fear.

"Your time has come. You must prepare yourself."

Knock it off. It's not funny. Pa's trying to sell me.

"You must bear the burden of your birth, Thierry. You must see beyond the appearance of those you meet. You must destroy the necromancer by any means necessary."

Destroy the necromancer? What did you say?

Charles didn't answer.

Stop it. It's no longer funny. What did you mean when you said destroy the necromancer?

Still, Charles remained silent. Thierry no longer felt the happy fizz of his magic. Where had he gone?

Thierry looked up just in time to see tendrils of a cloud cover the crescent moon, like fingers of a hand, grasping for its luminescence.

Time's up, the sky seemed to be saying. *Darkness is coming.*

Thierry had no time to react to his morbid imaginings because a foul-smelling rag closed over his mouth and nose. The choking odor made his head spin. Darkness closed in on the edges of his vision.

"Got 'im," someone said from behind him. A deep voice. Alpha but not his father. Thierry felt the point of a blade at his throat. "Come along now."

"Get a gag on him. Hurry."

"Thought you said he couldn't talk."

"Who knows what he can do? He's Goddess cursed." That

was a sinister drawl Thierry knew only too well. His father had delivered his most poisonous words with it.

"Should I keep the knife on him?"

"Yes, but *hush.* The wife can't find out about this."

Whoever held him trussed his legs and arms. They dragged him some distance then threw him over the back of a horse. Someone mounted behind him, and they took off at a trot.

Charles? Where are they taking me?

Charles didn't answer

Pa had help, that much was plain. They were probably the usual riffraff: the drunks and degenerates his father called friends.

There was no way Pa would get away with selling Thierry to a merchant or a smith in town. Ma would do anything in her power to get him back.

No...if Pa wanted to get rid of him for good—because he was omega born, because he was different, because he'd had the misfortune to watch his best friend die—he'd have to sell him to someone passing through.

His father thought him powerless and weak.

Thierry bit the inside of his cheek to keep from crying.

Claude thought him worthless, but Thierry told himself Charles was right. Things had only started for him. Now was the time, his time. Charles just said that.

My time has come. I must prepare myself.

Thierry had no notion of direction. Wherever they finally stopped, the man mounted behind him let Thierry go. He fell from the horse headfirst and saw stars.

"*Careful*!" Thierry's father cried out. "We'll get nothing if you kill him."

"Who's this trader that wants your boy?" someone asked.

"What if the sheriff gets word what we're about?" asked another man.

Was that hesitation that Thierry heard?

"What's this trader going to do with him anyway?" asked the first.

Thierry waited breathlessly for his father's response.

"Whatever he wants." Pa gave a mocking laugh. "It's his business after he pays me for 'im."

Thierry gulped down nausea. If ever there was a time to scream, this was it, but even if he could, there was no one to hear him. Not even Charles, apparently.

He would not cry. He would not surrender. And he would not forget his father's work this night.

From the sound, Thierry assumed his father's party waited on the trade road. He smelled horses first, then the scent of tobacco and unwashed men. Someone approached.

Thierry sat bound, still hooded while his father transacted business. Then someone hoisted him onto the back of a wagon. They pulled his hood off.

"Hello." An unknown human eyed him warily. "Master said he was buying an omega. He needs a look at you before he pays. Wait, Master—"

Whatever the man was going to say, the arrival of several riders carrying torches forestalled him.

"Claude Guillard, you evil bastard. You're not selling Thierry to anyone."

The sheriff stepped down from his horse while the others with him stayed mounted.

"Untie the lad. There's been a mistake."

"No mistake," Claude argued. "He's my son. I can sell him to whoever I want."

"He's only a week shy of his majority." The sheriff turned to the buyer, a smooth-faced man whose demeanor didn't strike Thierry as argumentative. "As an omega—"

"It's not an omega. It's a lad," said the human who'd taken his hood off.

"I assure you," the sheriff said, "he's an omega. He's well

known in these parts. He's protected. In a week, he could claim his right to leave, and you'd have to allow it or face imprisonment. This man is cheating you."

Whatever the sheriff said, Thierry was certain that the trader knew what he was getting.

As for Thierry's right to leave...

Thierry doubted he'd have been given his freedom. Whether the merchant purchased Thierry to draw attention to his wares or he had plans to sell him on to a menagerie, Thierry wasn't stupid.

Pa's companions had wisely melted into the forest, leaving Claude alone to take the blame for this night's work.

"A mistake has obviously been made." The young merchant laid a hand over his heart while his companion glared at Claude. "I thank you for your intervention, Sheriff. I do not like to be cheated."

Thierry watched as they mounted their wagon. Hoofbeats clip-clopped as they drove into the night.

The sheriff glared at Claude. "Go home to your missus. I'll take over from here."

"As you like." His father said through gritted teeth. "Thierry, come,"

"I'll be keeping Thierry with me." The sheriff jerked his head for Thierry. "He'll need to answer some questions."

Pa shot Thierry a murderous look. "The lad's mute. I'm taking him with me."

"No, you aren't. And as I'm quite certain it will take me a week to get to the bottom of things here, don't expect Thierry back unless it's of his own free will."

"You bastard. You can't do that." Claude clenched his fists. "The lad's mine. There's work to be done at the farm."

"That may be, but I have a use for him too." The sheriff eyed Thierry. "It's the Crown's business. You can go to the shadowlands, Claude, and if you ever lay a single finger on Amelie again, I'll see you rot in prison for life."

"You old bastard. You won't be sheriff much longer, and then we'll see."

"See him home, lads."

"Mount up, sir. You've caused all the trouble you're going to this night." The soldiers, who had up until then been as still as statues, harried Claude to his horse and then away. The sheriff dismounted. Thierry eyed him warily.

"I wasn't lying, son. I have need of someone exactly like you. I warn you, it's a dangerous job but one only you are fit to do. Will you come with me and hear me out?"

What was this? Out of the frying pan and straight into the fire?

Why had Charles said those strange things? Where had he gone?

Charles was never silent.

Thierry was only a farm boy, not even considered an adult. Who would be there to guide him now if Charles was gone?

Thierry's father was a scoundrel, but the sheriff had saved him. He trusted the sheriff and believed the man when he said he had a job for him.

Thierry nodded, putting his fate in the sheriff's hands if only for a week.

The man smiled. "Thank you. You're a good lad."

If only his father ever once had said those words.

He hadn't, though. He'd treated Thierry with disdain. With hatred that grew with every passing day. Thierry loved his mother and siblings. He loved the farm. But he wouldn't go back while his father lived.

That was a vow.

Thierry followed the sheriff to town.

CHAPTER 4

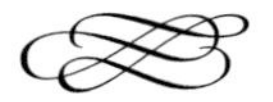

Several people waited for them when they arrived in Amivienne, Jean and Jules among them. They ran forward to wrap Thierry in their embrace.

"Goddess, I'm glad to see you," said Jules. "Are you all right?"

Thierry nodded.

"We've got to run home and tell Ma." Jean motioned for Jules.

"Don't know what's going to happen now," Jules gave Thierry a last squeeze and let him go. "Ma was angrier than I've ever seen. She's talking about leaving and taking the girls with her. You shouldn't come home until we know what's going to happen."

He wouldn't go back there again. Never while Pa lived.

"Sheriff Lavigne will help you," said Jean. "May the Goddess bless you, little brother."

Thierry embraced his older brothers before watching darkness swallow the two men. Would he ever see any of his siblings again?

"Bad business," said the sheriff. "Those two have promised to look after your mother. Goddess knows how your father will behave if he drinks on the way home."

Thierry closed his eyes. He'd been a disappointment to his parents, a flit in school, and he'd let Charles get killed. He felt as though he'd never put a foot right in his life, and now he was the cause of the biggest fight his parents had ever had.

"Don't take this on yourself. The fault lies with your father," the sheriff muttered darkly. "He's always been greedy and foolish. I don't know what Amelie ever saw in him. I'll protect your family from his schemes."

Thierry nodded.

"Now, come with me. We must discuss important matters, and there are people I'd like you to meet. Too much time has been wasted already."

Instead of walking, the sheriff offered him a mount. He wasn't a good rider, but they moved through the empty streets at a slow pace. Accompanying Sheriff Lavigne, a sense of freedom stole over Thierry. He didn't have to return to the farm. His father no longer had any say over him. He hardly knew how to feel.

What was he meant to do for the sheriff, and what would he do in the future? Where did he see himself in a week when he was legally free to choose his own path? In a month? In a year?

Could this be the beginning of a new life?

Without speech, he was limited, but he could read and write. He was fit. Strong. He'd learned to fight, having scuffled with his older brothers and schoolmates who'd tried to bully him. If the sheriff had use for him, perhaps that would suit? He would see. Amivienne was close enough to home that if his siblings wanted to keep in touch, they could meet. He could watch over Ma from there.

They rode past the taverns on the main road, past the Academy. Past all Thierry knew of civilization. The sheriff veered off on a small, well-trodden path into the woods beyond even that.

A full hour passed before they stopped outside an ancient fortress with a stone wall surrounding it. A grand gate stood sentry at the entrance, carved with the Goddess and the phases of the moon.

Thierry's heart stuttered with surprise.

What is this? he tried asking Charles.

No voice answered. The sparkle of Charles's magic had been entirely absent since he'd spoken those eerie words about the burden of Thierry's birth.

Where was he? Was this a joke, or had he left for good?

Had he been silenced somehow?

Had he finally passed between the worlds where Thierry couldn't hear him anymore? Goddess. What would Thierry do without him?

The sheriff dismounted and pulled a rope by the gate. Several bells chimed at once. The work of mages, Thierry thought. He felt the tingle of magic in the air, unfamiliar but controlled, so not the work of witches.

Was there a second magic academy he didn't know about?

Thierry didn't have the time to wonder because a woman opened the gate. She wore a red, hooded gown and a white wimple. Thierry had heard about the red-garbed sisters often enough to place her as a Sister of the Merciful Moon Temple. Theirs was a secretive sect, a temple of unmated omega priestesses who devoted their lives to charitable acts. Thierry had no idea that the Merciful Moon Temple was so close to his home.

"I am Sister Selene." She swept her hand out to usher them inside. "Please follow me. Mother Luna is very anxious to talk to you."

Thierry dismounted and, guiding his horse by the reins, followed the woman and the sheriff into a courtyard, or more properly, a bailey between a curtain wall and what looked to be an ancient keep. This wasn't at all what he had imagined their temple would be. The sisters must be making use of one of the many ancient fortresses that used to guard the trade route before the country was united under the Regnault kings.

Many of the old buildings were said to be in disrepair, abandoned by trade-rich families who had rallied around the Regnault banner and now lived at court in Avimasse.

Given the gate and some obviously new construction, the sisters had been making themselves at home there for some time.

They followed Selene to the keep in silence. Nothing stirred around them but chickens until two more red-cloaked sisters materialized from the shadows. One took their horses, and the other joined Selene. Side by side, they led him and the sheriff into the great hall.

The enormous room featured a dais at one end with an altar and ceremonial gear. The sisters led them past that and into another room where a group of sisters gathered around an old wooden trestle table. At its head sat a woman wearing both a red hood and a red wimple. Around her neck, she wore a large and costly looking medallion—the moon surrounded by its phases—probably signifying her status as high priestess.

Thierry thought the sheriff would draw the sisters' attention first, but instead, all the women turned to look specifically at him. Magic scintillated like the glow of candlelight among them.

The sheriff said, "This is the young omega I told you about."

"Merciful Goddess." The high priestess—presumably Mother Luna—eyed him with surprise. "Welcome. You are, in truth, a sight for sore eyes."

The other ladies murmured excitedly among themselves. No one had ever reacted to him as they did, first with pleasure and not dismay. He didn't entirely trust their welcome.

"Sheriff, have you discussed the situation with this young man?" Mother Luna asked.

"His name is Thierry, Mother Luna. I felt it best to wait until we arrived to broach the subject. I fear he cannot speak for himself."

"Ah, yes. Since that awful encounter in the forest." She narrowed her gaze. "Don't be afraid, Thierry. Come here."

Mother Luna held her hands out to him. Bright magic fizzed from her like Charles's had, shiny and clean. Charles said that most omegas hid their magic. They could pull ambient magic inside them until that wasn't easily detected either. How did Mother Luna *radiate* magic?

He walked toward her and placed his hands in hers.

"I'm sure there is much you don't understand," she said as if reading his thoughts. "But because the situation is dire, there won't be time for long-winded explanations."

Thierry glanced toward the sheriff, who nodded. "She's right, lad. There's a murderer targeting the sisters in the forest."

Thierry frowned. A murderer? He'd heard nothing about murders. Who had this murderer killed? He widened his eyes.

"One of my novices were slain," Mother Luna said, "along with a priestess of the Order. There have been other close calls. I should start from the beginning—"

Thierry nodded eagerly.

"The Order of the Merciful Moon provides temporal aid to the people living in Hemlock Forest. We visit the sick, the elderly, and other isolated souls here. Until recently, we've been able to go about our mission in peace, equally revered by those in need and the outlaws who ply their questionable trade. Now there is someone—*something*—new in the forest. Death magic. Ill intent."

"We can't solve this the usual way." The sheriff couldn't hide his concern. "So far, all my men and I have done is chase shadows."

Thierry turned to the priestess, miming for something to write with.

"This way." She led them to a second table where she'd obviously been working earlier. It bore a half-burned candle and several letters, a bottle of ink, and a quill. There were also other items he recognized: an athame, herbs, crystals, a map, and scrying tools.

He wrote, "You're mages!"

Her eyes widened. She glanced toward the sheriff and back to Thierry.

"How do you know we're not witches?"

He wrote, "I sense your magic. Normally, omegas hide—"

Since Charles's death, there were many things he hadn't been able to *unsee*.

"That's true." She pulled the parchment from him before he could finish. Ink dripped onto her table where his quill hovered. "And for a good reason that we needn't go into."

He nodded and took the paper back. "What do you want from me?"

"We plan to set a trap, Thierry," the sheriff said. "This murderer is targeting the sisters."

Thierry began to see. He wrote, "You want me for bait?"

The sheriff gave a slow nod. "Whoever is doing this has shown a preference for the sisters. We need to bait our trap with an omega, dressed in the red robes of the sisters."

"It's not without risk," Mother Luna admitted.

"I volunteered," Selene clasped her hands together, "but Mother Luna refused to allow any of the sisters to take part in this scheme."

"Because it's too dangerous." Mother Luna laid her hand on Selene's shoulder. "I agreed to consider the proposal that we send a soldier out dressed in our robes, but Thierry's just a boy. An omega boy. Do you know how rare he is?"

"I know," the sheriff admitted. "I also know he's clever and resourceful. He's a fighter. Thierry knows the forest, and my best, stealthiest men will be right beside him, watching his every move."

As glad as Thierry was to hear the sheriff thought him capable, he wasn't prepared to face an enemy he knew nothing about.

"How does this monster kill?" Thierry had seen monsters. He wanted to know what he was up against.

"We don't exactly know." The sheriff lowered his gaze.

Mother Luna said, "The girls were all found lying on the forest path near a cairn we use as a point of reference. They appeared to be sleeping, but they were dead and"—she lowered her voice—"drained of all magic."

Thierry's heart sank.

"Whoever is doing this," she continued, "knows omegas have magic and how to extract it. I've not spoken of this to anyone outside my sisters and the sheriff, but based on the evidence, I fear this is the work of a necromancer."

Thierry already had nightmares about death magic.

Did this mean the necromancer who had killed Charles was back?

Did it mean these people wanted him to bait a trap for someone who could drain an omega's magic and leave them a soulless, lifeless husk?

Could this be the mage that killed Charles?

Charles said he was a necromancer. His beast had done his killing for him. That, Thierry knew, had been unplanned.

Had the necromancer learned to steal his victims' magic since Charles's death?

Charles, oh, Charles, where are you when I need you?

"Whoever is doing this is leaving a trail of terrible grief behind him," said the sheriff. "I thought about your circumstances. How helpless you must have felt after Charles died, and I wondered if you would be willing to act as bait to catch this new monster?"

Mother Luna paled. "Sheriff—"

"The boy can say no." The sheriff's gaze bored into him so

deeply that Thierry's head hurt. "No one will hold refusal against you, Thierry. But this beast goes after young omegas, and you're the only male omega in anyone's memory. Unlike the sisters, you're strong. You know how to fight, which is to our advantage. You can hide from this challenge or embrace it. What say you?"

Thierry glanced around at all the anxious faces. The sisters were of every age from preteen novices to doddering old women. All of them were clearly afraid they might be next, not to mention the omega girls whose families made their homes in the woods. They deserved his protection.

On the other hand, he could be facing down the mage who haunted his nightmares, along with the many brutal men and outlaws that Hemlock Forest shielded.

Goddess knew what else waited in the dense undergrowth. He'd spent his whole life tending a farm, learning the woods beyond, and making small trips into Amivienne. He wasn't stupid enough to think he knew what lay in the thickest heart of Hemlock Forest. He'd be facing that filthy magic again.

Thierry was no mage, but he could tell the difference now. Some magic was bright and healing, and some was…decidedly not that.

How he wished that Charles was there to ask.

He picked up his quill and wrote, "When do we begin?"

The sheriff's tension eased. "We'll set things up for tomorrow night. You stay here with the sisters while I retrieve my knights and experienced trackers. We may be sending you into the forest, but you won't be alone, Thierry, I promise. My men and I will be with you every step of the way."

Thierry nodded his thanks.

How would that work, though? They must mean to go along out of sight in order to catch the rogue mage when he attacked. Thierry looked to Mother Luna, who was frowning. She was right to be concerned. No true mage would be fooled by a decoy. They'd sense the soldiers' presence and take measures to keep them busy while they got what they wanted from Thierry.

Thierry pictured being drained of magic. Physical torture. Death.

I have to try.

Maybe the sheriff was right, and he was strong enough or clever enough to prevail or at least escape again. Or maybe he was sacrificing himself for the greater good. He should have died at the hands of the necromancer instead of Charles anyway. Maybe on this adventure destiny would finish what it started.

Either way, Thierry would give everything he had for the murdered girls, for Charles, and for the chance to say he'd done something to help at last. He would give every bit of his strength to eliminate this threat to vulnerable omegas everywhere.

As if a great weight had lifted off him, as if he'd somehow suddenly become a part of something far greater and more powerful than himself, he sighed with relief.

He had no voice, but that didn't matter anymore.

He knew who he was and what he had to do, and it was enough.

CHAPTER 5

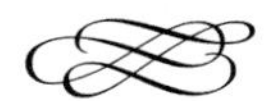

The following night, they dressed Thierry in the muslin robe, white wimple, and red cloak of the Sisters of the Merciful Moon. They pinched his cheeks and instructed him to bite his lips until they were dark pink and swollen. Catching a glimpse of himself in Mother Luna's scrying bowl, he thought he made a pretty good girl. He'd studied the demure way the other sisters walked, deliberately imitating their shorter steps and lowered gaze all day.

While he'd done that, the sheriff's men arrived in parties of two and three to avoid detection. Some were knights, and some were practiced trackers. Those alphas trained in shifted form.

All were robustly confident they would catch this mage and any other threat to Amivienne's peace, but Thierry didn't for a minute believe their ruse would be easy. He could see Mother Luna shared his anxiety.

As day faded into twilight, Mother Luna sat with him on a quiet bench before her private shrine to the Goddess. She stayed silent, like him, but her presence in that moment spoke of how worried she was.

She had loaned him a beautiful set of meditation stones, and he counted them off now, one by one, not really knowing the words to use but simply acknowledging that the Goddess had a plan for him, and he would go where She led him.

"I'll bet you didn't see this coming." Charles's voice startled a gasp out of him.

Where have you been? For Goddess's sake, I've been begging for your help!

Mother Luna looked up, suddenly alert. "Who is your friend?"

Thierry widened his eyes. *Can she hear you too?*

"She feels my magic, I think," said Charles. "I don't know if she can hear me."

"I guess you can't answer, can you?" The high priestess gave him a smile. "Your friend's magic is very...vivid."

Thierry nodded. *Where did you go, Charles? I worried I'd never hear your voice again.*

"I don't know," Charles answered. "One minute I was talking to you, and the next I was nowhere. It felt like my magic had frozen, and I couldn't break the ice. I'm sorry."

Do you know what I'm about to do? Thierry asked.

"Yes, you numpty. I don't think I was supposed to influence your decision. Well, I can have my say now. Stop this at once! You're going to get yourself killed."

Probably.

"Then why would you do this? You make a lovely Merciful Sister, but please don't throw your life away playing bait for this madman. Tell them you've changed your mind. They don't know what they're up against. He has as many undead beasts as he chooses to make now. The bastard has perfected his art."

So you think we're hunting the necromancer who killed you?

"I know it's him. He's back, Thierry."

How did he elude the law all these years?

"I don't know! Mages are bound by law to report death

magic users. This man has to be extremely powerful and very highly placed to have eluded the League of Ethical Magic."

Or he has their support.

"It could be both. You mustn't go."

He murdered you in cold blood and crowed about it as if he'd done something marvelous. I've seen his face. If it's our necromancer, only I can identify him.

Thierry wiped a tear from his eye. He'd forgotten Mother Luna was beside him. He startled when her arm wrapped around his shoulders.

"Your friend's fear for you is great," she observed. "Is it the young mage who was killed?"

Thierry nodded.

"You have a tremendous gift. He speaks to you?"

Thierry nodded again. What good did that do him, though, when he was unable to repeat what Charles said?

"Does your friend offer any clues to the necromancer's identity?"

Thierry shook his head.

"Any ideas on how to find and stop him?" she asked hopefully.

Thierry shook his head again, and this time, he lowered his gaze to the hands in his lap. He didn't want to see the pity in her eyes. He didn't want to know if she believed he was going to his death.

"Thierry, your inability to speak began after the murder, am I correct?"

He nodded.

"That means one of two things. This necromancer cast some sort of spell to silence you—"

Thierry shook his head. The necromancer never knew he was there. He'd be dead if the man had seen him. Sensed him.

"If that's not the case, then the magic in your omega nature is protecting you."

"That must be it," Charles said gleefully. "Your magic drew my attention before I knew what it was. Your omega nature must have hidden your magic and all the magic around you—including mine—to create some kind of void the necromancer couldn't penetrate. There's no spell, Titou. You're mute because you've chosen not to reveal our secrets."

No. He'd tried to speak. He'd tried hard. It was awfully inconvenient to be mute when everyone equated his silence with lunacy or stupidity. Tears spilled from Thierry's eyes.

"Sometimes we make choices we're not aware of," Mother Luna said gently. "Losing one's ability to speak after a traumatic incident isn't uncommon. In your case, it was probably instinctive. If you can't speak, you don't have to tell a tragic story."

"But if tonight's scheme fails..." Charles's voice trailed off. "Please don't do this."

Thierry bent over and wept into his hands.

Mother Luna patted his back. "I didn't tell you these things to make you unhappy, Thierry. Just remember when you have need of your voice, it will be there. You can overcome the fear that keeps you from speaking your truth whenever you choose to have your say."

Easy for you to say, he thought bitterly. He'd been *thirteen* when Charles was killed. He'd just received his first kiss. He'd looked forward to a simple country life of love and laughter with his best friend. Neither of them had imagined it would be their last hour together.

He'd held that night inside himself, all the good and all the bad, as if to speak of it would shatter the world around him. As if he could keep the true horror of it away as long as he never told...

"There you are, Thierry." The sheriff's spurs rang on the stone floor. "It's time."

"Goddess guide you." Mother Luna hugged him tightly to

her. "And know you'll always have a place of refuge here should you want it."

Thierry rose on shaky legs. Was he really going to do this?

"You can still back out." Charles's magic seemed to sting him like sparks from a forge. "You don't have to do this."

Thierry drew his hood over his head to hide his anxiety.

His limbs trembled, so he clasped his hands together as he'd seen the sisters do. Outwardly, he tried to project the image of a demure young omega on a mission of mercy. Inside, he was screaming.

"You'll be going to Grandmother Ellis's cottage." Earlier that day, they'd had him memorize a detailed map of the many footpaths in the forest's interior, and now they gave him a basket of food. It was a good long way to the little house where Ellis and her woodcutter husband had lived out their lives. With him dead, she was alone but for the sisters. "She's very frail, and lately she's had a persistent cough. I've included a potion for her lungs. Please see that she drinks all of it. There's enough food for a few days."

Poor woman. Thierry nodded. He would see the sisters' good work done.

"Soon," said Mother Luna. "Because of you we'll be able to visit her again very soon."

One of the waylaid omegas had been on her way to Grandmother Ellis's cottage when she was killed. She'd been the first, and at the time, they'd had no clue how she'd been killed. Now, after two more deaths and some investigation, it was clear something sinister was at work.

And Thierry would be walking straight into it.

He took the basket and another hug from Mother Luna, which in turn got him hugs from all the other sisters, or handshakes, or in one case a hearty clap on the back that sent him stumbling.

Anyone who had ever considered omegas weak should see

these women. They had magic and went about the forest day and night without fear for themselves in order to do good. Only the threat of death magic caused them any concern for their safety.

As he took up the lantern that they gave him and opened its louvers to light his way, he was wholly committed to his quest. If he had to do this night after night, he would to keep these valiant omegas safe.

Behind him, the great wooden gates closed.

The only sound he heard was his own rapid breathing.

He took a single step and then another.

The sheriff and his men had assured him they would be a short distance behind him. The trackers had shifted and melted into the woods on either side of the footpath.

Thierry held on to the thought that he was not alone. That even if he couldn't see them, the sheriff and his men were watching his every move. They knew what waited in the darkness for him. Nothing could take him unaware.

He shifted the basket to the crook of his elbow and made himself study the narrow path the sisters had worn in the undergrowth. Here and there he heard small animals, mice or maybe voles, scuttling through the bushes. The heavy beat of wings told him there were owls in search of a meal.

No matter how hard he tried to be stealthy, each footstep echoed loudly.

His heart beat faster.

The forest was far too dark. An unnatural hush seemed to drape slowly over him. He told himself his clumsy footfalls made every other creature wary. Perhaps animals and insects froze as he walked by, just as he would when confronted by an unfamiliar sound near his home.

He made it to the first landmark. Then the second. The third, a lightning-struck tree, appeared against the sky like a man in dire pain. It was less obvious until he stood right beneath it, looking up, but he'd found it. He hurried on, convinced he was going the right way.

After several more minutes, Thierry smelled the sickly aroma of dark magic before he saw its effect—an oily mist—creep from the forest over the path at his feet.

Mother Luna had warned him of this. One could be lost in a mage's false fog. One could get turned around and go deeper into the forest than one intended and never be seen or heard from again.

"If it happens," she'd advised, "stay near one of the landmarks."

But he was, by his calculation, directly between the forked tree and the next landmark, an ancient cairn. He looked for a pile of stone with a spiral—the earliest-known symbol of the Goddess—etched on the largest. The question was...should he go forward toward the cairn or back to the forked tree? *Charles? I could use some assistance.*

"This fog is made of tainted magic. I can't see anything but you."

Well, then. Forward or back. I'd flip a coin if I had one.

Thierry closed his eyes to the frightening fog. Besides the tainted magic, there was other ambient magic in the air around them. He caught the scent of trees, silverleaf oak and walnut. Hemlock and beech and yew. He sensed the living, ancient magic within them, slow and ponderous, like the drip of cold sap. He felt the quickening of living things, all the animals that made their lives within the forest's boundaries, and smiled.

No wonder people fled to the forest for shelter. It welcomed his presence. There were things to fear here, surely, but nothing compared to the darkness wrought by the necromancer. The forest itself wished to be free of the encroaching darkness.

"What are you doing?" asked Charles.

I'm listening.

"That's lovely, sweetheart, but how are we going to find our way in this sinister fog?"

I've thought of a way to go forward.

"Have you? Because this isn't the time to guess and get lost. Something is bound to eat you, and believe me, you won't find it pleasant."

That's what I love about you, Charles. You always clarify things for me.

When Thierry opened his eyes again, he decided to test the theory that the empty path would feel different from the vegetation all around him. He took a small step and then another, letting his sense of magic guide the way. With each move, he feared he'd walk face-first into the rough bark of one of the ancient trees, but he didn't. He was lucky enough to stay on his feet, and he moved forward, following the unseen path. Presumably he would find the pile of rocks he was looking for this way unless the necromancer confronted him right here. His way was slow going.

He wished he knew he hadn't lost his escort.

Despite his lamp, he could barely see his hand in front of his face.

"This is how he kills the omegas, isn't it?" Charles asked bleakly. "They get lost in the fog, and his beasts hold them at bay. Then the necromancer sucks them dry of magic and—"

Shh. Stay as close to me as you can, please. I need to feel where the magic isn't.

"As you wish." Charles huffed, "I still think we were mad to come."

You like an adventure. Admit it.

A twig snapped suspiciously close by. Thierry froze.

A low, ominous growl came from some distance ahead. Friend or foe, he wondered. Was it one of the sheriff's men or something more sinister? He dropped his basket and lamp in favor of slipping his knife from his boot. The louvers closed, and his lantern winked out. Thierry had been trained to hunt since he was a toddler, but he couldn't hope to move as silently as an alpha wolf. His blasted cloak rustled for one thing. He closed his eyes again and reached out for the essence of life around him. There were two wolves close by. More than one man coming stealthily along the path behind him.

Something else—something he couldn't identify—headed straight for him, crashing through the underbrush like a newborn dear. Whatever it was, it was huge. It stank of death and the aftermath of storms. The fragrance of spent magic. Whatever it was, it wasn't worried about making noise.

Indecision wrapped him up like the fog. If he ran, whatever the thing was would chase him. If he screamed for the sheriff's men, he could conceivably attract other, unwanted attention or alert their prey they were there for him.

Possibly the noisy intruder was only one of the outlaws he'd heard about, who robbed merchants as they moved from Amivienne to the next town and the next on their way to the capital city.

Thierry stepped toward the edge of the path. It was too much to hope he could remain unnoticed. Perhaps he could stay out of the way long enough for the sheriff's men to do their work.

Thierry asked the Goddess's blessing and took another step.

He felt more than heard a great shape move above him. Bigger than any bird, it seemed to swoop down—*oooph.*

An arm like iron banded around his chest, his feet left the ground, and the next thing he knew, he was swinging up and up, into the branches of a tree. Behind him, someone grunted, breathless with the effort of hoisting them both onto a sturdy tree branch. Whoever it was held onto a rope as thick as Thierry's wrist.

A raven landed beside them, wings flapping mightily enough

to stir the thick, still air. The foul fog began to dissipate, allowing him to see the sight below.

Thierry was too shocked to react before a callused hand clamped over his mouth as one of the wolves came into view. The tracker looked like a rock in a river of fog but moved like the apex predator he was.

A dreadful, misshapen beast burst onto the path not ten feet ahead, its crackling energy disbursing the fog as it stalked toward the wolf, glowing with an unholy luminescence Thierry remembered all too well.

The creature was huge, far bigger than the animal that had killed Charles, its enormous body made entirely of muscle. It appeared as if someone had combined the best parts of several animals: a bear, perhaps, with a lion's body, a wolf's thick coat, and ram's horns. It shook its great furry head, flinging foamy blood-flecked drool in all directions.

The wolf waited, biding his time.

Then four more beasts converged on it. They were far more *other* than the first. They juddered along unnaturally on limbs that seemed to be attached backward, straining with each movement like marionettes in the hands of a demented puppeteer.

Thierry wanted to warn the wolf, he even believed he could find his voice for it, but the rough hand of his captor tightened. Another wolf approached and two bloodied men.

A truly awful battle commenced.

The wolves were the first to die. It occurred to Thierry that with their strong senses the wolves could have fled when they first scented death magic, but they hadn't because of him. He gagged when the aroma of spilled blood filled his nose. It slid over his tongue, coppery and thick with the miasma of dark magic clinging to it.

He whimpered, closed his eyes, and pushed his face into his captor's neck.

The man sheltered Thierry while below dying men screamed with their last breaths. The wolves whimpered mournfully. Thierry sagged. Numbness swept over him.

The necromancer's beasts howled with delight. The forest trembled with fear as it seemed the mage was finally approaching. Fine, thought Thierry. After your beasts have done all the bloody work.

With a distant shout, the air rushed from Thierry's lungs. Death magic kicked up a whirlwind beneath them. Dust and leaves swirled upward. Thierry felt its physical pull as well as its esoteric draw. Did his captor feel that? Thierry shifted his gaze to the man's face. *Oh my.* An outlaw. He had to be.

Who else dressed in the forest's greens, armed himself with a bow and a quiver of arrows, and swung stealthily from tree to tree on ropes?

For a man who apparently lived rough, he smelled delicious. Like good magic, fir trees, wood smoke, and vetiver. Though his hands were callused, they were gentle. His face was fine boned and elegant, and he wore his raven black hair shoulder length. His moonlight pale eyes caught Thierry's gaze and held it. They studied each other for several seconds too long.

Directly beneath them, a large man crept through the still swirling fog followed by several others. Each carried a sword. Thierry hadn't sensed their presence, so they must all be mundane. But no...if he could sense even the trees...Was this some new, hidden magic he'd never beheld, keeping the truth from him until it was too late for him and the man who held him?

Thierry's whole body tensed.

"It's all right," his captor whispered. "They're mine."

The largest fighter leapt forward with an ax as big as Thierry. One of the great beasts charged, but the man struck its head off with a single, impossible blow. Gouts of blood arced out of the wound like some grisly fountain.

"Mate," the raven croaked. "Mate, mate, mate."

"Silence, hush," the outlaw hissed.

"Luc," the bird croaked. "*Kraa-kraa.*"

Below, the horrible fight continued. Thierry shivered.

"Sorry about the mess, sunshine, but it's the only way." The man spoke so low Thierry could barely hear the words. "You've got to strike off the head, or they keep on fighting."

Thierry gaped at him.

"Your escort is dead, I'm afraid."

Thierry felt his heart lurch. He shook his head.

The outlaw nodded. "My men were well behind me. I barely got to you in time."

Did they really have to die? Did these outlaws *have* to wait until everyone was dead to destroy the beasts, or was it simply convenient to rid the town of the sheriff who might stand in the way of their thieving?

A necromancer. An outlaw. Had he been rescued or was he in some new danger?

Wait. Thierry looked below. The mist had dissipated, giving an unrestricted view of the blood-soaked scene below. It was monstrous. Appalling. But as the air cleared, so did the residue of death magic.

"Stand down," the outlaw called to his men. "Likely the mage fled. Blast him for his cowardice."

The ax-wielder glanced up. "You want to face him?"

"Do you want more of the sisters to die?" The outlaw swore vividly. "I want the mage responsible for the murders in my forest to die bloody."

"Fine. You can put the omega down now. You've already scared the life out of her."

"No." The outlaw's arms tightened around Thierry. "I—I've got her."

Thierry and his captor glared at each other while the other men went to see if any of the beasts remained. Perhaps there was something to be done for the sheriff's men if any were still alive—

Thierry gave a violent jerk to free himself.

"Be still, Sister." The villain held him tightly. "We've just killed the beasts who attacked your escort. The least you can do is come along without fighting."

His captor started down then, carrying Thierry from branch to branch and leaping the last few feet until they were both on the ground. He held Thierry in a tight grip and began walking as though Thierry represented the spoils of war.

Thierry did his best not to look at the slain wolves or the decapitated beasts. He tried not to notice the blood staining the hem of his gown, his thin boots getting heavier and heavier.

He fought down nausea. The outlaw plodded on via one ingenious, misleading route after another. Where were they going? These men weren't heading to the Temple but farther into the woods.

Whoever the outlaw was, however good he smelled, he didn't seem to be heading in the right direction. Thierry tried to loosen the man's tight grip. He wanted to go back to the Temple. No, he wanted to go back in time to his childhood when Charles was alive and there was nothing in the forest scarier than wolves.

He dragged his feet. His captor lifted him off them.

Suddenly the events of the night were too much to bear.

Thierry's knees buckled and his body sagged, whether from fear or grief, he didn't know. What he did know was that he couldn't stand to be touched. Not now. Not after the things he'd seen. He shoved his captor hard enough to knock him down and crawl away, his chest heaving with the effort. The big lout who'd wielded the ax thought that was hilarious.

"She got you good, Luc." The man guffawed. "I can't wait to tell the lads you were bested by one of the sisters. If they could only see your face."

"Shut up, Peter. If you think you can do better—"

"I know I can. C'mon, Sister. I've got you." The man called Peter leaned down and hoisted Thierry over his shoulder. When Thierry tried to struggle, the brute administered a smart smack to his flank. Outraged, Thierry elbowed him in the ear.

"Don't touch her!"

"What?" Peter asked. "Why?"

"I—" Seemingly surprised by his outburst, the man shivered violently. "I—I don't know why."

"Luc, you hothead." The man guffawed. "Sister, you're going to have to do a lot better than that to get free of me."

"Come along quickly," said the one called Luc. "John is in dire need."

"Oh, aye." Peter picked up his pace until he was running as if he knew every inch of the terrain. The branches they shoved aside in their haste all seemed to spring back and whip Thierry's face. The raven flew low, darting between the branches and harrying the leader as if it was one of the men.

At least he could still feel Charles's presence.

Who are these people?

"I don't know. Probably outlaws."

What about the sheriff's men? Did he speak true? Are they all dead?

"They are, Titou. I'm sorry. We're on our own with this lot now."

Let's hope we haven't leapt from the fat to the fire.

CHAPTER 6

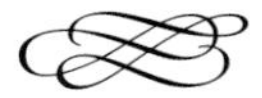

"Let the sister walk, Peter." Luc didn't want any of them touching her. "She must be feeling very undignified."

Luc had studied the forest's every nuance since his self-imposed exile from the luxurious life he'd known in Avimasse. He'd learned to use the forest as cover for his activities, and his men knew it almost as well as he did. They'd gone far enough off the well-marked footpath that the good sister had no choice but to follow them.

For three long years, Luc had carved out a life for himself here, meeting other rebellious, independent men who for some reason thought he should lead them. They had mapped every tree, every spring, every natural and manmade landmark in every direction. They knew the animals that lived within the forest's boundaries, but Luc had never seen anything like what they'd come up against lately.

Creatures out of some death mage's bestiary. Patchwork monsters seemingly put together by a madman. He'd never seen such evil up close before. He'd only recently learned the trick of killing them. If he hadn't, the good sister would now be lying dead on the path, beautifully pristine and composed in death.

He'd been out ahead of the hunting party when he'd realized what was coming. He'd barely made it in time to lift the sister out of harm's way before the beasts began their nasty work. Too bad he couldn't have saved the sheriff and his men. He was glum about that. It was a poor day's work.

Sister no-name was in shock, he surmised. When she'd shown she wouldn't bolt, Peter had released her. She walked beside Luc now, saying nothing.

"You don't talk much," Luc mused. "Have you made a vow of silence? That's not a requirement of your order that I know of."

The sister lowered her soft dark eyes and continued moving without giving him an answer. She was frightened of them, he guessed. And she could probably tell she was far from the path she was supposed to follow.

"Nothing?" Luc nudged her gently. "Don't be afraid. Even outlaws are grateful for the kindness your sect brings to the forest dwellers. Make no mistake, no man here will harm you on my watch."

She turned her face away.

The raven, Silence, dove down recklessly, no doubt showing off. Luc held his arm up, allowing the corvid to land.

"Mate, mate, mate."

"You could not be more wrong." Luc stroked the raven's feathers.

"Handsome Luc. Lovely Luc."

"Knock it off, Silence." Luc's cheeks heated, but if the sister heard, she gave no sign.

In truth, the sister's diffident response wasn't what Luc normally expected from the fair sex. He'd been a catch in the city. Even way out here at the end of the world, there was no shortage of wenches throwing themselves at him. He wasn't used to a maid who wouldn't even look his way.

"*Kraa-kraa*." The bird saw something—probably tasty—and took off.

Discreetly, Luc gave his tunic a sniff. They said you couldn't smell yourself, but he knew better, so he bathed regularly and cleaned his teeth. Perhaps it was because he hadn't shaved?

"Not long now, miss," said Peter. "If your feet hurt, I can carry you some more."

Luc gave Peter his most deadly glare. "No, you can't."

The girl shook her head rapidly while shrinking away from both of them.

Well, at least she wasn't any friendlier with Peter. That made Luc feel better. Perhaps the sister was simply young and skittish. She was probably new to the Order, fresh out of her novitiate. She probably hadn't heard that the outlaws of Hemlock Forest looked out for the Sisters of the Merciful Moon.

Luc didn't care precisely if she liked him. He only wished she knew he posed no threat to her physically or spiritually.

He preferred bedding men. It was a pity he'd been born in Rheilôme where the king had a narrow mind about things like that. In Helionne, they weren't such awful prudes anymore. Word was, Crown Prince Christopher had even *married* a man—a male omega—though that part had to be someone's idea of a joke.

There were no male omegas, more was the pity. Even if there were, Luc wouldn't be allowed to mate with one in Rheilôme anyway.

Still, he took heart from Christopher's courageous marriage. Things would change someday. If it was true that Helionne had a male consort, things would have to change everywhere eventually, wouldn't they?

All Luc could see of the girl was a pretty face. Pale skin, fine, straight nose, and lips most men would be only too happy to kiss. Perhaps her beauty had drawn the wrong sort of attention before she joined the sisterhood, and now she wanted to be left alone. He could honor that—would honor it gladly—if she'd only help his second-in-command, John.

Dogs barked, signaling that their party had finally made it to the clearing where his ragtag tribe of outlaws had cleared the land and begun building cottages to live in. They even had plots for growing food. Despite his accidental leadership status, he was proud of what they'd accomplished. At this time of day, his friends were gathered around a communal fire for a late night of drinking, no doubt, and waiting for him to return with good news.

Kelan played his fiddle while Hap kept time with his drum. A few of the women danced and made merry among the men who'd stayed behind to keep watch over John and his family.

Luc took charge of the sister, much to her dismay.

He towed her immediately to the tent where John's wife Serafina nursed him. She must be tired. She'd left her children with another family, and it was past time for her to reassure them.

Goddess grant them good news.

Inside the tent, Serafina kneeled next to John's cot, sleeping with her cheek on their joined hands. Luc took in the sight—John's pale, still face—with sorrow. He hoped he wasn't too late.

He glanced toward the sister, who stared back with wide eyes.

"Serefina," Luc said quietly.

"Hmm? You've brought help?" The woman startled awake. "Thank the Goddess."

Serafina gathered her skirts and rose to her feet with some difficulty. She'd had a hard day. Exhaustion shadowed her face.

"The sister will know what to do," he told her. The girl's face paled. Was that exhaustion or fright. "How is he?"

"Fever's bad. He's been delirious for a while now." They both turned to the red-cloaked omega and waited. When she didn't speak, Luc prompted her.

"Please, Sister. Can you help us?"

She blinked at him, her mouth drawn into a tight, inexplicably hard line. She pointed to her mouth and then her chest then mimed something. Writing?

"You can't speak?" Serafina asked gently. The sister shook her head.

"I understand you've taken vows—" Luc's patience thinned. "But there's a man dying here, and—"

"Wait." Serafina placed a hand on his arm. "Are you mute? Incapable of speech?"

The girl nodded gratefully. She mimed writing.

"I beg your pardon, Sister." Luc said with some chagrin. "My concern for my friend drove me to rudeness."

The sister didn't seem mollified. Perhaps she spent her days fending off questions from people who thought she was choosing not to answer. Luc strode to the door and flagged down one of his men. "Can you bring ink, a quill, and parchment from my quarters, please."

The girl seemed surprised he'd have such supplies. Yes, outlaws, by and large, didn't read, and parchment was a rare and costly commodity. She'd find him full of surprises if she learned more about him.

Wait. Was she some kind of spy? He needed to warn his men to keep their counsel around her, lest she take more than her person back to Amivienne and whoever was going to take over for the sheriff.

He needed the girl's aid, and he'd vowed to protect her order, but he wasn't about to bring the law down upon himself or his friends.

The lad he'd sent to gather his writing things returned, and they made a makeshift desk out of an old trunk. The sister fell to her knees and began right away, asking first: *What happened to him?*

"He felt tired two days ago, and then he complained of pain in his joints. Fever beset him, and then he began coughing." Serafina wrung her hands nervously as she answered. "He's been very still since this morning. Does it seem to you that his breathing is labored?"

The girl nodded. She frowned over what she'd heard. She wrote, *What have you done to treat him?*

"I have some skill with healing magic," Luc said, "but nothing I've tried has been successful. I'm not adept with healing potions or elixirs."

No. He'd been forced to study magic's history. It's laws. Not very useful.

"He can't shift. That's usually a sign that magic won't help." Serafina exchanged glances with Luc. "John pushes me away whenever I give him food or drink. I don't know what to do."

The girl wrote, *Bring me any herbs you have among you. Did you bring my basket?*

Luc nodded. "I think one of my men picked it up with your lamp."

She nodded. *Let me see what you have,* she wrote. *I will try to help him. May the Goddess grant me skill.*

"Thank you, Sister." Serafina took the girl's hand in hers. "That's all we can ask."

Luc spent the next hour scouring the camp for healing herbs, asking his men, their wives, and their unattached followers if they had anything the sister might use to aid his second-in-command.

After pooling their resources, he took the many pouches of powders, vials of oil, herbs, and dried plants to the sister. She knelt by the side of the trunk and studied what he'd given her. Taking her time, she carefully opened pouches and lifted stoppers and gave everything a sniff or a feel. She had an odd, expectant expression as she picked out one dried plant immediately: willow bark. Luc had seen that used for pain before.

The girl pointed to his knife and held her hand out. He must have been mad because he offered it to her, hilt first. It was a heavy, well-made blade with an unusually long, ornate hilt. she used its weight to smash the willow bark and stirred it with some other herbs in a wooden bowl along with some kind of yellow powder. She added hot water, let it steep, and then strained it through a cloth torn from her skirt. She held both hands over the bowl and closed her eyes.

Was she praying? Despite watching Mother Luna and her acolytes for years, it was fascinating to watch this girl. She worked with less certainty. He hoped she knew what she was doing. He wished he'd found one of Luna's older women this night.

When the girl finished, she urged Serafina to dab the liquid up with the bundle and drip it slowly into John's mouth while she made a poultice of eucalyptus and lavender to spread on his chest. As the night wore on, she bathed John's skin over and over with cool, rosemary-scented water. After a while, it seemed as though John rested more easily. But as the fever came down, John's cough worsened. His breathing grew labored again.

She mimed carrying her basket.

"Oh, right. Your things." Luc left the tent just as the sky lightened to the shadowy blue of predawn. It was his favorite time of day, and were it not for John's illness, he would have stayed by the fire for a bit to enjoy it.

"John?" Peter asked after their friend.

"Still struggling mightily," Luc admitted. "Do you have the sister's basket?"

"The lads left it at your place."

"Thank you."

Luc found the homely basket lying just inside the door to the little thatched cottage he'd built for himself. Even now, with all his worries for John, he felt inordinate pride to have built it with hands never meant for menial labor.

He took the basket to the girl, who found a vial inside and

unstoppered it to smell the contents. Again, she had that odd waiting expression on her face.

He had sensed magic in the air around her on and off during the night. It wasn't hers, he was certain, but it was strong enough for him to feel its power. It was focused magic, not ambient, which meant there had to be a mage involved. He glanced around the room suspiciously then left the tent and circled it, making sure there were none to eavesdrop on their work.

Odd, that hint of craft. It made him suspicious. As a practitioner, he'd sensed the girl's naturally occult omega magic, which was bright and powerful. But that didn't explain what he felt now. When he returned, that whisper of magic was gone, and the little priestess wouldn't meet his gaze.

"Have you been with the Order long?" he asked.

She shook her head, holding up the elixir. Her expression asked for permission to use it.

"Who created that?" he asked.

She pointed to her red cloak and mimed a heavy medallion.

"Mother Luna?"

She shrugged.

"Oh well. In for a penny," he mused as he watched her take the elixir—whatever it was—to his best friend's bedside. Goddess help her if John didn't make it. Luc would ruin her life, but sweet Serafina, who was as deadly with a blade as he, might very well kill her.

"Go rest," he told Serafina. "Spend time with your children. I'll keep watch for a while."

Serafina frowned. "But—"

"I'll come for you immediately if anything changes. You must take care of yourself in order to take care of the people you love."

She gave a sigh, but they clasped wrists, the gesture a silent vow of loyalty between them.

"Take care of him," she told them both before leaving.

The priestess barely looked up when she left.

Luc watched her patiently drip the contents of her vial, one drop at a time, into John's mouth.

"The man you are treating is my best friend," Luc admitted. "We've known each other since we were children."

She looked to him and nodded that she understood.

"My father never claimed me officially, but he saw me raised and educated. John was my companion and later my protector. I never made his job easy."

There was the quick twist of her lips, barely there and gone again. Apparently, she could well imagine him causing trouble. Fair enough.

"Three years ago, I…went too far. My father washed his hands of me. Despite having a wife and children and a job where he was respected and feared, John gathered his family and followed me here. If anything happens to him, my heart will shatter."

The sister's expression softened. He didn't want her pity. His story was common enough, except for the loyalty his friends had shown him. The sisters healed the sick—rich or poor, good or evil. But Luc wanted her to know how much John meant to him and everyone around them.

How much it would hurt to lose his friend.

She clasped her hands over her heart and then over John's. Her eyes seemed to say that she understood, that she would do everything she could.

It was the Goddess's will if John lived, not this slip of a girl's. Still, her understanding reassured Luc. Her very presence lit a fire inside him, warm and comforting and so natural he didn't know how he'd lived without it. The girl must have felt something too because her cheeks turned a delightful shade of pink. How strange to have his breath stolen by a girl's beauty—that was a first for him. A Sister of the Merciful Moon, no less.

Perhaps the oily magic earlier had tainted his mind.

She continued to sponge John's face and arms to keep him cool. Luc noticed she didn't struggle with his weight. She even lifted his thickly muscled torso and swiped the cloth over his back by herself. For such a puny thing, she was very strong.

Luc's admiration for her grew. He enjoyed being surprised, and this mute girl was surprising indeed. As she worked and he waited, that frisson of magic he'd been feeling seemed to come and go. Once or twice, he checked outside again, but no one lingered there.

Life had taught him to be suspicious of everyone. To be wary of anything that seemed too good to be true like this silent sister with her herbs and potions and uncanny strength.

The threat to his forest home made him wary of all practitioners of the craft, for it was certain that a death magic user—a necromancer—had set up shop in their midst.

Luc didn't yet know how he'd fight such a thing.

Was it a coincidence that he'd rescued this stranger, this silent sister, in the forest now?

Did he believe in coincidences?

No. No, he did not.

CHAPTER 7

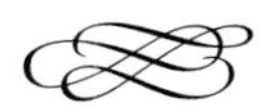

"Look out, Titou, he senses my magic."

Then leave for a bit. As long as I'm doing this right.

"You're doing marvelously for someone who doesn't know willow bark from a carrot."

How are you such a knowledgeable healer? You were in mage school.

"First of all, our housekeeper was a fine healer, and I learned a lot from her. Second, they teach healing in potions. It's part of our training."

Thank you. I'm pretty sure they'll kill me if he dies.

"They won't. It would be bad business to kill you since they could ransom you back to the Temple of the Merciful Moon. After they get paid, though, they might kill you."

Thank you, as always, for the encouraging words.

"I told you he sensed me. He's outside looking for the source of my magic."

Just go. I can take care of John for a while anyway.

"He's better now, to be sure. Take heart, Titou. I have no wish to see anyone die. Least of all a father whose children need him."

Do you think he'll live?

"It's as the Goddess wills, but I think if he makes it till midafternoon with no further crisis, he'll only gain strength after."

Thank you, Charles. I couldn't bear to let these people down.

"I know. I'll return later to check on you."

Relieved, Thierry continued to follow Charles's instructions. Bathe the patient, keep him cool, administer the willow bark potion every few hours, give him the sister's lung potion until it was used up, keep his head elevated with cushions to make breathing easier.

Wait and see. Wait and see.

How much of Thierry's life had he spent waiting for things outside his control? He dampened his hands with the rosemary water and cooled his face with them.

"Tired?"

Thierry looked up to find Luc had returned. He nodded.

"I appreciate all you're doing."

Thierry couldn't keep his lips from turning up. It wasn't a smile. He told himself he didn't smile at outlaws who kidnapped him. It was only inappropriate humor, the kind that made one laugh at funerals.

"You're very young, aren't you?" Luc asked. "Well, to me, you seem young. I suppose that makes me old. Where were you born?"

John coughed fitfully, and this time when Thierry raised his upper body to relieve him and cool the feverish skin of his back, Luc went around his other side to help.

"He's an armful, isn't he?" Luc asked. "I'm amazed you're strong enough to lift him."

Thierry lowered his gaze with what he hoped was maidenly modesty.

"Tell me, Sister, are you by any chance a practitioner?"

For the average alpha, that was an almost heretical question.

No omega was supposed to use magic. If Charles and Mother Luna were to be believed, hardly anyone believed omegas had magic at all.

Thierry glanced up to see the outlaw staring at him with nothing more suspicious than warmth and interest. Goddess. The look Luc was giving him took his breath. He couldn't have answered, even if he could speak.

Luc gave his head a shake. "I must be more tired than I realized. Of course you can't answer."

Thierry busied himself keeping John comfortable. He dripped a bit more liquid into John's mouth, just enough to moisten his lips and tongue and hopefully soothe what had to be a terribly sore throat.

"Luc," Peter poked his head in the door. "We need to see to the perimeter."

"Right. I must check the wards." Luc stood. "Will you be all right alone for a time, Sister?"

Thierry nodded.

He feared these hard men. Feared failing Luc's friend and being discovered as an imposter—an unnatural male omega—and not one of the wise Sisters of the Merciful Moon. And he feared what would happen if Luc discovered he had no training in potions or medicaments. But he feared the necromancer more.

Whatever was out there, if this small outlaw community had wards to prevent it from getting in, Luc was welcome to leave him for as long as he needed to secure them.

He must have appeared nervous because Luc patted his shoulder briefly. Magic sang between them, strangely powerful for such an idle touch. When Luc's eyes widened, Thierry knew he wasn't the only one who felt it. Luc licked his lips.

"Don't fret, Sister. You've done everything we've asked of you. The rest is up to the Goddess. None here will harm you." He lifted the tent's flap. "Ho, Silence!"

Thierry startled when the raven flew into the tent.

"Look after the sister, will you?"

The raven bobbed its head and croaked, "Mate, mate, mate."

"Make sure she doesn't get into any trouble."

The raven turned to look at him. It was uncanny and almost as if he'd understood what Luc had said.

Thierry shivered as he watched the two big alphas leave. Peter stalked, and Luc swaggered as if the trees should take up their roots and get out of their way.

He's a handsome one. And he knows it too, doesn't he?

Thierry'd had to keep himself utterly still to ignore Luc's touch, the sound of his voice, his wonderful alpha musk. Thinking about him now made Thierry's cheeks hot and his belly tighten. What a dreadful thing, too, after the deaths of the sheriff—who'd always been so kind to him—and the brave men with him.

What kind of a person is attracted to his kidnapper?

Not someone Thierry was proud to be, for certain.

"What's wrong? I could hear you fretting from miles away," Charles asked.

What's wrong? Thierry narrowed his eyes. He wished he could see Charles since he was about to be very cross with him. *My father tried to sell me, I was nearly attacked by monsters, and I've been kidnapped by outlaws who are counting on me to heal someone when I don't have any idea how!*

"I understand how you feel—"

Really? He shoved his red cloak back and his sleeves up his forearms. *You understand how it feels to be the wrong brother, the wrong status, wrong no matter what I'm doing? To always be in the wrong place at the wrong time? You understand what it's like to be* bait?

Charles's nervous energy sparked unhappily around him. It felt as though Charles was trying to think of something to say but couldn't.

I never belong anywhere. I'm one of a kind and not in a good way. Everyone I know has made up their mind about me, but I have no idea who I am. You can't understand, Charles. Try as hard as you might, you'll never understand how very alone I always feel.

"I'm here." Charles's magic swirled around him, warm as a hug. "You're unique, and you're confused, but you're not alone."

"How are you doing that, omega?" The door burst open. Luc and Peter stepped inside. "I felt a stranger's magic in here just now. *Focused craft.* Tell me who it is, or I'll put you in chains."

The nerve of the man to come bursting into a sickroom making accusations. Thierry had done everything Luc had asked, and for what? To be incarcerated somehow, or as Charles suggested, ransomed?

For the first time since his father had dragged him from home, Thierry smiled. He crawled to the table where he snatched up paper and pen and wrote, *How dare you!* in big, blotchy letters.

"I want answers." Luc took Thierry's arm in a harsh grip and yanked him close enough that he could feel Luc's breath on his face. "Are you using magic?"

The bird flapped his wings in agitation.

"Hey, Luc. Hey, Luc," it kept repeating. "Mate, mate, mate!"

"Silence, fly." He pointed outside. "Watch yourself out there."

Thierry had never seen such affront on a bird's face, but the bird took wing.

Luc softened his grip.

"Sister, I do not want to be suspicious of anyone from the Order. I know Mother Luna well, and I'm aware you have your secrets." Somehow Luc went from captor to confidant. He slid first one hand, then both from Thierry's shoulders to his elbows in a soothing gesture. "But I'm responsible for the safety of this community. They are my priority. You need to tell me what you know of this transient magic so I can assess the threat it presents."

Thierry's head swam as he adjusted to Luc's heat and his touch. His breathing quickened. Luc's scent filled his nostrils. Goddess. How could such a man exist? He was so strong, built lean but with a grip like iron, but when he softened it—used it to soothe—he was utterly devastating. He had beautiful dark hair, pale eyes, flawless fair skin with a scratchy-looking morning beard that gave his outlaw status the ring of truth.

Luc had stolen Thierry's breath before he'd begun to manhandle him, and now that he had he was being gentle, stroking Thierry's skin, pulling him ever closer…

Thierry's body reacted predictably. His pulse kicked up. His heart hammered. Due to their proximity, it was only a matter of seconds before Thierry's cock grazed Luc's thigh. Goddess help him, Thierry didn't even try to avoid it.

Luc's gaze swept down in something like horror.

Thierry jerked away.

"Out," Luc barked at Peter. "Get out. I need to speak to the good sister alone."

Thierry didn't like the way Peter's back stiffened, but John had a timely coughing fit, and Thierry sagged to his knees beside John's cot in hopes of a distraction. Together, he and Luc lifted John until he breathed easier and they could lay him back on his pillows. John seemed to quiet. His breathing evened out.

"What are you?" Luc practically spat the words.

Thierry took a breath as if to speak, but of course, the words wouldn't come. He stood and turned to face the wall where he worked the frog closure on his cloak. He dropped that and lifted his robe over his head. The heavy garments fell to the ground behind him as he unwrapped the cloth around his shoulder-length hair. At last he turned to face Luc, hands clasped in front of him. He didn't try to speak. He didn't have to. What lay beneath his small clothes spoke for itself.

"I don't understand." Luc strode toward him angrily. "This has to be some sorcery. Are you a spy? Don't assume you'll be allowed to return to your masters. If my men don't lead you out of the forest, it will be an age before someone stumbles on your bleached bones."

Thierry lowered his gaze and let the man rant. What could he do? He didn't speak, couldn't, though for the first time since Charles's death, he wanted, *longed*, to have his say.

"Out with it." Luc grasped his wrists in a punishing grip. "You are no acolyte of Mother Luna's. Why were you with the sheriff and his men? Are there more coming? Did they hope to follow us back here and take us unaware?"

Thierry winced when Luc's fingers tightened. Despite the pain, his body vibrated with a heady energy. As if reacting to magic, his blood sparkled in his veins like fizzy wine, and the effect was equally intoxicating. He felt drunk with it. Was his voice really a choice? If so, he had to use it now. He had to tell this man to go to the shadowlands, and unhand him, and keep holding him, and...

"Tell me what I want to know, or so help me, boy, I'll beat the truth from you. Why did you come to my forest?"

"B-bait." Thierry mouthed the word more than spoke it aloud. His unused voice creaked like a rusty graveyard gate.

"To catch us? Were you after me?" He shook Thierry roughly. "Who sent you? Was it the king's men?"

Thierry shook his head until his neck ached.

"Who sent you?" Luc gritted his teeth. "Tell me, or I'll throw you to our dogs for sport."

"Bait..." Thierry croaked. "To catch the necrom—"

"Liar." Luc threw him into the corner where he landed on his bottom. Luc began to pace back and forth from the cot where John now lay peacefully asleep to the shadows where Thierry cowered. "You expect me to believe the sheriff—that Mother Luna—risked your life to catch a vicious killer?"

"You spoke!" Charles's magic exploded into the room.

Thierry didn't acknowledge him, but Luc caught his breath.

"I told you that you'd speak when you had something to say. You should see this from where I'm standing. I have an entirely new theory about omegas now."

Shut up, Charles.

"Did you know that when Luc touched you, you both lit up like fireflies? From what I've witnessed, alphas luminesce when in contact with their fated omegas."

No. What are you talking about?

"I told you I'm interested in omega magic, didn't I? It's hidden, but apparently it's like a…I don't know, a vault, maybe. Some alphas seem to be able to use their omega's magic somehow, or at least it affects them, because when Luc touches you, it's indescribable. You glow. We must consider the hypothesis that he's your true mate."

"What are you doing?" Luc demanded to know.

Oh no. Charles, the man just threatened to throw me to dogs.

"He's not going to do any such thing. Now that you can talk, you can explain. If it's hard, write everything down."

How will I explain the potions I made? I'm a farm hand, not a mage.

"Tell him about me, then. I don't mind."

They'll throw me in a lunatic asylum.

"Tell me what this magic is?" said Luc. "Answer, or else."

Thierry considered what Charles was saying. Luc's threats had a hollow sound to them. He didn't seem like a bad person. He couldn't be if he cared this much about his people.

"He'll believe you. He's simply sensing my magic. Tell him you're haunted by the ghost of your dead lover. Ooh. Yes!" Charles sounded delighted with the idea. "It'll be just like one of those books your sister Esme reads."

I will not tell him that.

"Tell him something. His dogs looked awfully hungry."

"If you can speak." Luc glared down at him. "You will tell me whose magic that is, boy. And now."

"I guess I can?" Thierry cleared his scratchy throat. "I haven't spoken. Not for years."

"You confuse me." Luc squatted before him, his thick thighs straining with the effort. Thierry tried not to look at anything below his chest, but the expression on his face was forbidding. Thierry kept his eyes on Luc's throat when he answered.

"I'm as confused…as you are." He had trouble pushing words out. His throat felt dry and sore and unused to creating sound. "Maybe could I have some water?"

Luc rose and crossed the room to pour him a cup of wine. "Here. This will loosen your tongue better than water."

Thierry took a grateful gulp. Almost immediately, warmth spread from his mouth to his throat and belly, his arms and legs. He sighed with relief.

"All my senses tell me you're omega," Luc whispered as if he feared. "Yet you're no girl. I've heard of male omegas. I never thought to meet one."

"Here I am." Thierry spread his hands. "I'm an anomaly."

"How old are you?"

"Eighteen. Almost."

"That's why you pass for a sister. You're still a boy."

"I'm not that young," Thierry snapped.

"All right. I didn't mean to wound your pride." Luc narrowed his eyes. "How did you come to be in the woods last night?"

"I told you. I was acting as bait to help the sheriff—" The minute the word was out of his mouth, the entire misadventure came back to him: his father's plans, the endless anxiety, the terror of walking through the dark woods alone to lure a necromancer, the awful beasts who charged him, and the misshapen, curse-spawned creatures that crawled forward to kill his escort.

Thierry shivered violently until Luc draped the red cloak over his shoulders.

"You're all right now," Luc hushed him. "You're safe."

Thierry could see the scene as if he were still there. He could smell the blood and hear the men's cries.

"They're truly all dead?"

"I'm sorry. By the time I got there, the beasts had already picked some of the sheriff's men off. That's when the last few made their stand." Luc gently reached out to swipe away Thierry's tears. His touch sent tingles over Thierry's face and down his spine. "You've had a bad time of it, haven't you?"

"Goddess, who will stop him?"

"Him?" Luc frowned.

"The necromancer behind all this. Who can stand against him if the sheriff's men could not?"

Luc bit his lip, unable or maybe unwilling to answer.

Thierry would not find answers here. The necromancer was too powerful. A band of outlaws wouldn't take on a powerful necromancer, even if they understood their lives were at stake. They were much more likely to leave the area to its fate and find fat purses to steal elsewhere. Even if Charles was right and Luc was his true mate, Luc wouldn't gamble his life away for Amivienne or for him.

"Seph," John croaked. Luc scrambled to his friend's bedside. "Seph? Where—"

"Goddess be praised, you're back with us." Luc sighed with relief. "I'll send someone to get Serafina right away."

Luc gave a whistle, and a boy of twelve or so peeked in.

"You need me?"

"Bring Serafina, please. Her husband asks for her."

The boy's smile widened, and he dashed off.

Luc turned to Thierry. "You and I still have much to discuss. Put on your habit, Sister."

"Right," Thierry rasped. He wound the wimple around his head and neck then donned the robe and cloak properly, pulling his hood up.

"I don't like asking you to return to your disguise, but I'm unsure what to tell my men."

"That must be a new experience for you." His little dig caught Luc off guard, and he laughed.

"You're too mouthy to be a mute *or* an acolyte of Mother Luna." He gave Thierry a playful poke. "Tone it down. And don't think I've forgotten about the magic that seems to follow you. You will tell me everything before long."

Thierry nodded just as Serafina burst into the shack.

"John? Oh, John. I thought we were going to lose you."

"Seph," the man croaked. "I'm fine, love."

That quickly, Luc seemed to forget Thierry's existence. He and Serafina converged on John, whose eyes were open and whose expression seemed as relieved as his wife's. Thierry guessed he'd turned a corner, thank the merciful Goddess.

John caressed his wife's face. "My treasure."

She wept on his chest while he stroked her hair.

"Don't think you can desert us that easily, you wastrel." Luc's voice sounded as rough as Thierry's. "How would I get along without you?"

Thierry glanced away.

While he was glad to see John recover, the affection between the three only served to remind Thierry how profoundly lonely he'd been, especially without Charles's lively presence.

What was to become of him now? He couldn't go back to the farm, despite his mother's and siblings' loyalty. He couldn't allow his father another crack at him, couldn't work and eat and sleep in a cottage with an alpha he could no longer trust. But where could he go that his omega status wouldn't cause curiosity, or superstition, or trouble he wasn't prepared to handle?

"I'm here," Charles reminded him. "I'll look out for you."

That should have been enough, but after feeling the outlaw's touch, looking deeply into his haunting, pale eyes, Thierry wanted more.

After a single fraught night, he wanted Luc, and that was impossible.

CHAPTER 8

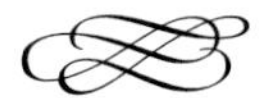

Luc left Serafina and the duplicitous omega to look after his friend. Despite his lies, the omega had done well for John, who had to be restrained from leaving his bed too soon.

What was he to do with the boy? Bait a second trap with him and hope he could prevail against a shadowy sorcerer using death magic? Take him back to Amivienne as if he didn't know they'd only try to trap the necromancer again, using the boy as bait?

In Luc's heart, he'd known what they were up against. The beasts they'd killed weren't natural, weren't even living. They were puppets, manipulated by an unknown enemy to Goddess knew what purpose.

He had to face the fact that he might not be able to fight this particular foe alone.

"Here you are. Mathilde says you're to eat this without argument." Peter offered him a plate of rabbit stew. "You seem troubled."

Luc glanced at the food, unmoved though he had gone without eating since the midday meal the day before. Upon that realization came a second. He hadn't bothered to give their guest food either, despite all he'd done.

"I've just realized I've been a terrible host. Give this to the sister, please. I'll get more for myself."

"If Mathilde thinks—"

"I'll tell her you're entirely blameless. Go on." Peter left.

Luc made his way to the fire where the oldest member of their little tribe, Mathilde, stirred something in a large kettle. She was a widow, a thin woman with long silver hair she wore braided over one shoulder. Her face was lined, but guessing her age was impossible. She could have been anywhere from forty to a hundred years old. A hard life had taken its toll on her, but she smiled often and had taken on the responsibility of directing meal preparation for the lot of them. Luc thought of her as a maternal stand-in as did many who knew her.

"I need another plate, Mathilde. I gave mine to the sister who helped save John."

"Oh, aye. Your boys took all my herbs and seasonings. You'll likely be sorry for it when you taste the stew."

"You can retrieve whatever Sister doesn't need once John leaves the sickroom."

"It's good you found aid in time. John had a terrible spell yesterday afternoon. I feared for him and Serafina. She might not survive losing her mate."

"She has the children." Though true mates were rare and grief was great, when one of a pair of fated mates passed, many a survivor had been known to take their life soon after.

"There's no replacement for the other half of your soul." Mathilde ladled stew onto a plank of stale bread for him. "Hard to go on when your heart is shattered."

Luc studied the old woman. "You speak as if you know from experience."

"I never had a true mate, but I know what grief is."

Luc felt ashamed because he'd led such a charmed life. Up

until now, all his troubles had been of the self-inflicted variety, and most had more to do with pride than people. Except for John and his half brother, Ethan, Luc hadn't formed many attachments, so he hadn't experienced loss firsthand. Still, he would have been devastated by the loss of his oldest friend.

He took a bite of his food but didn't savor it. He had an inkling of what grief must be like. He'd have done anything, gone to the shadowlands and back, to save John. He worked hard on behalf of the forest folk. Perhaps it was simply that he did know what failure felt like, and he hated it. If he'd failed to save John, his grief would have been unbearable.

"You look sour." Peter had returned while he was wool-gathering.

"Did our guest eat?" Luc wouldn't use the word *girl* anymore. Falsehoods came unnaturally to his tongue, and he hated himself after speaking them.

"She will. Serafina's taken her to rest at your place. The girl could barely keep her head up she's so tired."

"Is John still awake?"

Peter nodded. "He's asking for you."

"I'll take my meal with him, then." He placed his hand on Peter's shoulder. "You did well last night. I have more information about our enemy. We'll need to talk after I eat. Call a council."

Peter nodded. "It'll be as you say."

"Thank you. Get some rest. You've earned it."

Peter strode off, his lumbering gate scattering the chickens that pecked about. In the sky, Silence made swooping figure eights on the wind, keeping watch.

The omega rested in Luc's cottage. Probably in his bed. While that thought shot secret pleasure to Luc's balls, the farther Luc got away from the young man, the more lucid he felt. He could hardly conceive of a male omega. He didn't know what to do with one. Or rather, he did, but he needed to keep his mind on his more immediate problems.

Luc had seen reanimated creatures, but the night before, he'd seen the gruesome product of an unknown mage's growing madness. He'd never heard of anyone who could piece together animals like that. Not even the wildest theories held that one could bring something so unnatural into being. Necromancy, death magic, taken to its ultimate extreme.

High magic practitioners and scholars alike spoke of necromancy in hushed whispers. Those who studied magic were always curious. Circumventing natural law, raising the dead, could be seen as a pinnacle of achievement for some. Even though the practice was punishable by death, there were always mages who pursued it. And it always went terribly, horribly wrong.

In Rheilôme, the practice of magic was a right, not a privilege, as the king was highly covetous of the power it gave mages. Only three years before, the king and his high court magus pondered purging all written manuscripts and teachings dealing with death magic entirely. Such a thing was anathema to practitioners and scholars. Destroying books? Forbidding discourse? These things were the opposite of the aims of the esoteric community.

Death magic had proved dangerous in the hands of unscrupulous men before, therefore mages ruthlessly policed their own. They had to be vigilant, lest they all burn for the sins of one individual.

Any mage discovered practicing death magic found himself clapped in irons and sealed in the king's dungeon if not shoved into an iron coffin and thrown to the bottom of the Helionne Sea. Death magic could be dangerous business, and a rogue of such power must not be allowed to operate in Rheilôme unchallenged.

Luc had a bad feeling about this news.

It boded ill for his people, and their kingdom, and possibly even their world.

He entered John's hut and found his friend sitting up while Serafina spoon-fed him broth.

"Peter said you wanted to see me?" Luc hesitated. "I don't wish to intrude."

"Come." John's voice was still weak, but to hear him talking lifted Luc's spirits. "I wish to thank you for bringing me back from the shadowlands."

"I did nothing." Luc made himself a place on the trunk that their guest had turned into an impromptu desk. "You must thank the...sister."

"I plan to. Seph says the girl is painfully shy and mute. You should return her to the people as soon as possible."

"Well, that's—" Luc set down his barely touched stew. "That's what I need to talk to you about."

John and Serafina exchanged a glance. "Go on."

"I feel like a madman saying this." He took a deep breath. "The sister is an imposter. She's—he's a young man."

"What?" Seph gasped. "No. She's omega, I'd swear to it."

"He is omega. Apparently, Prince Christopher's mate isn't unique."

"A male omega. Here in Rheilôme?" John coughed then cleared his throat. "That seems like an omen. You're certain?"

"The imposter is definitely a male. I can't sense anything but omega from him. The sheriff hoped to use the boy to catch whoever is killing omegas in our forest."

"The man's an idiot." John coughed. Serafina rubbed soothing circles on his back. "We have no idea what we're up against, and he sends a boy out to lure it?"

"The men spoke of fighting off beasts from a nightmare," said Serafina. "Undead, unholy things. How do we know our strange guest wasn't the one manipulating them?"

"He wasn't." Luc knew that much at least.

"How can you be sure?" John asked. "Perhaps it's a clever illusion that makes you believe."

"I was with him at the time of the attack, touching his skin. He wasn't casting. Anyway, death magic feels different. It's noisome. He couldn't hide that from me, omega or no."

John nodded. Serafina worried her lip.

"This changes things," he told John honestly. "I despise the ruling class, but I won't sit by while death magic swallows up this part of the kingdom. I must return to the capital and ask for help."

"Your father won't see you. You know that, don't you?"

Luc shrugged. "I still have my half brother and contacts at the Royal Academy. Those I trust must know we have a necromancer practicing in our midst."

"That lot is so full of treachery." A fit of coughing softened the impact of John's words. "Have...you...forgotten what it's like at court?"

"I haven't forgotten, but people are building new lives here. Things are getting better." Luc stood and pulled his shoulders back. "I won't allow some upstart conjurer to destroy everything we've worked toward."

John turned to his wife. "He doesn't look much like his father, does he?"

"Not at all," she agreed with a smile. Neither John nor Serafina bore any love for Luc's father, but it had to be said Luc was more like him than his father's cherished heir. "I think he's right, John. We can't take on a necromancer by ourselves."

"I won't risk Seph or the children." John glanced Luc's way to make certain he heard the words. "I'm sorry, Luc, but I can't."

"I would never ask you to. I've arranged a council to discuss things. You'll have the opportunity to speak your piece, but no one is risking anything they aren't willing to lose."

"What about this boy omega?"

"He knows more than he's let on," said Luc. "I'll make him talk."

"So he's not mute?" Seph asked.

"He says he hasn't spoken in many years, and I believe him. His voice sounds terrible."

"I don't trust a man who hides behind a woman's guise," said Serafina.

"Nor do I," Luc admitted. "But there's no denying the fact that he did everything he could for John. I'll tread carefully."

"See that you do." John shot him a disgruntled look. "Don't be a fool for those pretty doe eyes, eh?"

Luc hid a smile. "You noticed those?"

"Yes, about that." Serafina gave her husband's arm a playful thwack. "I saw you making eyes at *the sister*."

"I did no such thing," John argued.

Luc left them to their play fight. He wasn't hungry anymore, but he took his dinner with him. No man in his position had the right to turn down good, honest fare. He entered his cottage without knocking, but the blatant show of strength turned out to be unnecessary. His guest was fast asleep. It was better that way. Open and gazing Luc's way, the boy's doe eyes were wondrous indeed. If Luc didn't wish to forget his responsibility to the people who'd entrusted their lives to him, he should not enjoy the burst of pure happiness he got from seeing the boy curled up in his bed.

An empty plate sat on the writing desk. Luc sat to likewise eat his meal in the first silence and peace afforded him in days. He had a major conundrum and little time to ponder it. The murdered omegas had been drained of their magic. That much Luna had confided in him. The most ancient and forbidden manuscripts did refer to magical cults where alphas stole a witch's magic—sometimes along with her virginity and her life—in ritual orgies of sex and greed. The practice had been universally condemned ages ago. The Worldwide League of

Ethical Craft had been established to closely scrutinize magic users in order to prohibit the resurgence of such a thing.

Was their foe experimenting along those lines? Any mage who wished to dabble in death magic would naturally need to work as far from the prying eyes of the League as possible. Hemlock Forest with its single trade road and vast dense foliage could prove useful for testing magical boundaries.

Luc had never been faced with such a thing. Never even conceived of a necromancer who would create terrifying experimental beasts—and leave murdered omegas—in the open for the world to see. Luc needed more information if he wanted to stop them.

That meant going to Avimasse.

Linens rustled behind him. He turned in time to see his guest rise. The blanket fell away to reveal the wide, muscled chest and well-developed arms the lad had hidden beneath his cloak.

"Tell me your name," Luc ordered.

"Thierry." Flushing deeply, he dropped his feet over the side of Luc's bed as he rose, visibly aroused. "Excuse me. I need to...er—"

"Go, but don't try to leave. My men and I will be forced to find you, and I promise the resulting accommodations won't be this luxurious."

"Should I dress?" He went to pick up his cloak and wimple.

Luc rose and went to his trunk where he found a simple tunic and breeches. "These might be more comfortable."

"Thank you."

Thierry turned away, but Luc couldn't help watching as he donned the humble gray-green garments. Thierry had a beautiful body, a far more masculine one than Luc had given him credit for. He obviously did hard work, but his lean, compact build was as lovely and graceful as an athlete's. Luc couldn't help wondering what it would be like to have all that country-bred goodness to play with. Strong arms to hold him. Powerful thighs wrapped around his hips.

Luc had enjoyed many, many beautiful men in his life, but he wanted Thierry with an urgency that surpassed anything he'd felt before. The desire to touch him was a physical ache, a craving. All his blood left his head in a dizzying dive straight to his cock.

Goddess, what are you up to?

Luc wanted more than to fuck the young man. He wanted to claim him. To own him. He could barely pummel his libido into submission before Thierry returned. The boy kept his eyes down as he sat on the bed, folded his hands, and let out a breath.

"Do you have questions?" he asked.

"Of course I do." Luc swallowed hard. "If we're to have any hope of prevailing against this threat, I need to know everything you know."

"Oh, well. That shouldn't take long. I know next to nothing. I meant questions about me."

Luc leaned back against his writing desk. "Have you heard of Prince Christopher of Helionne?"

Thierry shook his head. "Pa says gossip is for the idle."

"Prince Christopher is said to have married a male omega."

Thierry blinked slowly. "He did?"

"Truly," Luc assured him. "Merchants bring news as well as goods. The crown prince married in the spring."

Thierry's eyes widened. "I'm not the only one?"

"If the news is true, you aren't."

"Goddess. If Pa knew that, he wouldn't have sold me so cheaply."

Luc let out an unexpected growl. "Your father sold you?"

Thierry shrugged. "It's how I got into this mess in the first place."

"Explain," Luc ordered. "There's a council meeting soon, and

I need to know what happened to bring you here and everything you know about this ugly business."

"I'd have to go back a ways." Thierry scratched his chin. "And I'd be grateful if I only had to say it once."

"Fair enough." Luc nodded grimly. "Come with me. The council will be gathering soon."

Thierry stood and smoothed the tunic over his fine frame. He was barefoot. He'd been wearing soft slippers like those the sisters wore. Luc found him serviceable boots to wear. It didn't help that he looked nothing like the fragile omega Luc and his men had brought to treat John. Now, he looked like a captured spy. Time would tell how Luc's people responded to the news that they'd been duped.

It shouldn't matter. Luc told himself it couldn't matter how his men—how his little tribe—reacted to the stranger in their midst, but it did matter to him. Something deep within Luc said Thierry was important. Necessary, like breathing air or slaking his thirst. Something told him that Thierry was about to change his life, whether he liked it or not.

Thierry met his gaze. Pink crested his chiseled cheekbones. Lashes lowered over his fine brown eyes. Luc wanted desperately to kiss him, but it was Thierry who licked his lips.

No, Goddess. What was wrong with him?

The attraction had to be the madness of the moment. It had been a day of firsts. He'd never battled a necromancer's beasts before. He'd never met a male omega. He'd never known the pain of nearly losing his best friend. Perhaps his attraction was mathematical: the sum of danger and beauty and uncertainty equaling lust.

This could not be his true mate.

Luc held out his hand and watched as Thierry guilelessly took it. Magic sparked between them, seeming to rush from Thierry's fingers to his and back in a loop. Power thrummed through them—he felt it—their hearts beating with a single purpose.

"That's different," Thierry said in a voice hoarse with shock. "What—"

"What indeed," Luc cut his question off because he knew the answer. He knew, although he'd never expected to feel anything like it. "We have no time to pursue that now. Come with me."

Thierry nodded. He followed Luc, who burned all over from excitement, and dread, and shame.

Why now? Why him? Why would the Goddess send his fated one to this place of beginning from nothing where hunger and exposure and danger were all Luc could offer him?

They were in a fight for their lives, for the nature of magic and the right to define the world. How was he to keep his mate safe?

Goddess, what have you done?

CHAPTER 9

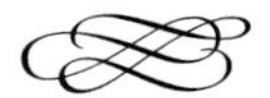

Thierry followed Luc as if in a trance.

Unlike when he'd first arrived, he got a good look at his surroundings. The clearing was larger than he'd thought with several humble thatched-roofed cottages and more in varying stages of completion. There were chickens and pens with pigs and goats. Women hung laundry on lines tied between trees, and men wrestled in an area cordoned off for training. Children played tag by running around the legs of unwary adults. They got an earful for their trouble. Everywhere Thierry saw a merry relentlessness. The setting sun cast long shadows between the trees and painted the children's faces. Firelight warmed Thierry's skin like a benediction.

There were signs of industry as well, weaving and bow-making and tanning hides. Luc's people dressed in homespun clothing that let them blend into the forest backdrop: men, women, and children alike. It was a clever gambit, especially at dusk. If they stepped off the paths and remained silent, Thierry wouldn't know them from the forest itself.

The closer they got to the central gathering area, the more noticeable the wary stares of Luc's people grew. It stood to reason. Not only was he now obviously a man, Luc had yet to let go of his hand.

Thierry should have hated their stares, yet with Luc's fingers interlocked with his the strange magic roaring between them seemed to wash every other discomfort away.

"I told you so," said Charles.

What?

"Can't you feel it?" Charles asked. "Luc's your Goddess-blessed mate. It's obvious from here."

Is that what this is? Because I feel dizzy and er...disturbingly energized.

Charles snorted. "Is that what they're calling it these days?"

Thierry heard Charles's unhappiness. He felt Charles's resignation.

You told me we weren't meant to be mates.

"After I *died*. It doesn't hurt any less."

I'm sorry.

"Don't be."

I really am sorry you're dead.

"I'm sorry your true mate's an utterly dashing outlaw."

You think so? I'm not displeased. Thierry couldn't have wiped the smile off his face if he'd tried.

"Oh, fine. Go ahead and gloat. I'm sure he's got some flaw. Terrible body odor or a tendency to snore. You know he farts. Everyone does. He'll stop hiding it from you the first moment he feels comfortable."

"What are you smiling about?" Luc asked suddenly. "You're about to be thrown to the wolves, quite literally."

"You said you'd throw me to the dogs."

"That was to scare you." Luc's smile faded, and he lowered his voice. "I hope you understand that you've gained entry to an outlaw settlement with the use of deceit. No one here will forgive that easily."

"I understand." Thierry would simply have to make himself

useful. That's how he'd managed to survive thus far. Why should this new life be any different?

Luc took a chair by the fire. He patted the one next to him. Thierry sat. More than a dozen men and several women drifted in and took their seats. It looked like they were mostly older. Good fighters and grandmothers who watched him with shrewd eyes.

Luc gave Thierry a reassuring nod then rose and lifted his hands until his people settled down. All eyes focused on Thierry as Luc told the group who he was and how he'd come to be there. Almost immediately, the muttering grew into an unhappy crescendo. Thierry tried to make himself smaller.

"He lied to all of us," said one woman. "How do we know he's telling the truth now?

"How'd you miss he's a man, eh?" one man grumbled. "Out of practice with the fair sex?"

"Thierry is omega." That got a disbelieving round of commentary.

"He's pulling the wool, Luc." The same man glared at Thierry. "Omegas are girls."

"We're women, you old lout." A woman with long, moonlight-hued hair corrected him.

"He speaks the truth." With Serafina's aid, John made his way to the circle. "The lad's an omega. There's no denying that fact."

John appeared displeased when he reached them. Was Thierry sitting in his normal place? He wished he could tell John that Luc had placed him there. He'd never have taken the man's seat had he known.

John took the empty seat on Luc's other side, much to Peter's dismay when he arrived a minute later.

"Thierry is a rarity. A male omega," said Luc, "There is precedent for this in the lore, and we've all heard that Prince Christopher of Helionne married a male omega in the spring. His consort bore him a child."

Some faces expressed surprise. Others remained openly hostile.

Thierry frowned up at Luc. Why wasn't he getting to the important part?

They were facing monsters.

"Thierry's status must remain a question for another time. I've asked him to tell us how he came to be in the woods with the sheriff of Amivienne and the hunting party. There is more to his story than even I know. I ask you to listen to him with open hearts and minds. What we face here is worse than I imagined."

Luc's words silenced them. Thierry could see why. Luc didn't seem the type to fear ordinary danger, and he had been visibly shaken by last night's encounter. At an encouraging nod from Luc, Thierry rose and explained everything, starting from the beginning. He told them about the mage whose risen beast killed Charles. About his inability to speak of it afterward, about his father's enmity toward him and his attempt to sell him. About the sheriff's rescue and his subsequent decision to act as bait.

"So since I'm omega and they knew I'd be better able to protect myself than most of the sisters, they asked for my help. The sisters are desperately afraid. There have been three omegas murdered so far. At first, I believed they had to be wrong. That someone was killing the women out of depravity, but after seeing the things I saw last night"—he shuddered—"I can honestly say no one knew what we were about to face."

"If you're not one of the sisters, how did you heal my husband?" asked Serafina.

"I had help," Thierry admitted. "I don't expect you to believe me, but my friend Charles told me what to do."

"Your dead friend?" Serafina asked.

"Yes," Thierry clarified. "The necromancer's beast killed him in body, but his magic—his spirit—seems to have remained behind."

Two of the council members burst into whispers on hearing this.

"No, wait. Charles's housekeeper is skilled at healing, and he learned potions at the Academy in Amivienne." Thierry spread his hands as if to say, *what could I do?* "He talked me through what I needed to do."

"See? He admits to dark deeds—possible necromancy—of his own," one man shouted. "I don't trust him."

"It worked, didn't it?" The old woman gave Thierry's detractor an eyeroll. "I'm not fussed."

"A necromancer's dead are mindless puppets," Luc pointed out. "They don't offer advice or healing remedies."

"We put our faith in you on false pretenses," another man muttered. "You wore the red cloak of the Order to deceive us."

"I know, and I'm sorry," Thierry offered. "Once the beasts attacked and Luc grabbed me, everything spun out of control."

"I thought I was losing my true mate." Serafina clasped John's hand between hers. "Perhaps we should look at Thierry's work as an act of good faith."

"I never would have done anything to harm him." Thierry glanced to Luc. "Charles is—was—terribly bright. And he was so certain we could help. I trust him."

"Except the once," Charles said bitterly.

Hush.

With a frown, Luc flicked his gaze toward Thierry.

"He definitely senses when we're speaking," said Charles.

Then don't. We can wait until later.

"Mages are curious by nature." Luc stood again to address the council. "That this fine young friend of Thierry's paid for his curiosity was a tragedy, but it might be to our gain. John is recovering. And apparently, we have an unseen ally."

More muttering and grumbling followed his statement.

"Are you so afraid of ghosts, Owen?" the old women asked. She shook her head in disgust. "Are you not all fierce, rebellious alpha outlaws?"

A couple nodded in agreement. One man shouted, "I'm not afraid!"

"Me either!" Another echoed his cry and then another. "Mathilde will drive him away with her evil eye if he's not on our side, and if he is—"

"We should get him something to drink." A laugh followed, and soon everyone had relaxed visibly.

"I still want my herbs back." Mathilde, Thierry guessed, winked at him. "I'm not much of a healer, but without them, the food will be foul."

"We'll get them back to you, Mathilde. I promise." Luc acknowledged her and thanked her for her support.

Then he clasped his hands behind his back and looked up at the fathomless indigo sky. The clearing grew quiet but for the bark of an occasional dog and the cry of a baby.

"I've asked you here because this business has me very concerned. We need to find out what's behind all this. I don't mean the beasts. Their only purpose is to kill. I mean we need to find the madman who created them. I'm certain he has more destruction planned. More victims in mind."

"But Luc—" John tried to rise but fell back into his seat with a wince. "How can we fight such a powerful mage?"

"Honestly? I don't know."

That got the council talking again. Everyone seemed to have an opinion. The oldest members were in favor of avoiding trouble. Some of the more fit wanted glory.

"I still have contacts within the Royal Academy and in the capital—"

"You'd be mad to return," Mathilde said flatly.

"Let me go." John stood.

"No, John," Serafina pleaded. "You're not well enough."

"I need to go, old friend," Luc told him. "These people will only speak to me."

"Is that enough to risk your life?" Mathilde asked.

"Luc—" Thierry felt alarm spin through his entire being. He'd barely met the man, and he couldn't, must not, lose him. In the single beat of two hearts, Luc had become the most important person in Thierry's world. "You could send me. I could—"

"No!" Everyone froze after Luc's sudden outburst. Luc tilted his head from side to side as if to relax his neck muscles. "There might be a minor complication. It seems Thierry is my Goddess-blessed mate."

Gasps and laughter followed this announcement.

"Settle down." Luc lifted his hands for quiet. "The thing is, I'm loath to put him in further danger."

"The choice isn't yours alone," Thierry reminded him.

"You would go against your alpha mate?"

The power behind Luc's words wiped all thought of rebellion from Thierry's heart. That too was new. But he'd never meekly submitted to his father or his alpha brothers. He had no intention of submitting willy-nilly now.

"I say you two should sleep on it." A lewd chuckle escaped the old woman's lips.

"That's enough from you, Mathilde." Luc pointed at her. She shrugged.

Peter cleared his throat. "At any other time, I'd be delighted by your news, but there's a rogue sorcerer killing people, and this boy"—he pointed to Thierry—"just happens into our camp and performs some perfunctory healing, and you believe him just like that? He could *be* the necromancer for all you know."

Every eye turned Thierry's way.

John's suffered a coughing fit, reclaiming everyone's attention.

"He shouldn't be here," Charles warned Thierry. "He needs hours more rest and tea made with willow bark and honey."

I doubt if saying that will help right now.

"You have reasons for your suspicion," Luc admitted. "We all have a right to think for ourselves. I don't know how to prove that what I say is true. I would not admire you so much—I would not seek your counsel—if you were gullible or acted rashly."

"I believe what you say," Mathilde said stoutly. "You already bicker like husbands."

Some laughed at this. Others scowled. One said, "Be quiet, witch."

"Be kind." Thierry glared at the man.

"My point is," Luc continued, "I'm glad to have people looking out for me, and if I'm wrong, I expect you to tell me. In the meantime, I will travel to the Royal Academy, for I believe it's the only place we'll find any answers."

"Why not the Academy at Amivienne?" Thierry asked. "If traveling to the capital is dangerous for you, why not discuss it with the mages here first?"

Luc sat, and it seemed he weighed his answer before speaking. "Do you know anything about the Worldwide League of Ethical Craft?"

Thierry shook his head.

"It's the body that governs the practice of magic, not only here but in the countries of Lyrienne, Helionne, and Calyxenne. There are members of the League in every jurisdiction, and if, as you say, someone has been dabbling in death magic for years, the Academy should have notified them already."

"I see what you mean." Thierry frowned. "The master of the Academy had to know what killed Charles. Death magic leaves a filthy residue behind."

"What's he saying?" an older man shouted from the other side of the fire. "Speak up, boy, so everyone can hear."

"I was just saying I learned to recognize death magic by its residue," Thierry shouted in reply.

"Oh, that," the man muttered. "You know a trick or two about magic, eh? Didn't you say you're an omega? How could you tell?"

"I'm a haunted omega, sir. I learned the hard way."

"Not funny." Charles's magic ruffled his hair.

"All right." Mathilde rose to her feet. "You've given us much to think about. John should be abed and so should you, Luc. You haven't slept in two days. We'll talk more later."

"Why do I feel like I'm being sent to the nursery?" asked Luc.

"It's not my fault some young people don't have the sense to sleep when they need to." Her expression brooked no argument.

"All right. Come, Thierry. You need rest as much or more than I do."

Peter spoke, "We should keep the imposter under guard, at least until we know he's not a spy."

There was suspicion there, Thierry thought. Jealousy?

"Peter," Luc said fondly. "I think you can trust me to guard him."

"It's not safe," Peter argued. "He could slip a knife between your ribs while you sleep."

"Then we can relieve him of it." Luc held out his hand, and Thierry gave him his knife, which he'd concealed in his cloak and now kept in his borrowed boot. "And I'll be sure to guard mine."

"I want that back," said Thierry. "My brother Jules gave it to me."

"Fine. Soon." Luc really did look exhausted. "Are you coming?"

"I can't. Not yet. Charles says John needs tea made with willow bark and honey. He needs to rest."

"I'll take care of him, Thierry." Serafina gave Thierry's shoulder a pat. "Since you taught me to recognize the herbs, I'll manage."

"Technically, that willow bark would be considered a spice," said Charles.

Thierry bid Serafina good night.

"You're not going to tell her?" Charles asked. "She can't go around calling everything herbs, you know."

Thierry took Luc's hand, and again, the tingle between them was profound like a knot tightening to bind them irrevocably together. Would things always be this strange when they touched?

"Oh, fine." Charles's magic took on the sharp feel of a million grains of sand, scouring Thierry's skin.

"*Ow.*"

Luc stared at him. "Something the matter?"

"Someone's having a fit of pique."

"It's what you get." Charles's sharp magic swirled around him and disappeared into the earth at his feet.

Luc blinked in confusion. "Don't tell me your ghost is jealous."

Having nothing to say, Thierry shut his mouth.

CHAPTER 10

They walked back to Luc's hut. Feeling an odd awareness of him, Luc kept hold of Thierry's hand. Was that all right with the boy? He seemed as dazed as he had been the night before when Luc had hoisted him to safety in the branches of a tree.

Goddess, what a lucky escape. Imagine if he'd come along seconds later and found his true mate in the throes of death. Luc shook off the shivers the thought gave him.

Luc had never expected to find his true mate, and given the complication of his desire for men, he had assumed he'd never mate with an omega. Yet along came Thierry, the beautiful, anomalous surprise. The Goddess was good. She'd blessed them as surely as she'd created them for each other.

But Thierry came along with new responsibilities at the exact moment when Luc's exciting—but so far charmed—life seemed to be crashing around his ears. The forest that he loved, the people whom he protected, were in grave danger. Their troubles and Thierry seemed likely connected.

They entered his homely living quarters where he took both of Thierry's hands in his and drew him to the bed.

"Please sit."

Thierry obediently sat, biting his lip, no doubt wondering what to expect.

"I hope you know having a mate is as new to me as it is to you." Luc laughed nervously. "I'm not entirely sure what to do with you."

"If it helps," Thierry offered earnestly, "I grew up on a farm. I have the basic idea. But it's probably different when the partners are both men—"

"Dear Goddess. No." Luc wanted to die. "I meant because we've only just met, and we're in the middle of a deadly magical crisis, and you...you're very young."

"I'm almost eighteen."

"Goddess give me strength." Luc scrubbed at his face to give himself time to think.

"My birthday is in"—Thierry counted on his fingers—"five days."

"And that's an excellent reason for us to take the time to get to know one another." Luc was only twenty-seven, but he felt generations older than his mate, who was very beautiful and who looked at him like he was some kind of god. Thierry presented temptation Luc had never before experienced. All Luc had to do was reach out and take what he'd been offered.

Oh dear Goddess, no. He was a rational man, not an animal.

"You take the bed," Luc ordered. "I'll light the fire and sleep on the floor."

"This bed is big enough for both of us," said Thierry. "Growing up, I slept with two of my brothers in a smaller one."

"It's fine. I don't mind." Luc really didn't need the temptation.

Thierry gave an eyeroll. "If we must sleep apart, then I'll take the floor. You need your rest if you're to lead your people with any hope of success."

"The thing is"—Luc pulled a chair away from his desk and

drew it over so he could sit facing Thierry—"I don't really lead them. We're more of a collective."

"Don't be silly. They look to you for guidance."

"I don't know why." Luc sighed. "Several of them are older than I am. Many have life experience I can't claim."

"Perhaps they see your heart." Thierry poked his chest. "You want what's best for them. You ask for their ideas. You don't lord about, ordering people to do things. You're a natural leader."

"You learned all this in one day?"

"Maybe it's the mate bond." Thierry picked up a blanket off the end of the cot and laid it out before starting a small fire in the hearth. Once it was crackling softly, he lay on his back and tucked his arm beneath his head. "Maybe that's how I see what's inside you so clearly."

"All right." Luc took off his boots and lay down facing the fire and his unexpected mate.

"I never thought I'd find a mate either," Thierry said. "Let alone one who is Goddess given."

"What about your young mage? Charles, was it?"

"He wanted me, and for a single night, I thought we might be together. If he'd lived, he'd have offered for me."

"I'm sorry you lost him." In the light of the fire, the boy's shoulder-length brown hair glowed with glints of red and gold.

"Charles deserved so much more. He was decent and bright and magically gifted. I would have been content to stay and work on the farm, but he had a real future."

"You want a simple life? A farm?"

"It's not as if I know anything different." Thierry pursed his lips. "I guess I made myself like it because I had no other options. What about you? People talk about thieves in the forest. I had no idea you were building a whole town."

"We're not thieves," Luc said gruffly.

"Oh. I'm sorry. I heard—"

"We're not *only* thieves." Luc rested his arm over his eyes. "Every day, merchants bring luxurious goods past little towns like Amivienne, heading for the capital where the highborn think nothing of spending an honest man's yearly wages on pepper."

Thierry turned his head. "Specifically pepper?"

"That was an example. Do you know where they get that money? From taxing the burghers and the shopkeepers and the farmers like your father."

"I've never seen pepper. What is it?"

"It's a spice." Luc laughed. "It makes you sneeze if you take too much of it."

"Did you know that the leaves and shoots of a plant are herbs, and the bark and seeds are spices?"

"I did know that," Luc answered.

"Charles told me. Honestly, Charles was so far above me his mother would never have let him offer for me. And of course, it's not even legal here for a man to mate with another man. He told me that in Helionne people are more modern. He said things are changing everywhere."

"They are."

"Charles was made of wonderful dreams," Thierry said wistfully. "I never wanted to ruin things for him, so I let him have them, but I foresaw a lifetime of farming and isolation in my future."

"Not anymore, I hope."

"Not anymore." Thierry lifted onto one elbow and peered up at him. "But I don't know what you're made of yet."

Luc studied the long, strong lines of Thierry's body. The breadth of his shoulders. The fetching curve of his ass.

Luc wasn't made of dreams, but neither was he made of stone. He covered his eyes with his arm again and sighed. What was he to do with a mate? He had nothing to offer. A shack in the middle of the woods and a one-way trip to the hangman if he and his little tribe were caught in the act of relieving merchants and tax men of some of their gold.

He doubted his father would let it get quite that far.

No, his father wouldn't let their blood be spilled for any reason, but imprisonment was a risk that Luc accepted. His people were willing to live and die with him, but how could he ask this lovely, lovely boy to do the same?

He owed his Goddess-given mate more than the life of a camp follower. He felt the pull of Thierry even now as if he'd been mesmerized. The desire to touch Thierry, to hold him, was as strong as blind, drunken lust but so elementally different.

His need for his mate wasn't about sating his cock. He would die if he couldn't be near him. He wanted to caress Thierry's forehead and smooth the hair that fell over his eyes, to make certain his blanket covered him properly, to keep watch so no harm could befall him. Luc wanted to hold his mate in his arms. It killed Luc to ignore those needs.

The boy's chest rose and fell slowly.

In sleep, he looked even younger than his years.

Luc was a proud man. He had principles. He had scruples. He stole from the rich, he stole from the king's tax collectors, but he didn't keep the money for himself. He distributed what he gained among people who had given up on life in the cities. Those who took refuge from high taxes, thankless work, and masters who treated them like serfs and not free men.

Luc had fled to the forest to be free of his father's expectations and those of the Royal Academy, the strictest school of magic in the world. He'd never seen himself as anything more than a rebel, a man who didn't give two shits about what happened to him, and now…

He'd found his true mate and the truth had found him.

I care very much what happens to me now.

This was the worst possible time for love. Luc was the worst possible choice for a wonder like Thierry. *The Goddess must have a plan or else She is surely having a laugh.*

"Is there anything I can do to help you sleep?" Thierry asked.

"Did I wake you?"

Thierry chuckled. "Your emotions apparently affect me when something's wrong."

"I have a lot on my mind," Luc prevaricated. "That's all."

Thierry didn't respond. Luc had a horrible thought. "Can you tell when I'm glossing over the truth?"

Thierry seemed to consider his answer. "It's your business what you choose to tell me."

"I'm sorry." Luc blew out a breath.

"You have your reasons."

"You're too forgiving. I will never lie to you, but I might omit things."

"You mean things like what will become of your people if anything happens to you?" Thierry turned to him, pupils swallowing the rich brown of his irises in the dim light. "And whether you'll figure out how to stop the necromancer before he kills someone else? And if you have what it takes to defeat him?"

"Something like that," Luc said dryly.

"You're frightened for the first time in your life because you have something new to lose. Do you really believe this is the worst possible time for the Goddess to have given you your true mate?"

Luc cleared his throat. "Keeping you in the dark isn't going to be easy, is it?"

"Tell me why you'd want to, and maybe I'll pretend."

Giving in to the temptation to move closer, Luc threw his legs over the side of the bed and went to his mate. He sat cross-legged by Thierry's side and gave up fighting the desire for connection. He clasped Thierry's hand between his own.

"I want to be worthy."

"Of what?" Thierry asked. "Me? You have nothing to worry about. You're worth ten of—"

"Don't say things like that. It hurts my heart to hear them."

Thierry's eyes widened. "All right."

"You are a gift from the Goddess, Thierry. Much longed for and badly needed. I want to be worthy of Her faith in me. I want to take good care of you. Keep you safe and well."

"I feel the same way. You're the alpha, but I'm no less grateful and no less concerned about my responsibility toward you."

"I didn't think of it that way."

"I'm wise beyond my years."

Luc snorted. "Don't make me laugh."

"No, really. My ma says that all the time."

"I imagine she does."

"What does that mean?" The lad puffed up like an angry kitten. "I'll have you know that I'm strong, and clever, and you're lucky to have me."

A smile found its way to Luc's lips. "That's more like it."

"Did you honestly provoke me so I'd say something nice about myself?"

"I did."

"Blast, you're going to be a typical alpha, aren't you? All wiser-than-thou and follow-along-blindly or else."

"I'm not that bad." Luc insinuated his arm beneath Thierry's neck and scooted his body as close as might be decent. He breathed in the sweat-and-sunshine scent of his mate's hair and found his hand. Thierry linked their fingers together.

This was better. He couldn't bear to go back to his bed, lose contact, and have his nerves jangling. His head ached when they weren't touching. He hoped that particular side effect of finding his true mate wouldn't last. Things could get awkward.

Luc didn't mind betraying his yearning for his mate. He felt tired and content, and yes, sleepy now that Thierry was close…

He filled his lungs with the sweet omega fragrance that said *mate,* and *mine,* and even *beloved,* though how could that be? He'd barely known the boy for a day.

"I know you well enough." The words left Luc on a sort of sigh.

"Me too," Thierry replied sleepily.

"Now give me a corner of that blanket and budge up since you're absorbing all the heat from the fire."

Thierry pulled the blanket over both of them as he dragged Luc under his spell and into their future, which still held all manner of worries that even his mate's soft skin and warm scent were no match for.

Please, he thought. *Please. Let me keep him. Let me be worthy.*

Though sleep found him, his dreams were troubled.

~

Mathilde delivered oat cakes and mugs of steaming nettle tea to Luc's door the following morning along with a cheeky leer.

"Don't even think it," he told her before going back inside where he left Thierry's share of food and a mug on the desk. He returned to Mathilde and closed his door behind him. "Thierry won't even be eighteen for four more days."

"Soon enough, I think, and you're his mate. What does it matter? The Goddess gave you a gift—"

"It's—I don't know. It's a line I draw." The outlaw on his shoulder was counting down the days, but his better nature made him queasy about claiming someone so young.

"Four days will bring the full moon. It could bring on the boy's first heat. You should prepare yourself for that, Luc. I may be an old woman, but even I know what happens when a Goddess-blessed omega is mated and the moon is full."

"We have bigger things to worry about." Though now, he'd worry about that too. "I plan to take Thierry to the Temple of the Merciful Moon to discuss the situation with Aunt Luna. She's probably worried sick."

"She won't have sent any of the sisters to the forest after Thierry, given the danger. I have to tell her what happened. Those poor men—the sheriff—their families should be informed."

"Will you do that?"

He shook his head. "After I talk with her, I'm heading to Avimasse. There are still a few people I can trust, and we need information. Can you let the others know?"

"The capital is no place for an outlaw, Luc. I hope you know what you're doing." Blue eyes bright in her weathered face, she nodded. "John isn't well enough yet—"

"I'll place Peter in charge until he is."

"There are those who won't understand why you'd leave under these circumstances. They'll worry it's because of your mate, that you're deserting us."

"You know better, I hope."

"Of course I do." She quirked her lips. "I'm not talking about me."

"I can't fight this necromancer unless I know more. I'll be back when I've learned something. We'll fight this monster side by side like always. Glory or shadows. Tell them that."

She brushed a stray lock of his hair behind his ear. "You are such a good boy."

"Oh, for Goddess's sake." He pulled away. "Thank you for breakfast."

"I'll pray for your safety and that of your mate."

"I'll pray for you as well."

"Bah." Mathilde turned away with a sniff that she wanted him to think was disdain. "I'm so old even death doesn't want me."

He let her go, but before he left his cottage to warn his best fighters what they were up against, he peeked inside his place.

Embers glowed in the hearth, putting out enough warmth to keep the boy cozy, and he'd have food when he woke, yet leaving Thierry alone was still painful. Luc forced himself to close the door between them though it was the last thing he wanted to do. He had much to get ready before they could leave.

Luc had a greater duty. He had people depending on him. He needed to return to his old life in order to fight this necromancer.

Luc had so much to lose the weight crushed his spirit, but he had Thierry now too.

He had Thierry, and he had to win.

CHAPTER 11

Thierry woke alone. Or rather he sensed nothing but a wisp of Charles's magic.

Are you there?

"I am." Charles didn't sound any happier than he had the night before. "I think I'll stay away when you're alone with Fluke."

Don't be mean.

"As you wish."

Don't be jealous of Luc. He's my Goddess blessed. Anyway, you know your mother would have never let us be together.

"She might have. I could have brought her around eventually."

No, never. It's time to stop lying to yourself. Your mother wanted far better things for you than me.

"He left you food." Charles's magic skittered aimlessly from one corner of the small room to another.

He did? Thierry rose from the floor. *How sweet.*

"You can speak to me normally, you know. Since you've been rescued and you've got your voice back."

Thierry knew he could do that, but he didn't want to.

I like that we can talk without others overhearing. Is it all right with you if I don't talk out loud?

Charles's magic settled around him. "Won't your Goddess-blessed mate get angry?"

So what if he does? This is our way, and you're important to me.

"All right." A bit of fizz let Thierry know that Charles's sour mood was lifting. "I like our way."

Me too.

Thierry drank his mug of tea and ate his oatcakes. It was plain fare, very much like the food he'd get at home. He got the feeling Luc wasn't born to this life or at least he hadn't been raised rough. He was too refined and too well spoken to have spent his whole life in the forest. Luc was a mystery Thierry looked forward to solving. For now, he pulled on his borrowed boots and left the hut, looking for the man himself.

"Luc's at John's cottage now, dear. Look for Peter," Mathilde called as soon as he set foot outside. "Luc didn't want to wake you."

"Thanks, Mathilde." He waved to the old woman and went on his way wearing a polite smile. He hadn't yet won anyone's approval—except maybe hers. He needed these people to like him. His position was made clearer when he spotted Peter's bulky form standing guard outside another of the freshly built cottages.

"Where do you think you're going?" Peter asked.

"I thought I'd visit with John to see how he's faring."

"Sorry." Peter blocked the way. "Grown-ups are talking. You'll have to come back later."

"Oh..." Should he press the issue or wait until later? He needed to find out what Luc had planned so he could get ready. He decided to be *meekly* insistent, but before he could say anything, the door opened, and Luc stuck his head out.

"Thierry? Is everything all right?" He glanced between Thierry and Peter. "What's going on here?"

"I was about to knock." Thierry smiled to smooth things over, but he doubted Peter appreciated the gesture. "How's John?"

"Come inside and see for yourself." Still studying Peter's face, Luc opened the door wide for Thierry.

John and Serafina looked well rested and relieved. John's color was back to normal, or—Thierry corrected himself—John's cheeks had color as opposed to the bloodless, clammy skin of the night before. That was good. Their cottage was identical to Luc's, except it bore Serafina's warm touch. Several colorful throws and bright cushions drew his eye. There were two small pallets against the wall, but he guessed the children were still staying with friends.

"It's good to see you looking well." Thierry put the back of his hand to John's forehead. "No fever."

"He's greatly improved." Serafina squeezed John's hand before rising to greet Thierry. "Have you eaten?"

"Yes, thank you." He turned to Luc. "Have you decided on a plan?"

"Yes, and it involves you. Come and sit." While Serafina saw to John, Luc took a chair at their table. Thierry took the chair facing him.

"You and I will return to the Temple of the Merciful Moon. I need to speak with Mother Luna and tell her what happened to your escort. I'm hoping you'll resume your ruse so I can escort you anonymously. How does that sound?"

"We can do that."

"Is it safe?" asked Serafina.

"The attacks have all occurred at night" Luc reasoned. "As long as we go during the day, we should be fine."

"Whatever you think best," said Thierry.

"I don't want you to worry," Luc told him.

"I'm the nitwit who allowed himself to be bait, remember?" Thierry grinned at his mate. "I have faith you'll keep me safe, Mate."

Mate. How Thierry loved that word. He loved belonging, which felt so much more powerful than being part of a family by an accident of birth ever had. He loved having someone of his own.

Thierry was new to feeling wanted. Feeling cared for and loved.

Luc—the very idea of having a mate—was a breadcrumb tossed into still water. All Thierry's thoughts and senses were minnows fighting over him.

He glanced up to find a knowing smile on Luc's face. "You're thinking about me?"

Thierry's face caught fire. They had an audience, and it didn't do to act like a lovesick fool, especially since he wanted credibility with Luc's men.

"I hung up your cloak." Serafina removed the red garment from the clothespress. "You might not be one of the Sisters of the Merciful Moon, but you certainly deserve to be called a healer. Thank you."

"It was Charles's doing. I barely know a cabbage from a rose."

"Whatever led you to us, it was the Goddess's blessing. May we be worthy." John held his hand out.

"Be well." Thierry took John's hand in both his own.

"Travel safely, my friends." They shook warmly.

"We will, John." Luc's hand felt like a brand on the small of Thierry's back. "Peter will look after things until you're ready to take the reins again."

"Aye. He's a good lad."

"Make sure you tell the sisters to stay away from the woods," Serafina advised. "We'll do what we can here to help—"

"Oh, I almost forgot." Thierry glanced toward Luc. "There's a Grandmother Ellis living somewhere on the path near where we were attacked. She's elderly and not well. The food and herbal preparation I gave you were meant for her. Is there anything you can do to see that she's cared for?"

"We don't know how to replace the preparation, but we can see that she gets food."

"Perhaps Charles can help me make another? I'll try if you have what we need. She has a worsening cough."

All the herbs they had available had been moved to John's home, so when he asked, Charles walked him through the process of making an elixir for a cough. He also taught Thierry how to activate it with magic, which took an hour during which Luc's impatience to leave bled through their mate bond like a strong whiff of smoke.

"Ready to go?" Luc asked when he'd at last stoppered the vial.

"Yes, thank you for waiting."

"Mrs. Ellis needs this." Luc softened his gaze. "I understand."

"Thank you." *And thank you, Charles, you're a knight in shining armor.*

"Just not yours." Charles's reply was one of resignation. "I'm sure I'll learn to exist with disappointment."

You know, most dead people would be glad to have friends.

"How many dead people do you know?" Charles's magic gave him a push.

"Whoa." Luc caught him. "What was that? Was that him? Did he just *shove* you?"

"Oh, for Goddess's sake."

"No, where is he?" Luc glanced around. "I'll teach him to shove my mate!"

"Exactly how is he going to do that?" asked Charles.

Not now, you.

"I asked you a question, *Mate*."

"Oh, here comes the alpha voice." Charles laughed gleefully. "Best not to tell him that never works on you."

"Both of you, *stop*!" Thierry could only see Luc's widened eyes, but he rarely raised his voice, so Charles should have been surprised as well. "I'm ready to go, Luc."

Luc said nothing but held his hand out. Thierry took it and allowed himself to be ushered from John and Serafina's cottage.

"I'm glad I'm not in your shoes, Luc," John called after them. "Your mate's got a bit of a temper."

Luc turned back at the door. "And yours doesn't?"

"You don't mind the row"—Serafina gave them a saucy smile—"if making up is sweet enough."

"Oh, ew." Charles's magic whirled dramatically up the chimney.

Ashes stirred in his wake.

Serafina asked, "Was that—"

"Yes." Thierry picked up his red cloak. "He enjoys a memorable exit. I hope to see you soon."

"Farewell." Serafina closed the door behind them.

They had to pass by Peter. Luc stopped to have a word.

"I'm entrusting you to look after our people until John is well. Can you do that?"

"'Course I can." Peter shot a glance at Thierry. "It's him I don't trust."

"I've no need for your advice as far as my mate goes." Luc leaned on the word to get his point across. "I expect you to be civil to him despite your misgivings. Understand?"

"Understood, sir."

Luc dismissed him, but to Thierry's senses he remained agitated over the man's earlier slight. Before Luc could say more, Thierry slipped his hand into Luc's.

"Leave it. I'm no threat, but he doesn't know that. You're not infallible. Be glad you have others to watch your back."

"I am glad, but when someone upsets you, honestly, I want to kill them and wear their rib cage as a crown."

Thierry cleared his throat to cover his delight.

"This is new for both of us," Thierry assured him. "And I feel the same. I'm tougher than I look. And stealthy. No one had better harm you while I'm around."

Luc put his arm around Thierry's shoulders and walked him back to his place where Thierry once again put on the robe, wimple, and red cloak of the Order of the Merciful Moon.

"I will never get over how pretty you are." Luc cupped his face. "Thank the Goddess you're not actually one of the sisters. I'm afraid I might transgress greatly."

"Very funny."

Luc tilted his head up. "I'm serious."

"All right." Thierry waited, holding his breath, hoping for a kiss, *the* kiss, the one from his true mate, the one that would make all other kisses—even though he'd only received one—pale by comparison.

That kiss did not come.

Instead, Luc's raven friend flew in the window.

"Mate, mate, mate," it warbled. "Luc. Mate."

"Goddess. He's been saying that since we met," said Thierry. "What an extraordinary bird."

"That's one word for him." Luc lifted his elbow, and Silence landed on his arm. "Come, meet Silence."

"That's his name?"

"It's what I call him, as he rarely shuts up." Luc stroked beneath his beak affectionately. "We met when I went to the Royal Academy. I think he felt sorry for me because I don't make friends easily."

"That's a flagrant falsehood based on my observations."

"It's different here. In the city, everyone knew who my father was and that he didn't regard me with favor."

"I see."

"Silence quite literally took me under his wing."

"He's wonderful."

"Speaking of which, I need him for something." He set the bird down on the table and got out his quill and ink before cutting a long strip of parchment. "Silence will take a message to my old mentor so he knows to expect us."

He carefully wrote and dried the ink then rolled up the parchment and attached it to one of Silence's legs. He said something quietly before lifting the bird and taking him outside. Thierry followed, excited to watch them.

"Take this to Master Cavendish," Thierry said. "Cavendish. Got it?"

The bird bobbed its sleek head. "Cavendish."

Together, Thierry and Luc watched the bird circle overhead and fly away to the north.

Rather, Thierry watched Luc watching his friend. The bond between the two was special, powerful. It was as mysterious as Thierry's bond with Charles or even their mate bond. For a single instant, Thierry got a glimpse of the way everything and everyone connected under the Goddess moon, and then he lost it as if it was simply too big to keep inside him.

Thierry threw off a trancelike state similar to the one that had held him in thrall before their almost kiss. Charles's kiss had been filled with kindness and hopes and dreams.

Would Luc's kiss be a lightning strike followed by a thunderclap of passion by which they'd be swept helplessly away? Thierry hoped so. His cheeks heated just imagining it, and he had to turn away to catch his breath.

Luc cupped his shoulders and drew him close, Thierry's back to Luc's chest.

He pressed a scruff-roughened cheek against Thierry's.

"It's not that I don't feel what's between us. I do," Luc whispered. "But my heart says this isn't the time to act on it. Do you trust me?"

"Of course I trust you." Thierry covered Luc's hands with his own, his arms forming an *X* over his chest like a vow.

"Then trust me to know when the time to claim you is right."

Thierry leaned back and let his head fall against Luc's shoulder. They stayed like that, with their hands clasped and their cheeks touching, for a minute more.

Luc's touch was medicine. It was sunshine, and clean water, and berries still warm from the heat of the day. It was an afternoon spent swimming in a cool pond when Thierry should have been at work. It was a night under the stars, bathing in the light of the Goddess moon.

Thierry never wanted to move again.

"Wherever this takes us, we go together," he vowed.

"Together," Luc agreed and pressed a kiss to his temple.

Luc let go first. Thierry didn't have the will. If there was anything to this alpha superiority business, it was the drive that made him move forward when an omega like Thierry would be content to curl up and relax.

Alphas were big-picture wolves. They were achievers, conquerors, warriors, kings. They didn't allow a perfect moment in the present to deter them from their goals as Thierry might, and they paid the price for their achievements with the heavy responsibility of leadership.

Even weak alphas like Thierry's father had goals. He had pride, the urge to dominate, and the nerve to see his schemes through despite what they cost him. Alphas never stopped, always rolling the dice for the next gamble and the next.

Luc was the better man. His goals were noble. Thierry could wager his heart on Luc, his life even. Faith was such a subtle thing, but he saw the truth in wonder. He had faith in his mate. Blind faith. He'd walk through fire to be with Luc and accept the consequences.

"It's a long walk to the Temple." Luc interrupted his thoughts. "Will you be all right in borrowed boots?"

He'd arrived wearing the standard slippers of the Order of the Merciful Moon. Though they were serviceable, every pebble and pinecone he'd stepped on had hurt his feet. The boots Luc had loaned him had thicker soles, plus they still bore the impressions of Luc's heels, high arches, and individual toes.

It was ridiculous, of course, but it felt as if he was wearing Luc's feet.

"Do you have an extra pair of socks?"

"I do." Luc pressed their foreheads together. "I like when you wear my clothes."

"Alpha nonsense," Thierry said fondly, even though he'd been thinking the same thing.

"We'll put the others in your basket along with some ordinary clothes for you."

"Thank you."

Thierry let Luc pack whatever he thought they'd need. He carried his basket, and Luc had a leather satchel with straps that went over his shoulders.

"Ready?" Luc asked.

"As I'll ever be." Thierry was loath to leave the serenity of Luc's forest home behind.

Things could have been so simple, but that would have required turning a blind eye to the danger they all faced at the hands of the necromancer. Luc wouldn't do that. Luc felt responsible for these people and all the others in Hemlock Forest.

Luc was Thierry's mate now, and with him came his responsibilities, his needs, his desire...Oh, desire was something Thierry couldn't wait to explore.

Together, they said goodbye to the confusing mob of Luc's friends, some of whom insisted on walking part of the way with them, but they would only accompany them so far before they had their own journeys to make.

Luc was his, and Thierry meant to go the distance wherever

life took them. He'd walk by his alpha's side into the shadowlands if he must.

He hoped it wouldn't come to that. Not before he got his kiss anyway. Luc laced their fingers together. So far, so good. They weren't dead.

So far...

CHAPTER 12

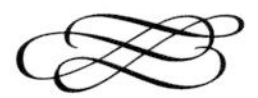

It was noon by the time Thierry and Luc arrived at the Temple of the Merciful Moon. They were greeted with mixed reactions. Many of the sisters had come to know and respect Sheriff Lavigne. He'd always been fair to everyone—championing omegas even before they had legal standing. He'd seen it as his responsibility to keep travelers safe in Hemlock Forest.

The sisters escorted Thierry and Luc to Mother Luna's office straightaway, though all they had to give her was terrible news.

"When you didn't return, I was afraid there had been another attack." Her face went pale when they entered alone—dressed as they were—to face her behind her highly polished desk. She sat heavily as they told her everything that had happened. "Oh, merciful Goddess, those poor men."

"They were picking off members of Thierry's escort in stealth. I arrived in time to conceal Thierry, but my men were too late to do more than slay the beasts after the fact. The bastard mage got away." As seemed typical, Luc was ready to bear the burden of guilt. "The creatures are dead, but their master doubtless thrives."

"I was afraid of that." She tapped her fingers on her desk. "I cannot fathom this. Why have the mages at the Academy in Amivienne not acted against this malevolent practitioner? I have written to Director Chaubert personally, and so far, I've received no response."

"Perhaps it's simply taking time for them to formulate a plan of action?" Thierry offered, although he knew nothing of the workings of mages.

"There are already plans in place for such a thing." Luc tightened his fists as he spoke. "The League set forth specific guidelines a century ago so something like this could never happen. If my men and I had only gotten there sooner, I'd have learned more. The sheriff and his men might still be alive."

"If not for you," Thierry argued, "I wouldn't be alive."

"He's right. You aren't to blame for the work of a madman." Mother Luna took in Luc's shabby woodsman's disguise. "What on earth are you wearing?"

"I'm incognito." He gave her a soft smile. "Just another wanderer, providing escort for one of the Merciful Sisters."

"You look like some nobleman's quaint idea of a peasant. But look at that smile. Those teeth never lived with famine." She stood. "Come here, and let me embrace you properly, Luc."

He did as she asked, towing Thierry with him. They each received a warm hug from the high priestess, who smelled like incense and honey and reminded Thierry a bit of his mother. Thierry blinked his burning eyes. Would he ever see his family again, or was he now cut off from them as his father wanted?

"How came you to rescue Thierry? Had you heard news of the murders?"

Luc nodded. "Bad news finds its way to my ears quickly. I was hoping to catch the bastard when I came upon the attack in progress. It was a ghastly scene. Only by the will of the Goddess did I arrive in time to save this one." Luc put his hand on Thierry's shoulder fondly.

She studied them. "The Goddess is good."

"May we be worthy," Thierry and Luc answered in unison.

"Lucas, do I sense—" She clasped her hands over her heart. "Is that a mate bond?"

Thierry was delighted to see Lucas blush to the roots of his black hair.

"It's true that Thierry is my Goddess given, but we haven't—er—sealed our union."

"Oh, this is blessed news. My word. Congratulations!" She hugged each of them again. "We must have a feast when you're ready to celebrate."

"Thank you, Mother Luna." Luc bit his lip. "In due time."

Thierry hid his laughter. This—*this*—was the best thing ever. Seeing Luc act as shy as a schoolboy in front of Mother Luna was a memory to cherish.

"Luc..." She seemed to hesitate, gave a quick glance at Thierry, and then said, "You realize the full moon is three days hence."

"Of course." Luc nodded grimly.

"What about it?" Thierry wanted to know.

"Wait for it." The bright fizz of Charles's magic seemed to ruffle Thierry's hair.

Mother Luna's quizzical expression showed that she registered Charles's magic somehow. She didn't acknowledge it, but her gaze followed him the way Thierry had learned to do.

"Should you fall pregnant, do you know how to care for yourself to ensure the safety of the child?"

"Should I fall...What?" Mother Luna and Luc stared at him as if they knew something he didn't.

"It's a likely outcome of your first heat with your Goddess blessed." Mother Luna acted as though everyone knew this. "Has no one ever talked to you about your omega nature?"

Was this a joke?

They were acting so serious. Ominously serious.

No. Oh no. He was omega, but he'd never considered the possible consequences. Who in their right mind would? He was a male. He had male parts. He couldn't get…but perhaps he could.

Darkness encroached from the periphery of Thierry's vision. He wasn't prepared to fall, but the floor came at his face, and that was all he knew until he woke to find Luc pale as a ghost and Mother Luna waving some noxious concoction beneath his nose.

"There, are you with us again?" she asked. "Luc very nearly lost control of his wolf."

"I did not." A threatening growl belied his words.

"Snap out of it, Luc. You don't want everyone to see you in fur with your small clothes dragging behind you. You're supposed to have better control."

"I admit nothing." Luc stroked Thierry's hair back from his face. "Hello, sweetling. Do you feel dizzy still?"

"Hello." Thierry's whole body reacted to Luc's dazzling smile.

"Let's get you up." Luc effortlessly lifted him and looked to Mother Luna for directions. "Perhaps if he could rest somewhere for a bit?"

"I'll show you to our guest rooms." She led them out of her office and down a long corridor. "The sisters and I live simply, but we keep quarters for state visitors and benefactors. Some are quite splendid."

"You get visitors often?" asked Thierry.

"Regularly. We even had the king's tax collector here for a time."

"So I heard," said Luc.

"Poor man." Mother Luna's chatelaine jingled with keys and small tools as she started up the stairs. "Apparently, he was set upon by thieves after he left us. It seems they stole all but ten percent of his gold."

"Oh dear," Luc said blandly. "What a shame he was robbed, but as the Goddess is satisfied with a tithe, how can a king expect more?"

"How indeed?" Thierry clearly heard her mutter. "You naughty boy."

Luc carried Thierry up a flight of stairs that turned on a landing and led to a more luxurious corridor. Here, the floor was covered with a thick runner in all shades of deep red, cobalt blue, and violet.

"In here, I think." She used a finely detailed key to open the door to a spacious room with a large bed, a sitting area with a low, cushioned couch, and a table and chairs for private dining. "The sisters will see that you have everything you need. You'll probably wish to wash the journey off. Luc, you know where the bathing rooms are."

A hot bath sounded like paradise to Thierry.

"May I have a few words with Thierry alone?" asked Mother Luna

Luc frowned. "I wish to stay with my mate."

"Not for this, I think. Thierry and I have omega business to discuss, and I would prefer it if you would find Selene and have her send Mayor Levain word of the attack on the sheriff and his men. We must inform their families and organize assistance for their widows," she fretted. "At least two of his men had young children. Tell Selene I will send word of the incident to Director Chaubert myself."

"I'll see it done."

"Don't worry, Luc." Her lips quirked into a gentle smile. "I'll take care of your mate."

He nodded, shot a last longing glance at Thierry, and slipped silently out the door.

"That one has always been stealthy as a cat." Mother Luna

helped Thierry to one of the two luxurious chairs at the small dining table. "Be warned, you'll never hear him sneak up on you."

"It seems you know Luc well?" he marveled. "How did you meet?"

"I caught him when he arrived into the world." She laughed at his expression. "Lucas's mother was my sister. Did he not tell you?"

Thierry's eyes widened. "He never said anything."

"He thinks he's protecting my reputation and the good name of the Order." Mother Luna was the aunt of a notorious outlaw. No wonder he'd been welcomed with open arms. Her expression grew wistful. "Verna died along with Luc's baby brother the following year."

"Oh no." It hurt Thierry's heart to imagine Luc as a motherless toddler. Thierry adored his mother. She'd been the only softness in his life. "What was she like?"

"Wild. Lovely." From her expression, her memories were fond but complicated. "She never did conform to Rheilôme society's rules, but she was well liked. Her heart was reckless, exactly like her son's, but alas, she didn't have his alpha status. Had Verna been born a boy and an alpha, she'd have remade the world."

"I wish I could have known her."

"I miss her." She sighed. "Thierry, have you discussed what it means to be omega with anyone? Your mother or sisters, perhaps?"

"Ah, no. Not really."

"I see." She pursed her lips. "That's normally the way omegas learn about their bodies. Omega mothers pass knowledge along to their daughters, or older sisters take up the mantle in the case when a mother isn't around."

Thierry blushed. "Pa wouldn't let anyone discuss my status.

He kept me isolated. I know a lot about farm work but not much else."

She placed her hand over his. "I knew the sheriff brought you to us because your father tried to sell you, but I had no idea there was such repression involved. Things must have been hard for you."

The table where they sat was placed beside a row of tall, narrow windows overlooking the kitchen gardens. The scene was familiar and serene—the sisters picking vegetables for the Order's table.

"I was lonely. I worked as hard as I could. My brothers protected me at school when I was young. After my friend Charles died, I was no longer allowed to attend."

"I'm so sorry."

"It's fine." He shrugged. "Charles was the clever one. He went to the Academy. I was going to end up on the farm anyway, so school wasn't as important."

"It's Charles's magic that follows you, isn't it?" She waved a hand as if to scatter gnats. "Obviously, the attack on him didn't drain him of his magic. It makes me wonder whether there's a different mage attacking omegas now, or if the same mage who killed Charles is growing in skill. To what end, though?"

"Luc thinks it's the same person."

"It is unlikely that two different death magic practitioners could escape the Academy's notice. Director Chaubert should have mages out searching for him. He should have notified the League by now."

"Are you certain he hasn't?"

"If he had, by now we'd be entertaining League members in this suite instead of you."

"Why do you think they're turning a blind eye? What reason could they have?"

She frowned. "I don't know."

"I've always wondered why Charles's murderer was never brought to justice."

"I've wondered about that too." She stared out the window. "But for now, that's alpha business. Ours is slightly more mundane. We need to talk about heats."

His face flamed. "Oh."

"Is your mother living?"

He nodded. "She is."

"Did she never discuss your omega body with you?"

"Ma had other things to do. There were seven of us." Despite an attempt at calm, his face heated again. "My body's no different from my brothers' bodies."

"This is wonderful," said Charles. "I wish I had snacks."

What do you know that I don't? Have you kept it from me on purpose?

"Let's say it never came up," he replied.

Mother Luna mused, "So if your mother never talked to you, I can stand in—"

"I can take care of myself, ma'am. I lived on a farm. I know what a heat is and where things are meant to go—except, you know—my mate is a man, so—" He kept his eyes on the garden where the sisters filled baskets with carrots, peas, and runner beans.

"There are some things common to every omega." She squeezed his arm reassuringly. "Including pregnancy."

Thierry choked. "With due respect, Mother Luna, if I had"—he squeezed his eyes shut—"something for a babe to come out of, I think I would know it."

"Not necessarily. Male omegas are very rare, Thierry, but they do exist. Ancient texts describe the lives of several. They inform us that all omega bear young. In fact, the Sisters of the Moon Temple assisted with the birth of the Princess Bella Aurora of Helionne. The omega earl bore Prince Christopher's healthy daughter only this year."

"But how? I mean, I don't have—"

"It's my understanding that what makes you omega will be noticeable when you require it." She coughed delicately. "This may seem vague, but your status as a male omega is so rare I've never seen one in my lifetime."

A hot-cold feeling crept all over his skin, and the rush of his pulse made his ears ring. At least he was sitting down. "I really could bear a child?"

Mother Luna nodded.

Did he want that? Yes. *Maybe.* Did Luc want children? There had been children in Luc's camp, so being an outlaw didn't stop outlaws from having families.

Would the babe be plain and sturdy like him? Or like Luc—elegant and stealthy and brilliant? Would their child have Luc's soft dark hair and pale eyes or Thierry's plainer mud brown hair and eyes?

A rush of longing filled him.

"This news of the prince's male omega mate comes at a strange time," said Mother Luna. "I wonder…"

When Mother Luna didn't continue, he prompted her. "What?"

"It seems like a sign, doesn't it? Maybe the Goddess is sending male omegas into the world for a reason." It took her a few seconds to shake off whatever had her deep in thought. "What matters now is that the full moon is only three days away, and since you've found your true mate, it will probably bring on your first heat."

"All right." Thierry felt excited and horrified at the same time.

"Heat, ha! And childbearing." Charles's magic, his very essence, seemed to explode in delight. "I bet you didn't see that coming. Oh Goddess, you should see your face."

"Charles," Mother Luna said sternly. The very air seemed to freeze around them.

"Ma'am?" whispered Charles.

"He's listening," Thierry told her.

"Are you an omega, Charles?"

"No ma'am."

"He isn't," Thierry answered for him.

"Then you are not needed for this discussion." Wherever Charles's magic came from, it had met its match in Mother Luna. She smiled, but it didn't reach her eyes. "Please don't make me confine you to a jar like a lightning bug."

Charles melted away like a shadow at dawn.

"Where were we?" Mother Luna said brightly. "Ah, yes. We were talking about heats."

Thierry wished he could disappear into the shadows as easily as Charles had. Instead, he listened dutifully to everything Luc's aunt had to say. There wasn't much to the topic that he didn't already know except that he could fall pregnant and bear young as soon as Luc claimed him. He had a hard time catching his breath for a few minutes.

"There, there. Get hold of yourself." Luna poured him a drink from a decanter filled with amber-colored liquid. The taste was so strong it burned his throat and nostrils. "All straight in your head now?"

He nodded weakly.

"All right, then. You must ask me any further questions you have as they arise."

"When pigs fly, ma'am." Thierry gave the only answer she deserved.

She laughed as though he wasn't serious. Goddess. For the first time, he saw his future clearly. Instead of the great indecipherable, unknown fate that being the only omega of his kind had led him to believe was all he deserved, he could have a life that he wanted.

He could have his mate, children, a home, *everything* if he was brave enough to take it.

"Where did you say the private baths were?" he asked weakly.

"Come. I'll show you." She rose, and he followed, still wearing the red robes of the Sisters of the Merciful Moon. "A nice hot bath may be just what you need."

"It's a start." What he needed was Luc's strong arms around him. Of everything he'd learned since the night his father had dragged him away, the fact he was most certain of was that he and Luc were meant to be together, bound by nature and spirit and immutable will.

Luc had said that this was a terrible time to meet his Goddess-blessed mate. With his body apparently at the mercy of his nature and a mad necromancer on the loose, Thierry had to admit he might be right.

CHAPTER 13

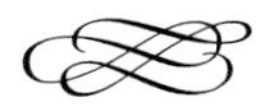

Placing bathing rooms off the kitchen was practical so the sisters didn't have to carry heated water far. Private stalls each contained pegs for hanging garments, a large copper tub, and a wooden bench. There was a shelf for homely soaps and bottles of herbs to scent the water.

Mother Luna had one of the novices prepare his bath with hot water and dried verbena. The novice brought him soap that she assured him was finer milled than the soap the sisters used.

"Mother Luna says you're to have the best." What Thierry could see of the girl's face was fiery red. "She says you've found your fated one. Congratulations, sir. May the Goddess bless your union."

"May I be worthy." He took a linen towel from her and waited for her to leave.

"May I ask, sir. What does it feel like to find your mate?"

"It feels"—he closed his eyes—"like going from winter into spring."

She bowed her head. "Sounds lovely."

"It's astonishing but also a bit frightening. So much is new."

"Thierry?" Luc knocked. "May I come in?"

"Is it all right?" He looked to the girl for permission.

"Of course, sir. I'll just—" She opened the door for Luc and pushed past him as though being pursued.

"I think we scandalized Amelia," Luc said.

"You know her?"

"I'm a frequent visitor, so I know most of the sisters. That's why I was trying to capture the killer. Losing Sister Meredith was a terrible blow to Mother Luna."

"Your aunt. She told me of your relationship. She adores you."

Luc buffed his nails on his jerkin. "Because I'm adorable. Haven't you noticed?"

"I did notice." Thierry glanced at the bathwater, which gave off sweetly fragrant steam. "It seems a waste that this whole lovely bath is only for me."

Fingers caught his jaw. "You would share it with me?"

"Of course. I'm used to sharing with all my brothers and sisters. Do you wish to go first?"

Luc smirked. "That's not entirely what I had in mind, sweetheart."

"Oh." Thierry's face heated as soon as he understood. "Excellent idea, Mate. That way, neither of us would have to bathe in cold water."

"Aye, we *could* share while it's hot." Luc's gentle fingers caressed his jaw. "But I still believe we must go slow. We're not exactly in the position to—"

"Mother Luna told me about the full moon," Thierry blurted.

"What did she tell you?"

"That I'll go into heat and probably bear a child from our… um…union. Why wait if it's only three days?" Thierry pulled his shirt over his head and hung it on a peg. When he turned, he caught Luc's audible swallow. "Like something you see?"

"It's possible you won't." Luc cleared his throat. "Go into

heat, I mean. There's a chance we haven't been together long enough, or—"

"And if I did?" Thierry wasn't stupid. His parents had seven children. He was aware—since his talk with Mother Luna—that he'd grow as mindless with need as his mother did sometimes, and it would require all of Luc's patience and stamina to see him through. While he didn't care to think of himself as unable to control himself, the Goddess made him an omega for a reason. He hoped. "What then?"

"You're my mate." Luc's voice roughened. "What do you think? I'd ride into the shadowlands for you."

"That might be fun." Thierry shot him a grin.

"You're a vixen, not a wolf." Luc's expression lost all solemnity.

"Maybe I've been waiting all my life to act vixenish, and here we are."

"Here we are." Luc leaned toward him. Thierry strained toward Luc. It didn't matter who initiated their kiss, but as soon as they touched, they wrapped their arms around each other and let their passion fly.

Luc plundered Thierry's mouth with dizzying force. Thierry had to grasp Luc's shoulders because after the morning he'd had and Mother Luna's amber liquid courage, he wasn't any too steady on his feet.

"You've been drinking?" Luc pulled back. "Not fair. You taste delicious."

"Mother Luna gave me something."

"My wily aunt."

"Please." Thierry pulled him back. "Kiss me some more."

"Soon, Mate. I promise." Luc stepped back and wrapped both hands around the back of his neck. "Things are so chaotic, there's a murderer on the loose, and you've not yet come of age..."

"Three days," Thierry argued.

"Yes." Luc caught his hands. "Three days in which anything could happen. It's not safe to lose focus right now."

"Don't you want me?" Thierry couldn't help how his voice sounded. Small. Uncertain. Wholly different from the image he wanted to project.

"Oh, sweetling." Luc's gaze lifted to the ceiling. "If you only knew how much."

"What are you going to do if Mother Luna is right, and I go into heat? Will you lock me away like a lunatic until it's over just to satisfy your desire to be a gentleman?"

"I will always put your needs first." Luc gripped his upper arms tightly. "You are the most important thing—person—in my life. I need to do right by you. Do you hate me for wanting to wait until your heat?"

"No." Thierry blew out a breath. "Of course not."

"Get in your bath while it's still hot." Luc knelt to help Thierry shuck his boots before he removed the rest of his clothes. He didn't look Thierry's way once he was naked. Luc thought him too young. Wasn't that just *great.*

Thierry stepped into the tub, and Luc slipped out the door to give him privacy.

Maybe Thierry was too young for his mate. Too unsophisticated. Luc could have his choice of omega women and any man who was inclined to enjoy other men.

Given Thierry's ignorance of some pretty vital facts of life—and his omega body—perhaps Luc needed time to get used to the idea that he was mated to Thierry. Ignorance wasn't necessarily attractive.

Thierry spread his fingers over his taut, muscled belly.

There was nothing soft about him. Nothing that seemed nurturing or maternal in nature. No wide hips, big breasts, or softness to welcome small children into his lap.

Thierry wasn't exactly an alpha warrior like Luc, but he was a man, he was strong, and he had muscles honed from years of backbreaking toil. He tried to imagine himself with child and couldn't. Such a thing simply could not be possible.

He slid down until he was up to his neck in soothing warmth.

The fragrance of the water made him sleepy.

He closed his eyes and relived the kiss he and Luc had shared. How amazing, holding Luc so close, kissing lips softer than Thierry had imagined they could be. For a hard man, Luc's mouth was soft, his kisses tender and giving. His hands had crept around Thierry's waist and pulled him into a hard body, into a cock that thickened with every beat of their hearts. Thierry's cock had risen in answer, and even now it throbbed beneath the water as though waiting for its mate's return.

Thierry gave it a hesitant stroke but pulled his hand away quickly. He'd brought himself off plenty of times before, but here, with the sisters bustling about the kitchen to prepare supper, he couldn't do it. What if he made some rhythmic splashing noise that they could interpret correctly as him taking himself in hand? They'd be horrified, and he would die of shame. No, his cock must remain untouched, but no matter how mundane and boring he made his thoughts, the blasted thing stayed stiff.

The end result was a quicker bath than he'd have liked and a lump under the towel he was wearing when Luc returned with a change of clothes. Luc's eyes widened. Thierry flushed to his toes. As he had before, Luc looked away.

"Wear these." He practically threw the clothes at Thierry.

"Thank you, Luc."

"I'll be—" Luc pointed helplessly toward the door. "Out. Somewhere. Aunt Luna wants me to describe what we saw again in detail."

At last, a cock killer. "Wait outside. I'll come with you."

"All right." Luc seemed reluctant to tear his gaze from Thierry's body, making it difficult to decide whether he should change in front of him or not. After a minute, he shrugged and dropped his towel.

"I should—" Luc fled the room.

"He's going to give himself apoplexy," Charles said.

Were you watching me bathe?

"At least I wanted to see you naked."

Do you mind not doing that ever again?

"Oh, all right." Charles huffed. "Just so you know, I haven't before. I wanted to talk to you. What happened after Mother Luna made me leave?"

We talked. Well, she talked, and I listened. If you knew about all this, why didn't you tell me?

"It isn't as if we had gotten around to that. I only kissed you once."

True.

"I would have said something eventually if we'd grown closer. Frankly, I'm surprised you didn't know."

How would I? Pa thought I was a freak. Imagine if he knew I'd go into heat someday.

A painful thought struck him.

He and his siblings had all learned to block out Ma's cries of need and delight. Sometimes he'd pitied Ma for her weakness. Sometimes he'd hated her for wanting Pa so badly. His parents weren't Goddess blessed. Why hadn't she chosen a more temperate alpha?

Was he to become like his mother? A slave to his body and a slave to his alpha? What if Luc's luck was poor, or his clever mind failed him, or his ambitions were thwarted? Would Luc grow bitter and angry like Pa, who used Ma every heat and then blamed her for their many offspring? Would Thierry keep going back for more if there was nothing of kindness, of love, left between them?

Would Luc take him for granted like Pa did Ma?

"You're awfully still," Charles observed. "What's going on in your head?"

Heats. I don't ever want to need anyone that badly.

"You're thinking about your ma and pa?"

Thierry didn't answer.

"Your pa's a special kind of stupid." Charles's magic wrapped around him. "He prides himself on his ignorance. Luc will never be like him."

How can you be so sure?

"He's your Goddess blessed. Luc will always put you first."

Isn't it too soon to tell if that's true?

"Titou, I know that after what we went through you've had a hard time believing you deserve good things, but believe in Luc. He's good all the way to his soul."

How do you know?

"I just know, all right?" Charles's magic jangled along Thierry's skin. "I don't have to love the fact for it to be true."

Charles hovered until Thierry finished dressing but didn't stick around after. He was gone by the time Luc knocked on the door.

"Almost ready?" Luc asked.

"One second more." He shoved his feet into his boots and ran to the door.

Despite his offer to help, the sisters pushed Thierry out of the kitchen before emptying his bathwater. Luc led him back to their borrowed room. There was food on the table for them—a simple meal of fresh bread, cheese, and fruit along with a decanter of wine.

Thierry found Luc daunting in this new situation, so while they ate, he let Luc do the talking.

"What do you think?" Luc asked.

"About what?" Thierry had been woolgathering.

"About going to Avimasse with me."

"Oh. It's fine. I've never been there. Is it very crowded?"

"Very. It might be difficult for you since you're used to being outdoors."

"I want to go," Thierry reassured him. "I never imagined I'd get to travel so far from home. What's it like?"

"It's bigger than ten cities of Amivienne's size put together. People from all over the world come to do business and go to school there. Lyrienne, Helionne, and Calyxenne keep embassies in Avimasse, and the largest school of magic in the world sits right next to the palace. You must see the marketplace. It's a feast for the senses. There's no food you can't get day or night."

"Sounds like you miss living there."

Luc shook his head. "That's not my life anymore."

"Couldn't you go back?"

Luc studied their wedge of cheese. "The reasons I left haven't changed, so no, I can't."

"If things changed and you were able to go back, would you?"

"I might." Luc's expression lightened. "But only if I could take a certain farm boy with me. Would you come?"

"What? And leave everything I have in Amivienne behind?"

"Yes." Luc's expression was unreadable. "Would you follow me to the big, bad city where you know no one?"

"Anywhere." Thierry smiled. "I would go *anywhere* with you. Isn't that strange? It's as if I hardly know myself anymore unless we're together."

"I understand." Luc filled Thierry's goblet. "I never imagined I'd find my true mate. The way I've been living, with fewer than a hundred people deep in Hemlock Forest, what were the chances you'd happen along?"

"I doubt the Goddess gambles."

Luc took a swallow of his wine. "I don't suppose she does."

Thierry picked up his goblet. He'd eaten enough that the

wine wouldn't fall on an empty stomach. Despite the rich red color, its taste was fruity on his tongue, sweet and robust.

"Like the wine?" Luc asked. "The sisters make it from their own grapes."

"It's delicious." Despite what he'd believed, it went to his head as quickly as Mother Luna's liquor had earlier. "I normally don't drink very much. This is twice in one day."

"What a reprobate. Perhaps you need to sleep. You've had a very great adventure, little wolf."

"Yes." Thierry's skin heated when he considered the large bed. "Will you join me?"

"I'm afraid not, sweetling. I have business to attend to with Mother Luna. You rest now, and when I get back, I'll tell you all about the ruse I have planned, all right?"

"Mm-hmm." Thierry finished his wine with a sigh and let his mate lead him to the bed. Luc knelt to help with Thierry's boots.

"You don't have to do that," Thierry protested. "I always take my boots off at home."

"What if I want to?" Luc's voice was honeyed. "What if I enjoy serving you or removing your clothes, what then?"

Thierry's cock stirred. He leaned back on his elbows and looked up, emboldened by the sisters' sweet wine. "Then have at it."

Luc settled Thierry in and pulled the covers over him.

"Goodnight." He kissed Thierry's forehead.

"You can call me Titou if you like?"

"Is that the nickname your family calls you?"

Thierry nodded. "Charles too."

Luc made a moue of distaste. "Perhaps I'll think of something else, then. Something that's just ours."

"All right." Luc made him absurdly happy. "I'd like that."

"I'll think on it, then. You do the same."

"What does one call the other half of one's heart, I wonder?"

Thierry nodded sleepily. Luc leaned over for one last kiss and then left the room.

The warmth of his lips remained as Thierry drifted into a shallow half sleep, tired but awake enough to worry about what would happen next.

"It's all right," he told himself. Or maybe that was Charles talking. "I won't let anything happen to you."

Yep. That was Charles, doing his best to reassure even though he knew little more than Thierry of the capital city. Thierry had never been as certain as Charles about anything, and now look where they were.

Avimasse seemed like a long way away.

CHAPTER 14

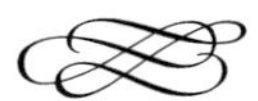

Luc spent most of the following day acquiring a wagon and a nag to pull it. From the sisters, he borrowed two empty barrels, three crates, and enough straw and blankets to make him look like a poor traveler with a wagon of farm goods to sell. If they did nothing to draw attention to themselves, they could be in the city by tomorrow's full moon.

He returned to their borrowed quarters with food and drink, but it was midafternoon and Thierry was napping. Luc ate his meal while it was hot. He should have ordered Thierry to do the same, but he looked so pale and peaceful lying with his hair spread over the pillow, each breath emerging from his lips like a sigh.

Luc had spent part of the day with his aunt, learning more than he ever expected to know about mate bonding with his omega while Thierry insisted on making himself useful in the kitchens. Thierry rarely left Luc's thoughts. Luc had a gift for knowing where in the vast temple complex he'd find him. Imagining life with a mate turned out to be both thrilling and scary, let alone one who was his Goddess blessed.

He'd never understood how important—how necessary—

Thierry would become to him. He had gone from caring only about himself and his needs to putting another person first. From their first touch, when he'd gotten lucky and pulled Thierry to safety, to seeing his beauty in daylight, to watching him sleep right now, so sweet...so *perfect*. If anyone had told Luc he'd feel these emotions, he'd have called them a liar and a fool.

He had been alone for a long time. Maybe too long.

He'd thought nothing of the risks he took. Flouting convention in a strictly defined society, turning his back on everything he'd been raised to believe, and choosing a life of danger on the outskirts of the law to appease his notion of fair play.

Before Thierry, he'd run as fast and as far as he could. But as if he were on an invisible tether, finding his fated one had jerked him to a sudden, painful halt.

Luc would not risk his mate's life with the mischief he was used to causing, but he couldn't extricate himself so easily from his responsibilities either. People depended on him— families, widows, old men, and orphans who had joined him on the promise of making a new society. Those whom poverty defined and whom the king and all his noblemen thought nothing of using and discarding.

How could he be the man he was and still protect the mate he loved?

Luna had advised him to take things one step at a time. The most pressing concern was their murderous necromancer. So far, she had received no reply to her queries and pleas for aid from the Academy at Amivienne. That was not good news.

Instinct told Luc that they must circumvent the local authorities and bring the news directly to his old contacts at the Royal Academy. Only the League of Ethical Craft had mages strong enough to deal with such a powerful, abusive practitioner.

Would they believe all he'd seen? He'd had a reputation—even when he'd been toeing his father's line—for chaos and rebellion. He had a strongly worded letter from Mother Luna and Thierry as a witness if it came to that.

Until the League was aware of the situation and Luc had their promise they would act on it, Hemlock Forest would never be safe.

"Luc?" Thierry turned over and blinked his eyes open. "What time is it?"

"Gone midnight." Luc crossed the room and sat on the bed beside his mate. "You must have been very tired."

"Still am." Luc's boy could barely keep his eyes open.

"There's supper."

Thierry snuggled deeper into the blankets. "I'd have to get up."

"It will keep."

"Mmm." Thierry took his hand.

"Go back to sleep, sweetling. We'll be leaving early." Luc wrapped his hands around Thierry's and kissed the knuckles tenderly.

Thierry smacked his lips. "Bed's big enough for two."

"I'll take the couch."

"You'll be cold come morning."

"There are enough blankets."

"You're such a…" Thierry's voice died away.

"Sleep well, my love." Luc kissed him on the forehead.

Goddess, Thierry's skin felt soft. His lips were right there for the taking. They had a long day of travel ahead of them and in two nights, the full moon would rise in the sky. Luc could slide between the covers with Thierry and hardly be blamed for what happened once he was there.

No, no, no. He wouldn't. What if Thierry didn't enter his heat this moon?

Was it really such a big deal to wait for Thierry's first heat? What difference did that make? Why did it matter so much?

Maybe because he'd spent a lot of time around humans.

There was no human equivalent to wolf mating. Luc had seen firsthand the difficulties faced by those who mated too young. So much of Thierry's appeal connected with his boyish nature, country charm, optimism, and innocence. Luc didn't trust himself to know whether Thierry was ready for a mate bond, and fatherhood, and all that went with it.

Luc's gut was very clear. He would not break his own poxy, self-imposed rules.

The couch, he discovered, had been made for its looks, not its comfort. It was too small, Luc's feet hung over on one end, and his head seemed to rest at an odd angle, one he knew he'd regret come morning.

It took a while for him to quiet his mind and...other parts of his body.

He needed to contact Cavendish, to decide what he would tell him. He hoped he'd get to visit with Ethan while he was there. It wouldn't hurt to enlist the aid of the crown prince.

"What was that?" Thierry sat up suddenly.

Luc listened. *Thud, thud, thud.* "Someone is pounding on a door."

He rose and shoved his feet into his boots. "Stay here."

"Like fire I will." Thierry leapt from his bed and followed Luc until the two stood together at the top of the stairs.

Several of the sisters must have been awakened because Luc heard their frightened whispers.

"What time is it?" Thierry asked in a low voice.

"Too late for visitors."

They crept down to the landing as Mother Luna confronted the intruders.

"Do you have any idea what time it is?" Mother Luna's voice rose in outrage.

"You're hiding him, aren't you? You omega bitches are hiding my son."

Thierry shoved his sleeves to his elbows and started down the stairs. Luc caught him.

“Let Luna handle this. She’s not without resources.”

“I can’t. That’s Pa.” Thierry’s shoulders sagged. “‘He’s here because of me.”

“I won’t allow you to—”

“You won’t *allow*?” Thierry’s eyes widened. “You’re my mate, not my keeper. Let me go.”

“What if it’s not safe?”

“It’s my father, Luc. He’s here to shame me or to try to drag me back so he can sell me to the next trader. I’ve had enough of him to last a lifetime. I’ve got this. Let me go.”

“I’ll come with you. If your father brought men with him—”

“They won’t hurt me. Not this time.” Thierry met Luc’s gaze with a maturity and grit Luc didn’t expect. “I need to do this on my own, alpha. Do you trust me?”

Luc trusted him. Of course he did. It was Thierry’s father whom he didn’t trust. He wanted to go downstairs and revisit every single humiliation and hurt on the man who’d tried to ruin his precious mate’s life, but it wouldn’t do to treat Thierry like a child and not an equal.

Helplessly, Luc forced himself to let go of Thierry’s arm.

Thierry marched downstairs, giving Luc a reassuring glance before he disappeared from sight. Helplessly, Luc crept down after him, intending to intervene only if things turned ugly.

Selene stopped him with a finger to her lips. She pushed him behind the Temple’s massive entry doors so they could watch through a sliding spyhole.

There were three men in the courtyard, and they argued with Mother Luna, who looked as put together and serene in her red robes as always. The men wore shabby clothing and belligerent expressions. One seemed to be having trouble keeping his balance. Torches cast monstrous shadows over their angry faces.

Thierry moved to Mother Luna's side and stopped, hands fisted on his hips.

"What in the Goddess's name are you doing, Pa? Go home," he demanded.

"You're coming with me, you brat." One of the men stalked forward and grabbed Thierry's arm.

Luc gave a growl. His wolf begged to be let loose.

"Hush." Selene's disapproval reined him in. For now.

"Don't touch me, Pa." Thierry easily broke his father's grip on him.

Thierry's father was an unremarkable-looking alpha, large in the way of big brutes who go to fat in their later years. He was ugly, inside and out. Luc's wolf paced inside him, enraged that Luc did nothing to stop the old alpha. Luc could barely hold him back.

"You're still my child for two more days." He looked to the others for agreement. "You won't be taking refuge behind a bunch of weak omegas while I have breath."

"I'm not *your* anything," Thierry said angrily. "You tried to sell me."

"It's my right, you worthless boy. It's my right to get some compensation for being saddled with a disappointment like you."

Luna said, "Claude Guillard, I've sent word to the sheriff's men. Leave now before this situation gets any worse."

"Don't talk to your betters, omega." Claude glared at her. "The sheriff's dead. Much help he'll be to you."

Several of the other sisters gasped with outrage.

"It happened again, didn't it, boy?" Thierry's father taunted. "You went into the woods with somebody and came back alone and babbling about sorcery." His dark, angry gaze landed on Luna. "This boy is an abomination. I'm here to make certain he doesn't get anyone else killed."

"Thierry is under the Goddess's protection," stated Mother

Luna. "And mine. If you try to take him, be prepared to fight me."

"Bah." The old man advanced on her. "Useless omega bitch. You can't take what's mine!"

"If you won't let him go," said one man, "we'll take him by force."

Claude agreed, "Aye! Let's get him, lads."

Claude surged forward alongside the other two men. Luc would have shifted, but a mighty pull on his magic stopped him —shocked him—as if an invisible fist had punched through his chest and grabbed hold of his heart. He gasped and staggered and fell against the door.

"Enough!" Thierry shouted. Magic concussed the air. Thierry's father and the other two men flew backward. They landed like scattered leaves, stunned.

"He's a mage," one mumbled.

"Can't be," Claude rolled like a beetle on his back. "He's omega."

"The Goddess protects her own." Luna's eyes seemed too bright, and the air crackled with her anger. "The Sisters of the Merciful Moon will not accede to your demands. Leave and don't come back."

"You said it'd just be women, Claude." One of them scrambled to his feet.

"You didn't say nothing about mages." The second man fled with his friend.

"Ingrates." Claude staggered to his feet. "Unnatural, unholy—"

"Pa, you're dead to me. Don't come after me, or you're going to be sorrier than you already are." Thierry turned his back and walked toward Luc, who waited for him, dazed by what he'd seen.

What he could feel roiling inside him.

Luna turned. Her shocked gaze locked with Luc's.

Had Thierry borrowed Luc's magic? If he had, he'd only taken it because he'd needed it to protect himself. But how? In all his studies at the Royal Academy, no one had even hinted that an omega could do that.

Thierry practically fell into Luc's arms. Luc got a hand under his knees to catch him as he lost consciousness. Luna directed him to the kitchens where he laid his mate on a worktable.

"Selene, please get Marta. Tell her we'll need her expertise."

Selene took off, robes rustling.

"What's happening to him?" asked Luc. "Is he going to be all right?"

"Is Thierry a practitioner?"

Luc didn't know. "He's probably capable of absorbing magic like any other omega. I don't know if he makes use of it."

"I wonder…" She laid her hand on Thierry's cheek. "Though Thierry's friend's body died the night that the necromancer attacked him, the occult part of Charles remains. I'm guessing Thierry was able to…absorb Charles's esoteric body—or hide it safely away—until the threat passed."

"That's…not possible."

"Do you have another explanation?"

"Charles is a shade. A vibrant one but a shade nonetheless."

"Have you ever heard of a shade who retains their magic?"

Luc hadn't.

He studied his Goddess-given mate's pale features as if he'd find the answers there.

"He used my magic to defend himself." He met Luna's worried gaze. "It felt as if he reached into my body and ripped a handful of magic free."

Luna frowned. "That's an interesting observation."

He gave an exasperated laugh. "Only you would greet that statement so coolly."

"Magic is an enigma. We understand only a tiny fraction of what it is or how to use it."

"If anyone in the community learns what he did—"

"I will quash any rumors immediately. Three drunk alphas attacked and were repelled. I will tell anyone who asks that the men triggered our wards and misunderstood where the protective magic came from."

"Thank you." Luc let out a breath of relief.

"Thierry is rare, though. People at the Royal Academy will be suspicious of him. They'll argue that he's cursed, as his father believes, or they'll want to study him."

"I've requested a meeting with Cavendish. I'll make sure it's somewhere neutral." Though he'd have liked to show Thierry the ancient building, Aunt Luna was right. It was too dangerous until they knew how the mages would approach him.

"He's shown he's capable of protecting himself, but don't let your guard down around anyone. Thierry's life might depend on keeping the things he can do a secret."

"I understand." Thierry was more than he had bargained for, but he was *magnificent*. Luc would not begrudge him the use of his magic or any other thing he possessed, not if his mate needed it to protect himself.

Thierry was welcome to all of Luc. Everything he owned, everything he was, he would gladly share with his Goddess-given mate.

Yet this new knowledge made their journey to the capital doubly dangerous. Thierry was a rare and powerful male omega. He could do something that no one else was capable of. His gifts would make him a delicious prize for the necromancer they were after, and Goddess help them if Thierry wound up in his hands.

Luc would be a fool not to see the danger, and Luc was no fool.

CHAPTER 15

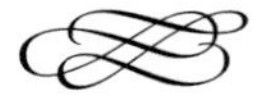

Thierry's head hurt when he woke to find several worried faces peering down at him. Why was he lying on a table in the kitchen? Had he fainted? "What is it?"

"How are you? Do you remember what happened?" Luc pressed Thierry's hand between both of his.

"Of course. My father was here, trying to cause trouble as usual." He was too embarrassed to ask exactly what went wrong. "Did he leave?"

"You don't remember anything else?" asked Mother Luna.

Thierry lifted to his elbows. "Not really. I remember Pa shouting at me. I remember he called me his property. He wanted to take me back and sell me off to some other merchant or tradesman."

"I would never have allowed that to happen," Luc said gently. "You're my heart, sweetling."

"Not in front of the *sisters,*" Thierry hissed. In truth, there was only Mother Luna, Selene, and Marta there, and all three looked like they were watching puppies cuddle.

"There's nothing wrong with being in love." Taciturn Sister Marta sniffed. "Best medicine in the world."

"Now I have your measure, old softie," Luc chided.

"What's the last thing you remember?" Mother Luna asked Thierry.

"My father was coming at me with the look he gets when he's going to hit me."

"That whoreson." Luc's face mottled with rage.

"Pa loses control when he's drunk." Thierry reached for Luc's hand. "Even when he doesn't shift, he's vicious. I wish I'd let you come with me. He'd think twice about going after me if he knew you'd be by my side."

Luc pressed a kiss to his forehead. "I wish I'd been there."

"I thought I could handle him. I'm a fool."

"Thierry, you did something extraordinary," said Mother Luna. Thierry turned to Luc, who nodded. He didn't remember much after his father had charged him.

"You reached into my chest, grabbed my magic, and sent your father and his lackeys packing," Luc said with wonder. "You truly don't remember?"

"No. How?" Thierry swung his legs over the side of the table. "You must have done it."

"No, my extraordinary omega, that was all you." Luc wrapped his arms around Thierry, but instead of letting him set his feet on the floor, Luc whirled around until Thierry felt like he was flying. Luc laughed. "You were able to do something that I've never heard of any omega doing before. You're amazing. I have an *amazing* mate!"

Laughing and face heating, Thierry begged to be put down.

"Do you suppose it's because he's a male omega?" asked Selene. "You're a practitioner, Mother Luna. If you had a fated mate—"

"I don't know." Mother Luna looked dazed. "We must make a new study of the archives. There are reasons that someone might want to conceal the truth of this."

"In Rheilôme, omega practitioners are rare, and most go into a life of service to the Goddess," said Marta. "That's why I entered the Order. I felt my gifts as a healer were better used on all those in need rather than members of my immediate family. Of course, I never found my fated one."

"I—" Selene gave a stricken cry. "Oh, Mother Luna. What did I do?"

Marta wrapped her arm around Sister Selene. "It will be all right, Selene. Come. Since the boy appears well, we can talk elsewhere."

Thierry watched her lead the sobbing Selene from the room. He turned to Mother Luna, who shrugged.

"Being an omega means making difficult choices," she said. "An omega who is able to use magic and not merely absorb it or store it is in a double bind. Many alphas regard their omega mates, even Goddess-blessed mates, as little more than glorified housekeepers. They occupy the traditional role of the chatelaine and mother and are expected to allow their alpha to make all the decisions. An alpha's word is law and not to be questioned by those beneath him."

"Omegas should not be considered beneath alphas." Thierry didn't think he could be that kind of mate. Thank heavens Luc didn't seem to be that kind of alpha.

"You have nothing to worry about. I vow I'll always value your counsel." Luc kissed his hand to seal the bargain.

"Because you already know I'd never accept you if you didn't," Thierry said.

"Obviously." Luc laughed, but he rubbed his chest ruefully. "I don't want control over my mate, but if I did, I think I'd be very sorry."

"Mmm." Thierry leaned against him.

"I will be looking into what happened this night," Luna offered. "There must be something in the historical records. At least the Lyrienne records. You're a rare man, Thierry, but there have been other male omegas. I will start there. Should we find that this is the result of any fated mate bond between an omega practitioner and an alpha, as rare as that may be...this could change things."

"In the meantime," said Luc. "Thierry and I have two hours before dawn. I mean to leave at first light. We should sleep until then if we can. You look exhausted, darling."

Luc tipped Thierry's chin up with a finger and kissed him.

"All right. Good night, Mother Luna."

"Sweet dreams."

Luc said good night to Mother Luna as well, and they started up the stairs.

"Wait," she called to them. "Your father now knows you are able to use magic, and I doubt he'll keep quiet about it. It might make you an especially good target for the necromancer."

"Why especially?" asked Thierry.

"He's killing Sisters of the Merciful Moon," said Luc. "He knows the odds are good that some are omega practitioners. If he wants powerful magic, he need look no further than you."

"Best to stay cautious." Mother Luna came to the foot of the stairs and looked up at them. "Keep to the road and try to make it to Avimasse before dark."

"Will you be all right here?" Luc turned to her. "Please follow your own advice and keep the sisters out of Hemlock Forest while I'm away."

"We must work where our help is needed, Luc. You know that. The Goddess protects us."

"The necromancer has killed three of you already."

"We always have a choice, Luc. We do not wish to stay home, protected, while others suffer."

"Aunt Luna—"

"We will take extra precautions, I promise you. Find help and get answers. Return as soon as you can so we may put this danger behind us."

"You know I will."

"The rest is up to the Goddess." She smiled fondly. "Go in safety, nephew. If I don't see you before you leave, please know my love and gratitude go with you."

Luc put his hand on the small of Thierry's back as they climbed the rest of the stairs. Once they were in their room, Thierry disrobed and slipped between the covers of the bed without speaking. He needed to think about the things he'd heard. The things they said he'd done to repel his pa's assault.

"Do you really think I took your magic?"

"You surely did." Luc sounded proud of him. Instead of making his way to the couch on the other side of the room, he lay down on top of the covers beside Thierry. "It still stings a bit if you want to know."

"I'm sorry."

"Never be sorry for protecting yourself."

"But what if I took too much? What if I hurt you, and we don't know it yet?"

"You didn't." Luc insinuated his arm beneath Thierry's neck. "Come here."

"I would never hurt you." Thierry turned on his side and rested his head close to his mate's. Luc stroked his hair. "I had no idea I could take your magic like that."

"I think you might be unusually strong and not just because you're a man. I think perhaps you've been hiding how strong you really are."

"How could I do that and not know?"

"Instinct, maybe? Knowledge that your father would cut you off at the knees rather than see you grow beyond his height?"

"When you put it like that…"

"Makes sense, eh?"

"He really is bollocks. Honestly, I don't know how my mother put up with him all these years. She bore him *seven* children."

"What number are you?"

"Four. Right in the middle."

"I wish I could meet your family. There has to be something to them, or you wouldn't be such a wonderful man."

"*Psht.*" Thierry tried to roll over.

"Your father cares only about what he wants. You are kind, and selfless, and loving. Who taught you to be so likable?"

"Ma, maybe. I did spend most of my waking hours in the fields and at the edges of the forest. I like nature."

"Nature can be cruel too. You, my dear mate"—Luc kissed his nose and moved down to his neck—"are a delightful enigma."

Thierry squirmed helplessly. "Stop it. That tickles."

Luc lifted his head. "I plan to spend my life solving the puzzle of you."

"I hope so."

"Know it. It is so." Luc pulled Thierry back into his arms. "Sleep now. We have a long day's journey ahead of us."

Thierry's whole body felt flushed and energized. How could Luc think he'd sleep when Luc was lying beside him, when his heat and his nearness played along Thierry's nerves like drummers at the midsummer bonfires.

He sensed magic whenever he closed his eyes around Luc, only he couldn't tell anymore if it was Luc's magic or his own. They felt like one and the same, as though every time he was near Luc, the barriers between them eroded a little bit.

Was this the mate bond or because he might be a practitioner? Was that possible? How had he never sensed that part of himself until now?

"I thought I knew everything about you," Charles interrupted his musings. "Obviously, you've been holding back."

Not on purpose.

"But it's exciting! You just reached out and used your mate's magic. It's unusual, that's for sure."

Charles...you don't think I ever did that to you, do you?

"What, used my magic? No. Based on Luc's expression when it happened, I'd have known if you had."

So you don't think I borrowed your magic when the necromancer sent his beast after us?

"Are you worried that's why I—" Charles's magic warmed him. "You didn't take my magic, Thierry. You were lucky, and I wasn't. Please don't make it more than that."

"This is awkward," said Luc. "Can you consider the bedroom off-limits, Charles? There must be somewhere that my mate and I can be alone."

Thierry closed his eyes. "Oh my Goddess."

"He has a point," Charles admitted. "Tell him I'm going."

"Luc—"

"It's not too much to ask," Luc pointed out reasonably. "I'm willing to share you otherwise."

Thierry opened his eyes to glare at his mate. "You'll *share* me?"

"That did it," Charles remarked. "I'm going now."

"*You'll* share me?" Thierry asked again.

"I meant—"

"Oh, alpha, my alpha." Thierry raised his arms as if in worship. "You do not own me."

"That's my cue." Charles's magic winked out as if he'd never been there.

Luc's eyes widened. "Thierry, for Goddess's sake. I'm tired. I only meant—"

"You can't share me, Luc, because you don't own me."

"You just called me '*my* alpha.'"

"Don't pick my words apart. We are a team. We are partners. I can have friends."

"Not in our bed, you can't," Luc said amiably. He no doubt found it all amusing, but Thierry felt odd and confused, and… absorbed somehow. As if the barriers breaking down between them left him unable to see who he was anymore.

"I—"

"Let's walk away from the argument right now and sleep on this, all right? I promise I'll be more coherent in the morning." A minute or two passed. "Can we revisit you saying, 'Oh alpha, my alpha' again sometime? That was pretty—"

Thierry dug his elbow into Luc's ribs. "Shut up."

"Sleep, sweetling."

Thierry liked being called sweetling. He didn't even mind when Luc called him "my sweetling," but one had to draw the line somewhere. It was like his mother had said when the twins had started toddling around and getting into things: "We must start as we mean to go on."

Thierry liked having Luc's arm around him.

He liked the soft whuffle of breath against his temple after Luc drifted off.

He liked Luc's warmth, his goodness, his humor.

We must start as we mean to go on.

This was a good start indeed.

CHAPTER 16

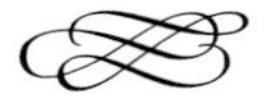

Luc and Thierry asked Charles to stay behind while they were gone. Having an unseen ally able to watch over Hemlock Forest and the Temple of the Merciful Moon seemed wise, and privately, Luc wanted time alone with his mate.

Luc had the horse hitched up and ready to go when Thierry joined him. He wore the robes and cloak of the Order again along with his borrowed boots. In the unforgiving blue light of predawn, Luc's young mate looked tired. He carried pastries wrapped in paper and a mug of tea that sent plumes of steam into the cold air.

"Ready?" Luc asked.

"I'm a farmer, Luc. I start every day at this time."

"Even in winter?" asked Luc

"It's hard to make livestock understand you don't feel like feeding them when it's cold."

Luc chuckled. "I'm indeed lucky to have such a hardy, stalwart mate."

"I'll make you very proud then. Unless I see a spider."

Luc took the reins and climbed onto the wagon's bench seat. Thierry climbed up beside him.

"Are you certain you don't wish to sleep in the wagon for a bit while I drive?"

"And arrive in the capital city looking like a wench who's been tumbled on the drive in?" Thierry pulled the hood of his red cloak over his wimple. "I'd give the sisters a terrible name."

"Mmm." Luc's gaze heated. "The way you look, it won't take much to do that."

Thierry blinked in surprise.

Luc laughed at his expression. "Hasn't anyone ever told you you're beautiful?"

"Your eyesight needs checking."

"Not at all," Luc assured him. "There's nothing wrong with my eyes. You look adorable this morning, even with smudges under your eyes from lack of sleep."

Thierry lowered his lashes, but Luc could tell he was pleased. He found it far easier to tease and cajole his mate than to face the journey ahead.

Luc waved to the few sisters up and about, clicked to the horse, and gave the reins a snap. The cart rolled forward, wheels squeaking. Luc steered the horse out of the temple complex and onto the merchant's road. The way was empty as far as he could see in either direction. That wouldn't last as merchants who'd paused their journeys to sleep liked to leave in the early hours.

Luc calculated that if they moved at their horse's moderate pace and stopped to rest as needed, they'd make the outskirts of Avimasse at dusk. He glanced over at his mate.

"Looking forward to the capital?"

"Not really." Thierry shook his head. "You'll think me such a rustic, but I don't enjoy Amivienne. If Avimasse is so much bigger—"

"If you miss a more natural setting," Luc offered, "there are wonderful parks in the city and a menagerie with rare animals from other lands."

Thierry clutched his arm. "Please don't let me end up in some cage labeled 'Male Omega.' That's long been a nightmare of mine."

Luc didn't take his plea lightly. "I give you my word."

"Tell me about your family," said Thierry. "I can tell that you're highborn from your speech. Why give up that life?"

Luc shrugged. "The nobles of Rheilôme lead strictly structured lives. One must rise at a certain hour, eat a certain type of food, ride at a time when one will be seen, change for lunch, change for dinner, adjourn and discuss topical events but nothing too meaningful."

"Sounds a bit like a farmer's life. Only we're dictated to by nature, and society seems to me the opposite of natural."

"You catch my meaning perfectly. It was boring as balls."

"No. You had the entire world to explore. You had the Royal Academy. You had books and crowds of strangers. I've never been bored, and I had none of that. Of course, I never wanted it."

"I wasn't permitted to go anywhere except the temple and school where the books I could read were restricted and the people I met were exactly like me."

"Oh, I can see how that would be awful." Thierry's expression filled with mischief.

"I should make you pull the wagon and let the horse sit up here."

"Honestly, I can understand why you weren't happy. Despite where you lived and all your resources, you were as isolated as I was."

"I had Aunt Luna, and she told me about her work. I told my father I wanted to be a healer, and he got furious. He contacted the Royal Academy and had my access restricted to the study of magical law. Bloody court mages. They do nothing but argue amongst themselves about the nature of magic."

"That sounds boring."

"Yes, well, for laughs, one month out of the year they get to argue with mages from other countries. They don't mate. Did you know that? They're required to stay unmated and celibate in order to keep their positions." A muscle in his jaw ticked. "Goddess knows they flout their own rules, openly taking lovers and having children out of wedlock."

Thierry wrinkled his nose. "That's what your father wanted for you?"

"Indeed."

"No wonder you fled. I'm surprised you didn't burn the place to the ground on the way out."

"Careful. You sound like an outlaw."

"What part of posing as a Sister of the Merciful Moon gave me away?"

"Eat your pastries," Luc reminded him. "We still have a long way to go."

As Luc drove, Thierry got excited over every little thing. There was a doe leading a fawn. A pair of hawks circled overhead. In the distance, they could see carrion birds.

Something large had died recently. Luc wished he could be certain it wasn't one of his friends. Luc felt torn. He should be there to protect the families that trusted him, but he was one of the few people with the resources to get help.

The horse clip-clopped along with little enthusiasm. Thierry eventually dozed, leaning against his shoulder.

They needed a rest at midday, so Luc veered onto the rutted path leading to a small inn that he knew. He pulled to a stop near the stables where a freckled boy of about eight offered to look after their horse. Luc was just in time to catch Thierry when he stumbled down.

"Whoa there. You're still drowsy." Luc pulled him close.

"Sorry." Pink flooded Thierry's cheeks. "I'm okay. Just stiff."

Luc saw no reason to let him go. "Oh, really?"

"Not like that." More blushing. "The stable boy is *staring* at us."

Ah. Well. That was enough like cold water to get him to let go.

It seemed harder to back away than he liked. Flushed and shy, his mate was most attractive. Pink was his best color. Luc wanted to see that pink flow over every part of Thierry's body. He wanted to lick it off him.

Lick and bite and suck…

Uh-oh. His mate smelled delicious. Every alpha in the place would notice and—on seeing him in disguise—assume he was an unmated female omega.

It was too soon for his heat. The moon wouldn't be full until the following day, but if Thierry's heat was coming on, lunch in a crowded tavern was out of the question.

He placed his hand over Thierry's forehead.

"What are you doing?" Thierry backed away.

"Checking if you're overwarm."

"I'm fine." Thierry knocked his hand away. "Only flushed from the sun."

Luc eyed him carefully. "You feel all right?"

"Of course. Let's go inside. I'm starving."

Cautiously, Luc followed his mate indoors.

Luc knew the owners of the place, a man and wife who kept a clean and wholesome respite for travelers. Rose was a good cook and her husband, Ander, shy and generous. Luc was both sorry and glad to see the tavern mostly empty—sorry for Ander's business but glad the room wasn't crowded.

The other customers, a pair of scholars with an open book between them, and a sleepy looking but well-dressed merchant, watched them enter with the interest of bored travelers.

"Luc." The owner greeted him by name before sketching

Thierry a half bow. "Sister, welcome to our humble establishment. Rose!"

"What?" Rose came out of the kitchen, wiping her hands on a towel. She smiled as soon as she saw him. "Oh, Luc, welcome."

"I told Sister Thistle we could dine privately. Do you mind?"

While they greeted each other, Thierry mouthed, *Sister Thistle?*

"Of course you may. Please follow me." Rose led them to a private dining room off the main tavern where she seated them near the fire. "I've got stew and freshly baked bread."

"Two, please, and ale for both of us."

Rose nodded. "Back in a tic."

Ander arrived a minute later, carrying mugs of ale.

"The place looks good," said Luc. "How are you doing?"

"Can't complain. The Stag's Head up the road continues to draw most of the trade, but their barmaids allow liberties, and Rosie would sooner break a rolling pin over a customer's head." The man shrugged. "So it goes."

"Admit it. You're as happy with your wife as a dog with two tails to wag."

"True enough." Ander put the mugs between them. "Where are you heading?"

"The capital."

"Oh, I see." Ander gave a glance back toward the kitchen. "Only I heard something disturbing about dark magic in the forest near Amivienne, and I wondered—"

"What you've heard is true," Luc lowered his voice. "But it's best not to repeat it. We can't have ordinary idiots hunting an unknown sorcerer. It's far too dangerous."

"It's true then. He's creating monsters?"

Luc nodded, meeting Thierry's gaze. "And he's killing omegas."

"Are we in danger here?" Ander's Adam's apple bobbed. "My Rose?"

"I couldn't say, but you're far enough from Amivienne. Stay close to the inn. Don't let Rose go anywhere alone and never at night."

"We'll do as you say." When his wife emerged from the kitchens, Ander dropped his worried expression. "You're in for a treat now."

"Here you go, Luc. Sister." She gave them each a steaming bowl of thick stew and a large hunk of freshly baked bread. "I hope this meets with your approval. Give a shout if you want more."

"Thank you."

Thierry nodded and clasped his hands together in a gesture of thanks. Rose and Ander looked to Luc with uncertainty.

"I'm afraid the sister doesn't speak," Luc told them. "She'll be delighted with the food. I always am."

"You're good for my ego," said Rose.

"You're bad for my breeches. I'll have to let them out if I eat all this."

"Bah. You're a tease." Smiling, Rose returned to the kitchen, but as soon as she left, Ander's too-bright smile disappeared.

"Is there anything I can do to help you catch this madman?" he asked.

Luc shook his head. "I'll alert my friend from the Royal Academy. It's up to them to neutralize this mage before he becomes too powerful to control."

"I'll ask the Goddess to bless your journey."

"Thank you." Luc accepted his offer gladly. "May the Goddess bless you both."

"May we be worthy," Ander replied before leaving them to eat.

Since they couldn't exactly chat, they ate quickly. Their meal was excellent. The stew was seasoned with warm spices and simmered in wine from the sun-drenched lands of northern Rheilôme. Luc enjoyed watching Thierry eat. His mate dabbed up every speck of gravy with his bread before laying down his napkin and leaning back in his chair.

"Sister Thistle approves," said Luc.

Thierry kicked his foot under the table while smiling sweetly.

"We should go if we want to make good time."

Thierry got up and followed Luc out of the private room. Luc turned to speak to Ander again.

"Remember what I said. Stay close to home and be alert."

"I will. Thank you for your business, as always."

"Thank you, friend." They clasped forearms. In the stable yard, the boy put the horse back in its traces while they waited.

"Good job, lad. Mind Ander and stay indoors at night." Luc gave him two coins for his trouble.

"Thank you, sir." The child doffed his cap.

Luc climbed up to the bench beside Thierry and took up the reins. It wasn't long before his mate again dozed against his arm. Happiness made Luc glow inside, and the bond that connected him to his mate warmed and comforted him. Alpha pride, Luc thought with some amusement. He was secretly delighted to make his mate comfortable.

Despite the fact that all Luc could see of Thierry was the hood of his cloak and his booted feet, a violent shiver of desire raced over his body. Leave it to the Goddess to bless him and satisfy—even enchant—him despite his conflicting desires.

Thierry was his. Beautiful, powerful, omega, and—*impossibly*—a man.

Whatever made Luc a likely recipient for such a gift had to be in his future; he'd done nothing in the past to warrant such a partner. Thierry deserved better than a bastard outlaw living in a shack in the woods, but Luc wasn't about to let him go. He'd die first.

He hoped the Goddess knew what She was doing.

By late afternoon, they were close to their destination. There were more wagons on the road heading both directions. The number of conveyances made the going slower. Horses or tired mules caused traffic to grind to a halt in places. Travelers sometimes exchanged greetings or even stopped to talk about market conditions or inns to be found. Luc decided to wake Thierry rather than leave him vulnerable in sleep while strangers stared.

He found a well and watered their horse while Thierry climbed down for his private business. They returned to the bench where Thierry primly arranged his skirts.

"Do I look all right?" Thierry adjusted his wimple and his hood.

"Perfect," Luc told him. "Though you're ruining the Sisters of the Merciful Moon with your saucy ways."

"Very funny."

"You think I'm joking?" Luc brushed a bit of straw from his mate's shoulder. "Did you have a good sleep?"

"Must be the air here. It smells like flowers. Did I hear voices?"

Luc nodded. "The road will be heavy with travelers until we arrive."

He got the horse moving while Thierry gawked at the land around them.

"Goddess, I've never seen so much lavender." Thierry strained around him to get a good glimpse of the other side of the road. "Is that the ocean?"

"Yes. This road hugs the coast from here on out. As for the flowers, these are a drop in the bucket. Central Rheilôme is famous for perfumes and wine. It's no exaggeration to say that the whole of the Grand River Valley is a patchwork of vineyards and perfumeries. You can't see it from the road, though. There are hills in the way."

"I never imagined such a thing."

"Unlike the south where you've lived, most of Rheilôme has a sunny, temperate climate. Wine and spirits distilled here are coveted throughout the civilized world. We grow olives, almonds, citrus, and flowers for perfumes."

"I've never seen the sea before," Thierry said excitedly. "I can see waves. The way the sun sparkles on the water is amazing!"

Luc smiled. "Yes, it is."

"Oh, if I lived here, I'd never get tired of looking at it."

And I will never get tired of looking at you, my heart.

"Imagine if I hadn't agreed to act as a decoy for the sisters. I swear, when we vanquish the necromancer, I'm keeping my red cloak. On feast days, I'll put it on and carry food to the people in the forest in gratitude for all this experience has given me."

"I'll go with you. We'll share the duty."

"Of course you will. Who knows when I'll need to be hoisted into a tree again?"

"I'd hoist you into a tree right now if we were free to do that sort of thing."

"Naughty alpha." Thierry's eyes sparkled as he clasped his hands together and declaimed, "Oh, *woe* betide me, for I'm not even eighteen!"

"Cheeky omega. Do you want to be spanked?"

"Is that a threat or..." Thierry's eyes widened. "Maybe?"

Luc might have swallowed his tongue. He couldn't breathe for a second, and when he did, it came as a sort of choked gasp with a laugh chaser.

Unfortunately, driving took more and more of Luc's concentration. An hour passed before they were able to see the highest of the city's spires, those of the Avimasse Temple of the Moon and the castle itself.

"The buildings are huge," Thierry breathed with awe. "How does everyone live chockablock on top of each other like that?"

"It's what they know."

Thierry frowned. "Where are all the trees?"

"What do you think they use to build things with?"

"Oh, no." His face fell. "That's not right. You said there'd be gardens."

"There are. You'll see when we're in the city proper. It's hard to tell from here, especially with night coming on."

"It's a little intimidating." Thierry looked to him. "How will we ever find what we're looking for?"

"I'm familiar with the place, remember? For now, sit up straight and let your hood cover your face. It's a fair distance, but from here on, traffic will be heavy, and there are thieves everywhere. We mustn't call attention to ourselves."

Thierry's brow furrowed. "It looks so close."

"Distances can be deceptive, sweetling."

From there, wagons multiplied like roaches. Traffic slowed. Thinning lanes and inspections by the king's men near the waterfront kept travelers in check and routed some smugglers, even though most of the gangs had men working directly for shipping companies. How else could gangs keep a stranglehold on the market for untaxed goods or items forbidden by current sumptuary laws?

It was a fact of life that wherever there were laws, there was an unlimited supply of men attempting to break them. In a city of the size of Avimasse, teeming crowds made it easy for outlaws to remain anonymous.

As Luc told his half brother every time they met, if he'd wanted to be an outlaw in truth, he'd have headed for the docks first thing and not the virgin forest.

Thierry took everything in, wide-eyed as any country bumpkin.

"I can't believe you left all this to gather drifters in the forest," he said.

"They aren't drifters," Luc explained. "Most are desperate men with families looking for a more independent way of life. They're tired of being under the yoke of powerful men who see them as little more than tools."

"You're my heroic ideal." Thierry nudged him with his knee. "Like an alpha from out of the old ballads, wearing shiny armor and fighting dragons."

Heroic? Er…no. "I'd be on the dragons' side in any fight."

"You know what I mean. You believe in being fair. Helping people. You're a hero."

Nah. If Luc were heroic, he would have noticed there was a murderer in the forest when the first sister died. He would have been able to save the sheriff and his men. He wouldn't have dragged his very young mate along on a journey into enemy territory.

He wouldn't be wishing that he'd stayed at home where he and Thierry could languish in bed while the world burned.

Luc wasn't heroic, but maybe he could do a bit better.

Maybe, since the Goddess had seen fit to give him such a magnificent mate, he'd be able to meet Her challenge and become worthy.

He'd have to. They'd come into the city proper, and it was time to do what they'd come for and warn the League that there was a death magic practitioner killing omegas in Hemlock Forest.

He hoped they didn't already know the truth of things.

If the League knew and they'd done nothing, their battle was already lost.

CHAPTER 17

Thierry had never seen such crowds. He had no knowledge of industrial factories that belched out smoke. The city was rife with both, and Goddess, did the place ever stink. It was worse than a barn, worse than a pigpen, worse than anything Thierry had ever smelled before.

Even at dusk there were more people than he'd seen in his entire life—humans and shifters working and walking and riding side by side. Filthy children ran in packs, begging for coins and food and trinkets; old men crouched and played homemade instruments in alleyways, hats turned up and waiting for tips. Hundreds of dogs roamed the streets, feeding from rubbish while feral cats stalked fat rats who seemed to have no fear whatsoever.

The smell of unwashed bodies permeated the air—stale clothes and urine and feces and slop. There were piles of garbage on every corner.

Thierry looked to Luc. "How do people live like this?"

"Oh, I know. It's foul here." Luc glanced around as if what he saw neither surprised nor revolted him. "It's worse at the wharf where they process fish."

Thierry couldn't imagine.

"This is the part of Avimasse artists don't paint," said Luc. "But I assure you, the area where we're going is nicer. For one thing, the houses aren't close together. And it's much cleaner."

A droplet fell onto Thierry's hand. He glanced up to see laundry draped over the balconies of the buildings above. In some cases, it hung from rope stretched between buildings.

Women shouted from their windows as they worked, the conversations mostly about children and chores. Occasionally, someone emptied a chamber pot right on the ground below where people were walking. Some men seemed to have a knack for avoiding the flow, and they pulled wives or girlfriends to safety with them.

Thierry didn't think he'd ever warm up to city life.

He had a headache, though he'd slept nearly all day, and his stomach was queasy. He blamed the malaise on the masses of people that clogged every street. How could anyone bear it? If he'd known what he was in for, he might not have been brave enough to come.

"Sweetling?" Luc asked. "Are you all right?"

"The city is all wrong." He shivered. "I can't catch my breath here."

"I'm so sorry. It's a mess, I know, but the place we're heading is near the palace. It's like night and day. You'll see."

That didn't reassure him.

"Not much farther now. You'll have a nice meal and sleep in a luxurious bed."

Thierry closed his eyes and let the rumble of the cart's wheels over the cobblestones jounce him. Beneath his voluminous cloak, he clung to Luc's hand, to Luc's soothing, familiar touch, to their mate bond. He jumped when a hawker whistled, jerked back when a fight broke out, leaned over the side of the wagon and lost what little he'd eaten since their noonday meal.

"Merciful Goddess." He was furiously ashamed of himself. "I

am normally tougher than this."

"I had no idea this would be so hard for you." Luc stroked circles into his back. "I'm so sorry."

Thierry shook his head. "It's hot here. I'm not used to it yet."

"I'll make this up to you," Luc promised. "We'll be staying with my half brother, Ethan, whose townhome is ridiculously luxurious. You will be cool and comfortable in less than an hour, I promise."

"It's all right, Luc. I'll be fine." *I hope.*

The drive took more than an hour. "Only a bit farther now."

As Luc had promised, this area of Avimasse was completely different. There were trees for one thing. Birds darted to and from branches overhead and onto the sidewalk between café tables and fancy dress shops and haberdasheries.

People there were dressed smartly, in a style that Thierry recognized as far more fashionable than the finest shops in Amivienne carried. The men's suits were cut shockingly close over thighs and buttocks, and the women's décolletage would have been indiscreet where he'd come from. They all wore gloves and hats. Several younger ladies carried tiny, preposterous dog companions, forcing the maids who scurried alongside them to carry their purchases.

Luc steered away from the busy commercial street onto an even quieter lane with large, stately homes.

"That's us." Luc nodded to one such house—three stories tall—painted white with grand columns holding a peaked roof over wide double doors. Luc pulled the wagon under the shade of a flowering plum tree and leapt from his seat before coming around to help Thierry, who felt weak as a kitten.

Luc led him up the few stairs to the front door and knocked.

The door opened. A smartly dressed older man said, "Tradesmen go around to the back."

The door closed.

"Come on." Luc cursed softly and knocked again. "Chalmers!

It's Luc—"

"Master Luc." The door opened again. "I beg your pardon. The eyes aren't what they were."

"Never mind, old friend. I thought Ethan would be expecting me. See that one of the grooms looks after our horse, please." Luc put his hand on the small of Thierry's back. "Is Ethan even in residence?"

"He's in his study, sir." Chalmers frowned at Thierry. "I was not aware we were expecting guests. Let me get Mrs. Quinn."

"No need. We should see Ethan straightaway."

Footsteps thundered down the stairs.

"Luc, you idiot." A tall alpha with broad shoulders barreled toward them. "Why didn't you tell me you were coming?"

"I sent Silence to Cavendish. I thought he'd tell you. Hasn't he been here?"

"He left his card earlier. I was out. And who's this?" Ethan studied Thierry. "One rarely sees Sisters of the Merciful Moon here in town. Is it true the Order still goes about Hemlock Forest healing people and such? You must be very brave, little thing, if that's your vocation."

Thierry didn't answer. He felt strangely uneasy with two such powerful alphas looming over him. He felt threatened, or… Was he losing control again? Oh Goddess. What if he stole more of Luc's magic? His hands and feet tingled.

"Is that magic?" Ethan asked. "Where is it coming from? You?"

Luc shook his head. "No. It's a long story."

"And I very badly want to hear it, but why don't we make the sister comfortable first. She looks a bit pale. Sister—"

"Thistle," said Luc. "I call her Sister Thistle."

"That's positively charming." He turned to the butler. "Chalmers, have Mrs. Quinn make Sister Thistle comfortable while my brother explains himself."

Before Thierry knew what was happening, an older human

woman came from the back of the house to help. She wore unrelieved gray and smelled of laundry soap and lemons. When she pressed her hand to his forehead—in the way of mothers everywhere—her hand was cool and soothing.

"Oh, you're burning up, dear. Let's get you to a guest room. Do you think you can make it up the stairs?"

Thierry nodded. He had no choice but to let her support him. Luc and his brother followed behind, muttering.

"I assume you've been on the road all day," said Ethan.

"It's a long journey."

"I saw the wagon. Couldn't you have hired a carriage?"

"Good way to draw unwanted attention."

"Why so hush-hush?"

"Wait." Instead of answering his half brother, Luc place a hand on Thierry's shoulder. "You should rest. I'll fill Ethan in."

Thierry gave a wan smile. "Thank you."

"Look after Sister Thistle, Mrs. Quinn. The Avimasse air nearly did her in."

"Oh, poor dear." Mrs. Quinn fussed over him. "What about sensitivity to light?"

"Yes, it's very bright. Even inside for some reason." Thierry glanced up and discovered a colorful glass skylight. He swayed backward when he tried to take it all in.

Luc stepped up to steady him, then he exchanged a glance with Ethan.

The two men stared at him. Ethan took out a handkerchief and held it to his nose.

"Tell me, my dear." The woman gently turned his face back toward hers. "Is your skin tingling at all? Are your nerves overset as though the least little thing will make you cry?"

Thierry nodded dizzily. She was right on all counts.

Obviously, this meant something to the woman—to all of them—he just didn't know what. Luc's nostrils flared. A muscle in his jaw tightened.

What was it? Did Luc know what was wrong with him?

The woman leaned in and whispered, "Does it seem as though your wolf is trying to tell you something?"

Thierry closed his eyes and examined his feelings. Oh yes. His wolf was mad with need. His wolf wanted…It needed…*Oh.*

Oh my.

Thierry's face caught fire.

"Oh, Luc. One of the sisters?" Ethan asked. "Does Mother Luna know?"

"It isn't what you think."

"Since when do you care what I think?" Ethan gave Luc a sharp slap on the back, said something to Mrs. Quinn that Thierry couldn't hear, and started back down the stairs. "We'll talk later, then?"

Luc glared silently at his retreating back.

"Come, dear. Let me help you." Mrs. Quinn ushered Thierry into a bedroom so large and elegantly appointed Thierry was certain it had to be a mistake.

"Is this all for me?"

"Of course, dear. Best guest room in the place. You rest while I lay a cozy fire. Ethan will already have a bath on the way, but there's wash water in the basin and mint pastilles in the dish there if you're still not quite the thing."

"All right." Thierry blinked slowly while she chattered on about soaps and toiletries. He picked up a mint candy. If nothing else, getting the taste of sick out of his mouth was very refreshing. He took two more.

The walls featured a tiny floral design. Paintings of birds and blossoms hung in thick, gilded frames. Luxurious carpet cushioned his booted feet, and velvet hangings enclosed an imposing bed. Matching draperies hung around the windows where wood shutters had been left open to let in sunshine and fresh air.

The furnishings included a large wardrobe, a chest of drawers, and a small table with a mirror where Thierry supposed ladies did their hair and adorned themselves with jewels. There was no sitting area. Only a single door, to what, Thierry couldn't guess. The room had to be for visiting nobles. Even the benefactors' rooms at the Temple of the Merciful Moon weren't this fine.

"Let me close these," said Mrs. Quinn, "and then you can rest, yes?"

Thierry glimpsed trees outside the windows before she drew the drapes closed, one by one, shutting out the moonlit night. At least he'd seen proof there were trees. "All right then, dear. Let's get you out of those clothes."

Thierry's heart gave a lurch. Should he brazen things out? Should he flee?

He couldn't disrobe. He wore the disguise for a reason. What if Mrs. Quinn wasn't meant to know he was a man? What if he gave himself away and they chucked him out along with Luc for bringing him?

All his father's direst warnings came back to him. *You're a freak. An abomination. If the wrong people find out what you are, you'll be taken away to be studied. Put in a menagerie.*

He turned away and pressed his face to the room's farthest corner, hands clutching his robes as if she'd try to tear them off him. His fear wasn't rational. Luc would never allow him to come to harm. But his thoughts were so scattered, and he was still shaken from the cacophony of the city streets, and he...he needed.

He *needed* with unprecedented urgency. He didn't think his own hands would work this time, and he wasn't sure how to ask for help without catching fire and burning to a crisp from shame, so he cowered in the corner and pressed his face against the wall like the frightened animal he apparently was...

The door opened and closed behind him.

"Mrs. Quinn, you may leave us." Luc's voice was throaty. The sound seemed to work itself inside Thierry, but he couldn't turn. Wouldn't. He didn't want anyone to see him this vulnerable, not even Luc, whom he trusted with his safety, his life.

This. This unexpected, unwanted exposure at his most helpless wasn't how he wanted Luc to see him ever. But there he was.

"Are you certain, Master Luc?"

"I'm positive. I'll handle this from here. Thank you."

"I'll send up a light tea and bone broth."

"That's an excellent idea. Have them place the tray outside. I'll retrieve things from there."

"Of course. If I may say, congratulations, sir."

"Thank you." Mrs. Quinn left the room silently—for a human—and then they were alone.

Long-seeming seconds passed before Luc placed his hands on Thierry's shoulders. His lips found the skin just under Thierry's ear.

"It's all right, sweetling, she's gone."

Thierry swallowed hard. "It's not the full moon until tomorrow."

"I know."

"Mother Luna said it might happen at the full moon. She never said anything about it jumping out at me like a—a highwayman."

"Oh. Stand and *deliver,* eh?" Luc's voice licked over Thierry's skin like wildfire. "Not a bad analogy."

"Hush, you." Thierry clung stubbornly to the corner, even when Luc tried to turn him around. "It's not funny."

"I'm sorry, sweetling. I don't know what you're feeling right now, but it certainly seems that you could be in heat." He punctuated his words with gentle kisses on the nape of Luc's neck. "Perhaps we should talk about it?"

Thierry covered his face with both hands.

He *couldn't* have some ordinary conversation about this.

Words were stubborn, misleading things, and at any rate, they seemed to be whirling around his brain like autumn leaves before a strong wind.

He barely knew anything anymore—not about his omega status and not about his body—but he was certain that words weren't necessary for this.

That words might even be beside the point.

He turned. "Don't talk. Promise me."

"Thierry—"

Thierry laid his fingers over Luc's mouth. "Hear my wolf's most ardent desire and promise me no words."

That seemed to rock Luc back on his heels. Thierry had surprised himself too, but even in his advanced state of confusion, he had a grip on one true thing. Heat was primal, animal, need. His human mind was not only unnecessary but might even work against him while he was in heat. This was between his and Luc's wolves, though their human bodies would accomplish the act. Thierry had no words for how much he wanted Luc. Trusted him. Loved him. He was Mate.

Mate, and home, and *alpha,* and Thierry needed him. He lifted both hands to Luc's square jaw and smoothed his high cheekbones with his thumbs.

Mate, mate. Beautiful, brave, alpha, mate.

Luc seemed to understand because he dipped his head to cover Thierry's mouth with his own. This kiss—Mate's kiss—wasn't like anything Thierry knew. Hot and greedy, Luc took, and Thierry's wolf yielded to him. Mate's kiss was mundane and magic twisted and sewn into a tapestry of perfection that depicted two halves of a heart coming together for the first time.

Luc's tongue swept out and parted his lips forcefully. It drove away any lingering doubt he had that this was Mate, and Mate was his, and kissing was the right thing to do.

He was Luc's omega. He was Luc's. He belonged to Luc, body and soul.

Thierry's pulse roared, and his cock strained against his smallclothes. He took his time and explored every single inch of the skin above Luc's collar with his fingers, but he resented Luc's clothes for covering the rest of his skin, so he began tearing them away, ridding Luc of his shapeless coat first and then his shirt. Luc unfastened Thierry's red cloak. He bent to grab the hem of Thierry's plain muslin gown and lifted it over his head. Luc let them fall to the floor.

Their eyes met. Luc's pupils narrowed to pinpoints. His eyes took on a distinctly canine appearance. They were the still, pale color of moonlit snow but rimmed with black, and they glowed hotly in an almost feral face.

Luc had to be a terrifying wolf. That was a good thing in a mate. Perhaps he'd let Thierry see him shift someday. Pride made Thierry want to growl. He made a subaudible, greedy sort of sound, which Luc answered with a growl of his own as he shed the rest of his clothes to stand naked and proud before him.

Thierry moaned in delight. *Mate is strong and fierce and beautiful.*

Thierry worked the fastenings of his smallclothes and sat down to tear off his boots. When he was finally naked too, Luc stalked toward him.

Oh yes. Heat was definitely between their wolves.

Luc didn't have to tell Thierry a thing. Thierry flung himself into his mate's arms and assumed his wolf knew what he was doing. He hoped Luc did too because whatever had his cock pounding was indescribable. Powerful. All consuming.

And whether he knew what he was doing or not, it was happening now.

CHAPTER 18

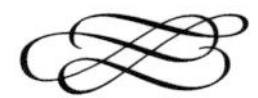

Thierry's wolf was going to be the death of Luc.

The moment they were naked, Thierry hurled himself at Luc and fell to his knees to scent Luc's cock. There wasn't the tiniest hint of shyness in his boy. Luc accepted Thierry's primal exploration, his mouth and his hands anywhere and everywhere. He adored the breathy little sounds that his lover didn't try to hide from him.

After a few precious minutes, Luc pulled Thierry back to his feet and returned the favor. Thierry had strong, lightly furred calves and hard thighs. Tight balls hung below a generously proportioned, rosy cock, and a bush of crisp brown hair arrowed up to the sweetest curved shell of a navel in his surprisingly muscled belly. Up and up, Luc looked, lifting his gaze to a well-formed chest with tightly pebbled nipples, broad shoulders, and half-certain eyes.

No words? How was Luc to do this without words?

He wanted to sing his lover's—his Goddess-blessed mate's—praises for the entire household, for the world to hear. He wanted to ask questions, to encourage. He wanted to know how much, how hard, how's this?

His mate was wonderful. He might be slim and youthful, but he was as strong as the steel in Luc's blade.

Luc cupped his balls. Thierry gave a low moan. Luc explored and shaped the heat of him with his hands, stroking up Thierry's cock and down again, drawing a bead of slick from him, a pearl of iridescent, incomparable beauty.

He lapped at the glistening head of Thierry's cock, tasting the briny, bitter flavor of *Mate* for the first time and glanced up to find a tender, raw expression on Thierry's face. A heartfelt, gut-deep welcome.

Goddess, the boy was made for Luc.

Thierry tangled his fingers in Luc's hair, tightening them almost painfully when Luc opened his mouth to take him in. The minor burn of pain went straight to Luc's cock. Thierry grunted with satisfaction.

Luc took him deeper to see if he could elicit a whine.

The greedy sound Thierry made lifted the hair at Luc's nape. He shifted his hold to Thierry's hips to take him deeper, offering himself up to Thierry's pleasure like a sacrifice.

Use me. Take me roughly. I'll be so strong for you. You can't hurt me.

Thierry jerked his hips forward. Luc smiled around his spit-soaked cock.

Mate, mine, omega. Mine, mine, mine.

Fingers tangled deeper into his hair. Luc relaxed his throat and encouraged his young wolf to fuck his mouth, and he hollowed his cheeks and sucked with each pull. A quick study, Thierry took his cue and quickened his pace. Though Luc's eyes watered, and he even gagged once or twice, his heart nearly burst from his chest with happiness.

He might even have crowed with delight when he felt Thierry's cock thicken, when Thierry's body stuttered, his legs gave way, and he let out a guttural moan while he released down Luc's throat.

That *sound* of satisfaction was so sweet, and Luc worked harder, squeezing out every single drop of cum until sensitivity made Thierry pull away from him.

He didn't go far. Luc opened his eyes to find Thierry leaning over him with his cheeks flushed and his eyes dazed with passion.

If Luc knew any very discreet artists, he'd commission a painting of Thierry with that exact expression—his pleasure spent, his body sated but still hinting at the gluttonous way he'd taken what he'd needed from Luc.

"Goddess, you're beautiful."

Thierry let out a sigh and—seeming to fold in on himself—draped his body over Luc's shoulder. Luc stood. Thierry was featherlight and practically boneless. Sated enough for now to leave alone on the bed for a few minutes.

"Rest now," Luc said before donning a dressing gown. As promised, outside the chamber door, he found a tray with snacks, tea, and a still-warm tankard of bone broth. Given this was Thierry's first heat, and Luc had no idea what to expect, he picked that up and brought it to Thierry's kiss-swollen lips.

"Drink this, dearest." Luc offered it carefully, holding it while his mate took his fill.

Thierry sipped obediently. The broth was gelatinous, meaty and salty, and seasoned with care if he knew Ethan's cook. Thierry's sudden smile didn't surprise him. He helped his mate up and gave him the tankard to finish while he poured a cup of tea for himself.

Luc's cock throbbed, still hard. He'd blown his mate because he'd wanted to and because he thought it might take the edge off Thierry's desperation, but he was not finished. Not by a long shot.

Luc told himself he was older, he was experienced, and he could wait for the next round, but watching Thierry lick his lips after finishing his drink made Luc's cock leak and harden almost painfully.

Goddess, he wanted his mate.

Luc pictured all the different ways he could pleasure his young lover with his hands and mouth and cock. Thierry gave Luc his mug with a considering look.

He stretched.

He arched his back and ran his hand down his chest, hips already restless, cock aroused and flushed again.

So much for taking the edge off. Apparently, his boy was made of edges.

Luc smiled wickedly down at him.

His boy might kill him, but he would be happy to die this way. He pulled Thierry up and crawled between his legs, covering Thierry with his body for the first time.

Thierry gasped in sharp surprise. "Warn a man, would you?"

"You didn't want words," Luc reminded him as he drew the blankets over them.

"Maybe one or two," he whined pitifully and pulled at Luc's robe. "'Brace yourself' would have been nice."

"You said you knew what was going to happen?" Luc flexed his hips cautiously. Now that he was about to take his mate, he didn't want to scare him off. "This all right?"

"Yes, except now that I've seen, um"—he flushed—"I don't know how you're going to fit it where um…"

"Do you need me to explain?"

"Maybe?" Thierry lowered his lashes. Luc brushed his cheek against Thierry's. Their beards crackled together.

"You'll accept me. Your body will soften and grow slick and guide me to your core, and when I'm there, you'll feel indescribable pleasure. I promise."

"I trust you." Thierry squeezed his eyes shut. "All right. Do it."

"While I adore your determination to sacrifice yourself…"

Luc laughed against his cheek. "I work at my own pace, little love."

"Go ahead, I'm ready." Thierry clenched all over.

Luc hid his amusement. It wouldn't do to irritate his little wolf or worse, embarrass him. Instead, Luc laid siege to his mate, kissing him until Thierry opened his lips, using his hands to gentle and sooth and arouse.

"Oh," Thierry gasped when Luc circled his nipple. "That's—*oh.*"

"Mm-hmm," Luc murmured. "Bet you'll like this too."

Luc took the pink nub into his mouth. He sucked and teased and stroked the flesh with his tongue. "Good?"

"Mmm." Thierry arched beneath him. "*Yessss.*"

Friction caused heat to coil in Luc's belly. He canted his hips, rutting over Thierry's taint until Thierry dug his hands into Luc's hair and tugged him down for frantic, filthy kisses.

Luc stroked Thierry's cock. He slid his hand down to cup Thierry's balls. He rubbed his mate's taint and circled his sweet virgin hole with careful, clever fingers. That untouched, puckered flesh had already softened a bit, so he worked it, running his fingers around the tight bud, insinuating a digit inside it in preparation for his cock.

"Ah." Thierry didn't seem to mind. He arched up and took Luc's finger deeper. Luc added another and watched as his fingers disappeared inside his mate's hot body, still attempting patience though he was dry-mouthed and desperate to feel his cock slide into him.

"Good?" Luc added a third finger.

"Oh yes." Thierry's head fell back. His slick aided Luc's movements as he searched for—

"Goddess!" Thierry shrieked.

"There it is." Luc smiled against Thierry's lips. "See? I told you. Pure pleasure. Want more?"

"Yes. Please, Mate."

"Truly?"

"Please, please. I want more, do it again, Mate. Please."

"You beg so sweetly, little love." He pressed his fingers to Thierry's sweet spot again. "I'd give you the world."

"Oh!" Thierry was proving to be a little shouty. "Mate. Please, *Alpha, please*."

"Shh. Do you want everyone to hear you?" Luc wouldn't have minded.

"Cover my mouth." Thierry blinked up at him. "Silence me like you did that first night."

Luc pulled away to look into his eyes. "Are you certain?"

"Yes, Mate. I want that."

"Then you shall have it." Biting his lip, Luc covered Thierry's mouth.

"Ready, love?" Luc lined himself up, the head of his cock at Thierry's hole. "Don't make a sound."

He found his way by touch and pushed in slowly. Thierry closed his eyes. Discomfort? Pain? Luc slowed, giving Thierry a chance to get used to the invasion bit by bit.

But Thierry wasn't made of patience. He wrapped his long, strong legs around Luc's hips and squeezed until Luc's cock bottomed out inside him. Flesh on flesh, Luc's balls slapped Thierry's pert buttocks. Thierry pulled air in through his nose. Luc rolled his hips, testing. Teasing. Trying to keep from spending the very first second he was seated inside his mate.

At last, he found that sacred spot inside Thierry and snapped his hips.

Thierry's head fell back on the pillows, his eyes rolled up, and he gave a stifled wail.

Got you now, sweetling.

Luc kissed wherever he could reach.

Their first coupling became a fevered race to the finish line. Thierry gave as good as he got, pushing up to accept each of Luc's thrusts, gripping with his thighs, clawing at Luc's back to urge him on. Luc gave more and went harder and delved deeper. They clung to each other as if trying to become one body, one heart, one mind.

Luc's wolf rode him hard, his voice deepening to grunts and growls. He stayed in control only by keeping his human mind on Thierry—his love, his mate, his Goddess-blessed one and only.

While Luc couldn't lose himself to his wolf, he did disappear into the bond they were creating together, a bond as strong and permanent and resilient and magical as their love was proving to be.

When Thierry surrendered to orgasm, Luc didn't hesitate.

He kissed his way to the junction of Thierry's neck and shoulder for the claiming bite and struck. The sweet cock in his hand pulsed. Thierry cried out, eyes wide with shock and pain as cum splashed across his beautiful belly. Time froze them in the act—sacred intimacy as old as the wolf itself—as infinite as the Goddess who made them.

Then Luc's pleasure barreled down his spine, and he slipped past all the barriers between them. He was inside Thierry, one with him when he released. As if a whole new breathtaking world opened to him, he saw them—two made one in flesh and soul.

As his heart calmed, he licked at Thierry's broken flesh to soothe him.

Thierry clung to him, kissing his face, his neck. Brushing his sweat-soaked hair from his eyes.

Their gazes met and held.

"You're mine now, Thierry. My omega mate, my love. I will honor and defend and provide for you as long as I have breath."

"Mmnh." Thierry nosed him in a decidedly feline manner. "You're mine, Luc. My alpha mate, my love. I will honor and defend and provide for you as long as I have breath. I will also cherish you. Luc, Goddess, how I love you."

"I love you too, dearest one." Luc kissed him deeply. "So much."

At last, I understand. It would kill me to lose you.

"Just because you're alpha, you don't always get the last word." Thierry shot him a saucy wink.

"Yes, I do." Luc was exhausted. Still, he needed to see to his mate. "Back in a second."

He went to the bath and returned with a damp linen cloth.

As he ran it over his lover's skin, he ticked off all the reasons he was so besotted. The sweet ticklish places beneath Thierry's ribs. His softening cock. The mysterious skin behind his balls. His slightly swollen hole, the virgin hole that was no more.

Mine, mine. Mate. My beautiful boy-mate. Rare, responsive, glorious mate.

Luc swallowed the shockingly possessive urge to claim Thierry again.

"Did you finish your broth?" he asked.

Thierry nodded and licked his lips.

Luc ruffled Thierry's wild hair. "Let's see what else we have, shall we?"

He offered the basket of pastries and watched as Thierry took one in each hand and stuffed his mouth with them.

"Oh Goddess, these are so good. Yum…mmph…so delicious. This one has cream!" He ate until there were none left and flushed deeply. "I guess I got hungry."

Luc's omega mate must have been starving since he insisted on talking with his mouth full.

Luc hid his smile. "Eat up. You need to keep up your strength. Do you want tea?"

Thierry wrinkled his nose. "Can I have more broth?"

"Of course. I'll ring for it." Luc rose and gave the bellpull a tug. "We should have them take care of your robes as well."

Luc picked them up off the floor and draped them over his arm.

"Our bath got cold. I'll get more hot water."

When the knock came, he gave the maid Thierry's things and asked for more broth and a fresh bath. The girl curtsied and scurried away. When he turned, Thierry emerged from beneath the blankets wearing a puzzled expression.

"Why are you so at ease with all this luxury?" he asked, sitting up. "You told me you're a nobleman's by-blow. Where I come from, people hide their indiscretions. They don't put them up in mansions."

"My father doesn't admit to any flaws of character, and there are none who can gainsay him." He shrugged. "I've always been treated as a member of the family, just not by him if that makes any sense."

"Mrs. Quinn called you *master*."

"I was raised side by side with Ethan. For half brothers, we're quite close."

"And you gave all this up to live in Hemlock Forest? Why?"

Luc poured himself a cup of tea, added sugar and cream, and bravely removed a half-eaten pastry from Thierry's hand.

"My mother was common but an exquisite beauty."

"That's not surprising." Thierry bit his lip. "You're beautiful."

Luc sat next to him and stretched out his legs. "Ethan, my father's legitimate son took his place in the world easily, but the standards were always higher for me. No matter what I did, there was a gap between what I could achieve and the things that were my brother's birthright. The unfairness of it all played havoc with me. I was angry all the time."

Thierry's hand covered his. "I'm sorry."

"You've not had it any easier. You're the only known male omega in Rheilôme. Perhaps that's why you and I understand each other so well. Neither of us—through any fault of our own—could ever be worthy in our fathers' eyes."

"You're right. That's true."

Luc let his fingers trail over Thierry's cheek. "How are you feeling?"

Thierry blushed. "Very well, thank you."

"It's likely you will feel better and worse in waves."

"Mother Luna explained things." He lowered his gaze. "I hated being helpless."

"I imagine it's not easy feeling out of control."

"It's horrible." Thierry huffed before looking away. "Not all of it. But—"

"For what it's worth, I will do everything in my power to give you what you need, whatever it is, whether I release or not. As your alpha, I'm meant to serve you in your heat, not use you for my pleasure. I promise you I will never hold your needs against you."

"Oh, how you will suffer for my sake." Thierry smiled shyly.

Luc snorted. "I admit, fucking you is pretty sweet."

"It might, uh, come up again. Very soon." Thierry's flush deepened. He lifted his hand and brushed Luc's hair back from his face. "You know, you have very delicate ears for an alpha."

"The better to hear you with, my dear." Luc turned his head so Thierry could look his fill. "See?"

"And you have the most beautiful eyes I've ever seen. When your cock is hard, the skin above and below your lashes darkens as if you've applied kohl."

"The better to see you with, my dear." Luc leaned over and fluttered his lashes against Thierry's cheek.

Everything tickled Thierry. Luc's boy was a bundle of delighted squeals and squirming and hot passion depending on what part of him you played with. Luc intended to learn every inch of him.

"Stop that." Thierry squirmed away and said playfully, "You have a mouth that just…ngh. When I see your mouth, I want to offer myself in submission to your wicked alpha ways."

"The better to suck your cock!" Luc pounced, pressing little nips and kisses along Thierry's collarbone and down his belly. He licked into Thierry's belly button and moved a bit lower to blow a noise that resembled a loud fart.

"Argh. Stop! No." Thierry caught him roughly by the hair. "Bad wolf!"

Luc lifted his head. Their gazes locked. Their wolves sized each other up.

Thierry tightened his grip in Luc's hair, which—honestly, hair-pulling had never excited Luc before, but Goddess have mercy. Now, it did. From the minute Thierry's fingers caught hold of him that first time...That bite of pain sent his pleasure higher and higher with every tug. Now he wanted it. Craved it.

He got hard at the sight of Thierry's plum-colored, swollen cock—so beautiful, and slick, and aching just for him. The slight pinch of pain at the roots of his hair wildly enhanced his desire.

"Are you trying to tell me something?" he asked his omega.

"Get to work, Alpha." Thierry dropped the empty pastry basket over the side of the bed and folded his arms behind his neck. "Your mate has need."

He'd created a monster. One that would surely kill him.

His Goddess had blessed and cursed him to live in joy.

This was love. This was *everything*.

How lucky could an outlaw wolf with a few tiny secrets be?

CHAPTER 19

Late the following day, Thierry splashed cold water on his face. There was no hiding the shadows smudged beneath his eyes or his unkempt hair or the debauched smile that wouldn't leave his face.

Luc looked no better, but the clothes he'd found somewhere were finer than anything Thierry had ever seen in Amivienne, and they fit him splendidly too. Almost as if they were made for him.

"Those are your clothes, aren't they?" he remarked. "They fit you like a second skin."

"They are." Luc frowned down at himself. "But I'm thinner than I was when I last ate Alice's cooking every day. Why?"

"It's a new and rather nice side to my outlaw mate."

"Shh. Don't get used to it." Luc put a finger to his lips as he stage-whispered, "And the outlaw part is a secret."

"I think I have some understanding of what the outlaw does." He remembered the tax collector who'd been robbed of all but ten percent of his gold after his visit to the Temple of the Merciful Moon. "Have you ever been caught?"

"Not yet." Luc gestured to a set of clothes on the bed. "I

brought some things I thought might fit my brawny farm-lad mate."

Luc held up the shirt. He was used to wearing shapeless garments with casing ties and tunics and rough breeches. He'd never worn anything his mother and Esme hadn't sewn for him.

He started to pull the shirt over his head and quickly got stuck.

"It's too small, I think."

"Let me help," Luc said warmly. "You have to undo the buttons if you want to put it on."

Thierry flushed. Buttons. Of course. The thing would be fitted once it was on.

"I see."

"I'll play valet, shall I. It will be like a game. When I help you on with your boots, I'll drop to my knees and—"

"Keep that plan in mind for later"—Thierry winced—"because my cock can't take much more just yet." His heat had driven them to ridiculous ends. Thierry was chafed, chapped swollen, and unlikely to feel playful for a day or two, even if he was gagging for release.

"I forgot, darling. I'm sorry." Luc settled the shirt on his shoulders before kissing the top of his head. "I'll ring for some of Mrs. Quinn's salve so—"

"Don't you dare!" Goddess, wouldn't that be fun? They'd have the entire staff laughing about his sore bits. "I'll be fine."

"Discomfort is not that uncommon after a heat. For both partners. Shall I pretend it's for me?"

"You'll do it whether I want you to or not," Thierry grumbled, having discovered his mate took no shortcuts in caring for him. "Why ask?"

"You're right, of course. I'll be a very bossy alpha when it comes to your health."

"It's just a little tender skin."

"But it's your skin, dearest. That makes it precious." Thierry let Luc harry him into breeches and a jacket with a leather vest and fine coat to go over it. These were bulkier than his normal clothes and far less comfortable, but when he saw himself in the mirror beside his mate, for the first time he thought he looked… worthy of him. He vowed to master blending in wherever he and Luc found themselves so he wouldn't ever embarrass his mate.

"What's that look?"

"We make a good pair." He wasn't about to tell Luc how insufficient he felt.

"Of course we do. The Goddess knows what she's doing."

"May I be worthy," Thierry offered. "Along those lines, is there anything I should know? Are manners very different here?"

Luc grinned. "Aside from not dashing to the guest bedroom to fuck for two full days after you arrive someplace, you mean?"

"Oh my Goddess—"

"Act naturally. You're polite, tidy, and loyal. They'll love you."

"Sounds like you're talking about a dog." Still flushing, Thierry allowed Luc to shove him out the door and down the stairs to face the day. Or what was left of it.

"Here you are." Ethan stared at the two of them with shock. "Wait—"

"Ethan, I'd like to introduce you to my omega mate, Thierry."

"But—"

"You thought I was despoiling one of the Sisters of the Merciful Moon Temple. Admit it. I still have the power to surprise you."

"I—" Ethan closed his mouth. "I need a drink, big brother. You?"

"Have you ever known me to turn one down?"

"No. What a lush you are." He turned to Chalmers. "We'll be in my study for a bit."

"Very good, Your Highness." Whether the man was surprised

to see a male omega instead of a Sister of the Order, he gave no sign.

"Wait." Thierry's head swiveled to look at Ethan, eyes wide with shock. "He said—"

"Later," Luc mouthed.

Later? Luc would explain why Chalmers had referred to Ethan as *Your Highness* later? The royal family was large, but if Ethan was a member, and Luc was his half brother...What did that mean?

Thierry held his tongue, but why would Luc wait to tell him? Did he want to fling his rustic mate in his family's faces as a form of rebellion? He'd rebelled by leaving school and becoming an outlaw. In a panic, Thierry followed Luc and his brother into a room with floor-to-ceiling books on three walls. On the fourth, a fire burned merrily in a fireplace large enough to roast an ox.

"Spill, Lucas. What have you done this time?"

"I've met my Goddess-blessed mate."

"Congratulations, brother," Ethan said heartily. "But he's—"

"A peasant?" Thierry supplied the word.

"I was going to say an omega," Ethan chided. "Which is far more interesting to me than whether you've handled a scythe, although that must be where all those lovely muscles originated."

"His eyes are in his face, brother." Luc huffed as he sat and crossed his legs.

"You're truly omega?" Ethan stared.

"All my life." Thierry perched on the edge of Luc's armchair, hands in his lap.

"Balls, what a treat. Father will swallow his tongue." Ethan moved to lean on the mantel. "Did you know Kit married a male omega?"

"I heard." Luc laid his hands over the arms of his chair. "I didn't believe it at first. I assumed they were only saying that because Prince Christopher wanted a male consort."

"But his mate gave birth, you said." Thierry remembered that as the news had pertained to him specifically. "So he must be omega, mustn't he?"

"He must." Ethan nodded. "He is. I was at the wedding. And then my brother shows up on my doorstep with *his* male omega mate, in heat no less. I was beginning to think I'd imagined you, but then Mrs. Quinn pointed out all the inhuman noises coming from the guest room and—"

"Oh Goddess," Thierry said weakly. "Oh my Goddess."

"Hush, Mate. My brother's being a cad because he thinks it's funny."

"I'm sorry, little wolf." Ethan had the grace to look chagrined. "It's simply that your kind is so rare. Only one or two male omegas have ever been recorded in the history books. There are more in the old tales, of course."

"I've hidden my status my whole life to avoid just such a moment," Thierry said dryly. "Perhaps there are others like me who don't want to be looked at like a new species of plant."

"Is that what you think?" Ethan's face fell. "Male omegas are said to be gifts from the Goddess. They bring change, and perhaps we need that now more than ever."

"I don't understand." Thierry was a little afraid to hear what Luc's brother meant, but he'd never been one to stick his head in the sand.

Or maybe he was...

How Charles would laugh at him now.

"Our father is old and set in his ways. He believes in a wolf hierarchy that keeps humans out of positions of power at every level. He has antiquated ideas about mating. For example, he'll positively combust when he sees Luc with you."

"Luc, what haven't you told me?"

"The king is our father," Luc said flatly. "Not to put too a fine point on it, Ethan is the crown prince. As the illegitimate son, Father intended me to be high court magus."

Thierry didn't understand. "Didn't you say Luc was your older brother?"

"Oh yes. He's older by six months." Ethan shrugged.

"Only a legitimate heir can ascend the throne," said Luc. "I never wanted to be king anyway. But there you have it. I'd rather be an outlaw than high court magus any day. I'd rather eat my liver."

"Even when I'm king?" Ethan asked. This seemed like an old argument because Luc waved the question away. "All right. It's not as pressing as your news, but we'll continue this at a later date. Tell me why you're here."

"I've come for your advice and aid." Luc explained everything that had happened in Hemlock Forest. Ethan sat very still. Only his tightened jaw gave away his feelings on the matter. "So far, it seems as though no one has informed the League."

"Hm. This is troubling." Ethan tapped his fingers on the mantel as if deep in thought. "Magic has, for centuries, been the purview of alphas. It stands to reason, given magic is intrinsic to the species, but it obviously gives us an unfair advantage in every aspect of life."

"We're apex predators, brother dear," said Luc. "That's our advantage. Magic is a bonus."

"Yes, but the more scholars learn about magic, the more they believe magic is inherent to the world we live in and *all* its inhabitants. As a master mage, you can correct me if I'm wrong, Luc, but—"

"Forgive me." Thierry turned to Luc. "Might there be something else you forgot to mention?"

Luc winced. "I was going to tell you."

"When? You're a master mage and the son of our king? Anything else? Can you fly? Breathe beneath the waves? Shoot fire from your buttocks?"

"All right. I've been reticent," Luc admitted. "At first, you and I barely knew each other, and I had to wonder if you'd been sent as a sort of spy."

"Spy. Well, I was spying. Not on you, though." Thierry frowned. "Charles always said he thought the tests for mage schools were skewed toward alpha wolves from noble backgrounds."

"Oh yes." Ethan agreed. "Almost all betas are turned away as having insufficient magic."

"Right. They're witches, allowed to practice what they can with ambient magic. Charles says that isn't right. He says that even omegas, who aren't supposed to have any magic, are powerful in some misunderstood way."

"His ideas are radical." said Ethan. "What do you make of his beliefs?"

"I know Charles. If he believes something is unfair, he'd fight for what's right. Omegas piqued his curiosity after—" Thierry shut his mouth.

"After what?" Ethan asked.

Thierry looked to Luc. Should he bare all, even though Ethan might think him mad?

They were no longer in tiny Amivienne where he could speculate with Mother Luna in relative anonymity. This was the crown prince. The man who would be king. What if he decided Thierry wasn't of sound mind or that he was part of the pervasive evil of Hemlock Forest simply because he'd had the bad luck to be in the wrong place at the wrong time? What would Ethan do to his brother's mate if he thought him mad?

"Tell him, Thierry," said Luc. "What you've seen is important."

So Thierry told him about Charles. About the magic circle and the beast and how Charles had died while he stayed hidden.

"Goddess," Ethan blanched. "I'm sorry for your loss, Thierry."

"It was a long time ago. And to be truthful, Charles's body was lost to us, but his spirit, his magic if you will, remains."

"Not possible," Ethan stated firmly.

"It's true." Luc stood and laid a hand on Thierry's shoulder. "I've felt him come and go from our presence the same way I'd feel you if I kept my eyes closed."

"Goddess." Ethan looked through them as he thought things over. "This is quite the tale."

"I still can't see the necromancer's purpose in all this." Luc narrowed his eyes. "He's used his puppets to kill. In the case of the murdered omegas, he drained his kills of their magic, but to what end? I know of no way to transfer magic from one user to another. It has been tried, of course—"

"First things first. There has to be someone covering his tracks with the League," said Ethan. "I can assure you that no mention of a necromancer prowling Hemlock Forest has crossed Father's desk or mine."

"I came to speak with Cavendish." Luc glanced at Thierry. "He's the one man I trust from my life at the Royal Academy. He never countenanced the use of death magic, even for academic research."

Death magic. Thierry shivered. Even the sound of it was revolting.

"I'll send for him straightaway. We'll get to the bottom of this, Thierry. Your friend will not have died in vain." Ethan strode to his desk and without sitting, picked up his quill.

"I'll be sure to tell Charles that," Thierry whispered for Luc's ears only. "When next I hear his disembodied voice in my head."

Luc eyed him. "Fucking has made you sharpish, little wolf. I like it."

"I do have alpha hearing," Ethan said without glancing up. "Chalmers will have someone run this to the Academy."

He got up and rang the bellpull. Chalmers came and took the

message. Ethan closed the door behind him and turned to them contemplatively.

"Luc, would you leave me with your mate for a bit?"

"Why?" Thierry's emotions swirled tumultuously.

"I have a few more questions for you, my very rare friend."

Thierry looked to Luc for…something. Not permission, he told himself.

Luc nodded. "He only wants to squeeze you for information about me. He won't hurt you."

"What don't you want him to know?" Thierry asked. "I'll lie about it."

Both Luc and Ethan laughed.

Luc said, "See why I adore my Goddess-blessed mate?"

"I do," Ethan agreed. "You've got an intelligent raven companion and an astonishing mate. Why do you have all the luck, brother?"

"I owe everything to honest living."

That time, it was Ethan and Thierry who nearly collapsed with mirth.

Luc left him alone with the crown prince of Rheilôme. The crown prince. *Goddess.*

"If Pa could see me now."

"From your story, I understand your father thought you cursed."

Thierry nodded. There was no point in going over that again.

"You'll need background. Luc's omega mother was a Lyrienne mystic and a secret magic practitioner. Father told me." He led Thierry back to the chairs by the fire and sat opposite him. "Cavendish knows, but I believe Father kept it from Luc."

"Do you expect me to keep it from him as well?"

"Would you?"

"No."

"Then I must give you permission to share anything we say

here." Ethan said easily. "As you can imagine, the old order is rife with secrets and lies and treachery. The fact that the magic aptitude tests are rigged against lesser alphas, betas, and humans and not even open to omegas is all of those things. I've long resented my father's efforts to avoid progress. I hate the arbitrary customs that keep Luc from taking his rightful place. He's a far more powerful alpha and practitioner than I am. And he's good. Courageous. As high court magus in my court he'd have the power to right these wrongs."

"But he'd have to be unmated."

"That's absolutely the first thing I would change. I've always looked up to my brother. I want to see him happy."

Thierry asked, "Why shouldn't he be king instead of high court magus?"

"Luc hates politics." Ethan shook his head. "He doesn't have the patience to wade through foreign negotiations. He'd take a knife to our allies if he had to host the many necessary banquets. Luc's not cut out to be king. I am not saying that because I am, although it's true, I am. I believe I'll be a brilliant king."

"You seem to have an open mind." That was probably a good thing in a king.

"That's good for a start, between us especially." When Ethan smiled, Thierry could clearly see his resemblance to his brother. "I'll try to earn your trust. You could aid me in bringing Luc around to my way of thinking."

"I won't manipulate my mate."

"I don't want you to. Just remind him that he's not really an outlaw at heart. He's simply doing what he believes is right. As king, I will find him a better way to help our people. He wants that deep down. He'll be glad to help them legitimately. Agreed?

"Agreed." Thierry saw no downside to that.

"All I want in this world is for my brother to come home. I want him beside me when I ascend the throne, in whatever capacity he wishes to serve, though he'd be such a very useful high court magus."

"He wanted to be a healer." Thierry thought back to their conversation. "He said your father wouldn't allow it."

"I *would* allow it if he still wants that. But I believe he's meant for bigger things. There should be no need for our people to flee into the forest."

"I wouldn't know about bigger things," Thierry said. "I'm only a farmer."

"You are a male omega, Thierry. A once-in-a-lifetime gift from the Goddess. It's not chance that brought you here to us, but destiny."

For the first time since he'd met Luc, words failed Thierry. He opened his mouth, but no sound came out.

"Trust me, little wolf. Tell me, is bringing Luc back here a lost cause?"

Thierry closed his eyes to think. Luc didn't love the forest, but he loved his people. He loved the opportunity to serve as their leader. He loved protecting them and watching their families grow.

"It's not a lost cause. Not if things change and he's no longer needed there."

Ethan seemed relieved to hear it. "It's selfish to wish he could be my second-in-command when he's independent and has his own people to lead. But I'll need a high court magus I can trust to watch my back, especially if I make changes to the status quo. There are those who will despise me for it. When I'm king, he can study anything he wants, do anything he chooses, as long as he agrees to stand with me."

Thierry considered him. "I heard little news while I worked in the fields on my father's farm. This may be insensitive. Is your father—"

"Father is not as well as he'd like people to believe. He's losing his memory. He has erratic moods. Physically, he's a shadow of the man he was two years ago. It has been a steady decline. His doctors tell me there's not much time left."

"That's another reason to broker peace between Luc and his father."

"May the Goddess grant it," murmured Ethan.

In the meantime, a necromancer was terrorizing the people in the forest around Amivienne. Thierry didn't envy his mate's brother. It had to be hard supporting a king in decline. Ethan certainly had a great deal to worry about.

Thierry, however, had only one thing: Luc.

He'd sworn to protect his mate whatever may come. Given a choice between his king and country or his mate, Thierry knew he'd choose Luc every single time. Thierry would go wherever Luc led him.

Hero or outlaw.

Perhaps now was a good time to be a little bit of both.

CHAPTER 20

Luc suggested a turn around the garden. It seemed to help take Thierry's mind off things, but the weather was unseasonably cold. Thierry wasn't dressed for a chilly, damp Avimasse morning. They barely made it to the first tree before he started shivering.

"What now?" asked Thierry.

"Now we wait for Cavendish." Luc hated waiting. Since there was no way to tell how high up their possible conspiracy went, and his brother had heard nothing of a necromancer working beneath the noses of Amivienne's Academy, they couldn't simply approach the Royal Academy directly. The League was apparently still ignorant as well.

By chance or by choice?

There were scholars in the highest echelons of magical philosophy who had expressed a desire to learn more about death magic. Even Luc had been curious. Magic was neutral, neither good nor bad. What a practitioner did with it gave it form and substance. A practitioner's intent gave it meaning.

Perhaps those looking the other way had decided it was time to explore death magic, believing that once the restrictions were loosened enough, there would be no stopping mages from exploring its uses, ethical or not. But Amivienne's necromancer had taken innocent lives, and Luc couldn't see any ethical person condoning it.

"What did my brother have to say?" he asked Thierry.

"He wants you back in what he calls your rightful place." Thierry was clearly trying to hide his shivers. Luc wrapped an arm around him and brought him close.

"I know he does. Let's go in where it's warmer."

Thierry went with him gladly. "It's colder here at this time of year than in Amivienne, isn't it?"

"We get the wind off the sea here. It comes from the north where it's colder."

"I wish Avimasse smelled better, though here it's not as bad as when we first arrived. I thought I'd never be able to breathe again."

"In retrospect, that might have been your heat. I've heard heats make an omega's senses more acute."

"I picked the wrong time to come to the city."

"I'm sorry, darling." Luc opened the kitchen door for his mate. "I couldn't leave you behind. Your first heat was bound to come with the moon, and I assumed you would need me."

"And come it did," Mrs. Quinn said blithely from the marble table where she kneaded bread. "Feeling better? What can I get you?"

"I'm fine, thank you," answered Thierry.

"More broth, please, Mrs. Quinn. And are there still pastries?" Luc wanted to make certain his mate kept up his strength. "Or cakes?"

"Of course." She studied Thierry's mate mark. "Well done, Master Luc. Congratulations again. When you're ready to share your news with family and friends, I'll see to everything."

"That won't be necessary, but thank you. We'll be returning to Amivienne shortly." And the last thing they needed right now was a public event. He turned to Thierry. "It will be some time before Cavendish arrives. You should rest while you can."

Thierry gave a nod and whispered, "You wore me out."

"Said the pot to the kettle," Luc teased. Thierry's fiery blush warmed him.

"Why don't you both go up." Mrs. Quinn gave Luc a nudge. "You haven't slept either. I'll have the maids leave a tray outside the door."

"Thank you. Perhaps that would be best."

As soon as the door to their bedroom closed, Luc took Thierry into his arms and plundered the sweet mouth he couldn't seem to get enough of. Thierry loved like he lived, without any artifice at all. Kisses blossomed like flowers between them. Some went off course, and Thierry giggled shyly. Luc let his lips slide to the boy's ear and the soft skin of his neck. Thierry's light cheek stubble caught against his. When he let go, Thierry seemed dazed.

"What was that for?" he asked.

"It has been entirely too long since I last kissed you." Luc couldn't help a tiny leer.

He wanted to sink into his mate, even though it'd been only hours since they'd last made love. He wanted to push him down and crawl inside him and never let him go.

"No…no." Thierry backed away, arms raised. "You have sex eyes."

Luc stalked him playfully. "What exactly are sex eyes?"

"Those right there." Thierry pointed at Luc's face. "Those are your sex eyes. You look like a hungry lion who wants to devour me."

"What if I do?"

"Argh." Thierry flopped onto the bed and groaned. "We can't. I'm all used up. There's nothing left. My cock will fall off if you so much as touch it."

"Hmm." Luc loomed over him. "I did ask Mrs. Quinn to put her very famous healing salve in our room."

Thierry sat up on his elbows. "Oh Goddess, she knows exactly why we need it."

"Of course she does. And that's fine. She's a genius when it comes to this sort of thing. Her salve is made from oil of almonds and herbs she won't divulge on pain of death. Why don't I massage a little of it into your skin, and we'll see if it helps?" He climbed into bed with his mate and began to undress him, boots first then breeches and smallclothes. He dropped Thierry's jacket on the floor but allowed him the modesty of his shirt. The day was cool, after all. He retrieved the pot of salve from the nightstand and pulled the cork out, giving the soothing concoction a sniff.

"Just as I remember." If he added his healing magic to the blend, his mate would feel much better. He should have thought of that earlier, but he'd never taken anyone's first heat before.

"I sense a trap." Thierry eyed him warily.

"Would I do anything treacherous to my beloved mate?" Luc dabbed a bit of the salve on Thierry's red skin. "It's my duty to make you feel good."

The soft surprise on his mate's face, the relief, was all he'd wanted, though he couldn't help giving Thierry's cock a stroke, just to make sure the salve warmed up.

"*Oh…*" Thierry moaned.

"Feel better?"

"Not—um—quite yet." Thierry's gaze turned teasing. "Perhaps you should massage my cock just a bit more."

"Your every wish is my command, darling."

"You spoil me."

"Not yet, but I plan to." Luc went to work, pleasuring his mate thoroughly.

Thierry was barely over his first heat, after all.

For now, their other problems could wait. At least until Cavendish replied to their cry for help.

~

Ethan ate dinner formally at the townhouse, even when he was alone in the city. An hour before the appointed time, Luc had reluctantly informed his mate that it was time to wash and dress. Now, he watched Thierry as the boy studied his reflection in the mirror.

"I look debauched," Thierry muttered. "Why are my lips so red?"

"The better to kiss me with, my dear." Luc wrapped his arms around him and nuzzled his neck from behind.

"Don't start." Thierry squirmed away. "I can barely walk as it is."

"The salve helped, didn't it?"

"The skin, not the muscles. I can't feel my legs. Is that normal? Why do you look so pleased with yourself?"

"Darling." Luc spun him around. "I'm pleased with my mate."

Thierry look up at him from beneath his lashes. "You're different from what I imagined you to be like when we first knew each other."

"How so?"

"You have this…playful side. Back home, you were always so serious."

"I feel safe here." It was true. He'd dropped his cares like a burden at the door because his family—even though he didn't bear their name—offered him protection. "I only wish my friends in the forest had such a place."

"*You* are their safe place, Luc."

Luc took his mate's words in. He questioned them then caught his breath.

"Goddess, you're right." Luc stepped away. "I must keep that in mind as we figure out what to do with this necromancer. As much as I wish things were different, now that you're no longer in heat, dallying with you—"

"I understand." Thierry cupped his jaw and pressed their lips together lightly. "We should wait for a better time."

Luc sighed. "I wish we were a normal couple. We could travel. Spend our days getting to know each other."

"I know all I need to know about you." Thierry caught both his hands. "I know that I want to stand by your side as long as I have breath. Luc, I'd follow you into the shadowlands if you asked me to."

"I would do the same." Luc's eyes burned. "You're everything to me. I hope you know that."

A soft knock on the door made Luc kiss Thierry's forehead and move away. "Yes?"

The maid said, "Mr. Chalmers says your guest has arrived, Master Luc."

"Thank you." He turned to Thierry and held out his hand. "Shall we?"

Thierry placed his hand in Luc's. "Let's go."

Cavendish and Ethan waited in the study. Though Luc hadn't seen him for years, his old professor had barely aged. He'd been a robust and athletic fifty back then with a touch of gray at his temples. The only difference Luc now observed was that far more silver glistened in his hair. Apparently, Ethan was filling him in because his expression was grim.

"Luc was right to come to me with this, wasn't he?" Ethan asked. "Surely the League would have responded had they been apprised of the situation."

"We've heard nothing of this." Cavendish turned to him and Thierry. "But congratulations are in order, aren't they? Before we get too deeply into business, please introduce me."

"Thierry, this is Drew Cavendish, my mentor from the Royal

Academy and the Rheilôme ambassador to the League of Ethical Mages. Drew, my Goddess-blessed mate."

"Goddess blessed?" With a catch in his breath, Drew greeted Thierry warmly. "It's a pleasure to meet you, my boy. A pleasure. But to answer the question, we've received no report of anyone using death magic around Amivienne in years. There was an incident in the region about five years ago. I believe a boy was killed?"

"Charles." Thierry paled.

"My mate witnessed his death." Luc took his hand protectively.

Cavendish narrowed his eyes. "I never heard of a witness."

"Someone must have hushed up his involvement. Thierry was rendered mute by the brutality of his friend's death. He couldn't answer questions, and his family didn't encourage him to interact with anyone afterward, but he witnessed the entire event"

"Hmm. At the time, I was told that a prank involving two students went awry, and one was killed."

"There was no prank, sir. And the mage involved wasn't a student. Though he wore the robes of the Amivienne Academy, Charles had never seen him before. Charles thought it a lark to spy on a mage at work."

"I see." Cavendish nodded. "I probably would have done the same. Young mages are curious on the whole."

"Charles didn't know what the man was doing until he made a blood sacrifice, and by then it was too late. The animal rose up after it died." Thierry had to clear his throat before he could go on. "He must have heard something because he sent the beast after us."

"How did you get away?" asked Cavendish.

"I—Goddess forgive me." Thierry clasped his hands. "I climbed a tree. Charles tried. He lost his grip. I almost had him, but he fell. I watched my best friend die horribly."

"Hush." Luc gathered him into his arms. "The fault belongs to the practitioner, sweetheart."

"Tell that to Charles's family." Thierry impatiently wiped his eyes. "To anyone in Amivienne."

"You hid in a tree? That's...impossible." A frown marred his old friend's forehead. "The mage should have sensed your presence. Why would he leave a witness alive?"

"Thierry's omega," Luc said as though that explained everything. "Come sit. There's much you don't know."

"Omega." Cavendish's eyes widened as he followed them to the chairs at the fireplace. "Of course he is, by the Goddess. I should have picked that up right away."

Thierry took one armchair and Luc's mentor the other. Luc and Ethan remained standing.

"Of course he's omega," Cavendish repeated. "How was that not obvious from the start? What is that other aroma? It distracts me."

"Oil of almonds?" Luc asked. "Myrrh?"

"Oh. Yes, that's it!" As if it had suddenly dawned on him why one might need such things, he flushed deeply. "Goddess, the full moon. Where are my manners?"

"It's nothing." Thierry kept his gaze lowered.

"So what do you make of this, Cavendish?" Luc redirected the conversation. "This mage has already killed several people that we know of."

"Three omegas very recently if I understand right?" He furrowed his brows.

"Plus, my escort, the sheriff and his men," said Thierry.

"So you think he's targeting omegas specifically? Is that because he assumes they're weak?"

"The Sisters of the Merciful Moon move freely in the forest. Perhaps it's a combination of things," Ethan offered.

"But why go back to Amivienne?" asked Thierry. "Do you

suppose it has to do with the Academy or the Merciful Moon Temple?"

"Why would you say that?"

"Because…" Thierry frowned. "Some of the omegas there are practitioners. Isn't that right? Luna is."

"Yes," Luc admitted. "But few people know that because omega practitioners hide their gifts, especially in Rheilôme."

"The practitioner community feels that omegas shouldn't be allowed magic. Is it bad for business or something?" Thierry's puzzled expression made the others laugh. "Oh, I know I'm not saying this right. Is it thought to be bad for society if omegas practice magic? It would change things."

Cavendish gasped. "Oh dear, you're absolutely right. Ethan, you must not allow the king to call the high council of mages until I've looked into this."

"Why?" Ethan asked. "How are we supposed to fight a powerful necromancer without our best mages?"

"You think the conspiracy reaches the high counsel?" asked Luc.

"Goddess, I hope not," said Cavendish, "but it's best to learn more before we make assumptions."

Luc and his brother exchanged frowns. "So this could be very bad."

Cavendish nodded. "Luc, you and Thierry must return as if nothing has changed. Inform Luna that the threat is very real. She's to do every single thing that she can to protect the sisters. She must keep them inside the temple walls."

"She'll never go for that," Luc argued. "You know how stubborn she is."

"Like Verna when she worked for the League," Cavendish said wryly. "I never met two more stubborn omegas."

Thierry's brows shot up. "How was she in the League when omegas can't be part of the practitioner community?"

"Lyrienne follows matrilineal custom, and they prize their

omega practitioners. Didn't Luc tell you he's half Lyrienne?" Thierry shook his head. "Well, I suspect that's why he's a bit of a rebel. It's only Rheilôme that's so backward thinking. After Verna died, Luna joined the Temple of the Merciful Moon in her sister's name."

"Mother was more worldly than her sister, or so I'm told," said Luc. "She enjoyed the finer things, and life in Rheilôme's court suited her. Luna meant to join a Lyrienne order, but after I was born, she chose to remain in Rheilôme."

"I see." Thierry bit his lip. "Do you think the necromancer or someone else is trying to discredit Luna in some way? Destroy her reputation, and you destroy the Order. No more refuge for practicing omegas."

"That was my thought as well." Cavendish nodded. "One possibility is that we have a madman exploring necromancy for his own gain. Another is that we have a conspiracy aiding acts of necromancy for some darker purpose."

"Putting omegas in their place?" asked Thierry grimly.

"It's widely known that I don't hold the same views my father does with regard to species and class and status." Ethan picked up a silver candlestick, studied it, then put it down negligently. "I don't see why humans can't work alongside wolves, and I don't believe the practice of magic must be restricted to the alpha elite. My first choice for high court magus is Luc because he shares my beliefs."

"Many in the practitioner community hold your views," Cavendish agreed. "But there are still a few in the old guard who would rather see things remain as they've been. And one of those people—one of the more outspoken ones—is Reginald Chaubert."

"I've heard that name," said Thierry. "Where have I heard that name?"

"Chaubert is the director of the Academy at Amivienne."

"If he's working with this necromancer," said Ethan, "it could have consequences far beyond the Order of the Merciful Moon. People are well aware of Luna's connection to the royal family. Destroying her reputation will cast a shadow over all of us."

"Wait," said Luc. "Are we saying that it's possible a necromancer in Amivienne is working against Ethan? Why? Because he's crown prince?"

"Not just me. He's killing in your forest, brother," Ethan said. "Didn't you worry you might be blamed for his crimes? Maybe the architect of the conspiracy seeks to kill two birds with one stone."

All the breath seemed to leave Luc's body.

He could see it play out. Discredit Luna, prove omegas need alpha protection, paint Luc as an outlaw—perhaps even blame him for the murders—he looked to Ethan.

"No one would blame you for my actions, though. You're the king's rightful heir, and I'm nobody."

"They would if I took your part." Ethan smiled at him. "And I would, obviously. Two birds. One stone."

"No," Thierry said aghast. "What can we do?"

"I'll contact the Lyrienne ambassador to the League," Cavendish said grimly, "and apprise him of the situation. I trust him. He'll offer help I'm sure."

"I need to get home," said Luc. "Luna and my people depend on me."

"You'd be putting your head in the noose," Ethan argued. "Better stay here. You can't be blamed for what the necromancer does while you're in the city."

"I can't protect myself at the cost of other people's lives." Luc shook his head. "Thierry will stay here. I want him safe."

"Like *fire* will I stay here while my mate goes off to battle an evil mage," Thierry said. "It's as if you never met me."

Ethan took a deep breath. "We rely on your guidance, Cavendish. You're League. You have a plan. What should we do?"

"Was that the royal we?" Luc asked. "Are you already—"

"Shut up." Ethan made a rude gesture.

"I have missed seeing you both more often," Cavendish said with a sad smile. "Luc and Thierry must warn Luna. Get her to see reason. Lock the gates behind you. No visitors. No one in or out of the temple complex."

"But my people—"

"You left Peter in charge," Thierry argued. "John must be well by now. Do you trust them?"

Did he? "They're my best men. They'll do anything that I would under the circumstances. I'd trust those two with my life." *Not yours though, beloved.* As if he'd heard Luc's thoughts, Thierry rose and kissed his cheek.

"Then we must do as Cavendish says," Thierry said with finality.

Luc took his hand. "Let's hope we can stop this madman before someone else is killed."

"We will." Cavendish stood. "Ethan, leave this to the League. As soon as the Lyrienne cohort can join me, we'll make our way to the Academy in Amivienne to sort things out. If Chaubert is guilty of some conspiracy, we'll put an end to it. You have my word."

"Thank you, Cavendish."

"No need to thank me. I have a soft spot for our next high court magus."

"I never said I'd do it," Luc grumbled.

"Nevertheless." The older man winked at him. "You'll do very, very well in the position."

"We were about to have supper," Ethan said, "I don't suppose you could stay."

"No time, Ethan." Cavendish offered his hand. They grasped each other's wrists. "This is urgent business, I fear."

"All right. Thank you."

"Anything for my future king." He turned to give Luc and Thierry a wink. "Congratulations again. This won't be the wedding trip I'd wish for you, but I'll see you soon. Together we'll sort this out, and you can take your young mate on a world tour, I promise."

"Thank you, sir." Thierry offered his hand. Luc's wolf wanted to tear his mate away from his old friend. Truly, jealousy was a new and uncomfortable emotion.

"Goodbye, Cavendish." Luc offered his hand.

Instead, the mage pulled Luc into his arms. The embrace was warm and paternal. Cavendish gripped his shoulders and set him away so they stood eye to eye. "It's good to see you happy. I'm very proud of you, Luc."

"Thank you, sir." Tears stung Luc's eyes. His father was a coarse man with a temper and the notion that gestures of affection made men weak. In part, that's why he and Ethan had always been close. At the Royal Academy, finally, he'd found his mentor—a father figure—in Drew Cavendish. His father's decision to restrict him to nothing more than a courtier, a pencil pusher, had destroyed his one happiness.

After they saw Cavendish out, Ethan laid his hand on Luc's shoulder.

"Dangerous work ahead, brother," he said.

"Yes." Ethan believed in a better world. He'd said he wanted Luc beside him while he created it. This threat—this evil necromancer—was part of a plot to ruin both their dreams.

Luc was grateful Ethan was the crown prince, not he. Luc was always going to be an outlaw at heart. He wanted the world they'd envisioned together, and he wasn't above destroying anyone who stood in their way.

"We should eat and get a good night's sleep," Luc told Ethan. "Thierry and I will leave as early as possible."

"Of course," Ethan agreed.

"We'll need fast horses."

"Done." Ethan frowned. "You won't exactly go unnoticed that way."

"We can't worry about that anymore." Luc wished Thierry would stay with Ethan, but he would make the same decision to stay with his mate if he were in Thierry's place. "Thierry needs comfortable riding clothes."

"I'll make sure you have everything you need."

"Then we'll go." Luc knew that Thierry's hopeful expression hid an anxious heart. Luc had no answers. They hadn't set this conspiracy in motion, but they were wrapped up in it anyway. They had to see things through.

They were stronger together.

They would succeed against any odds as long as they had each other.

They would succeed, or fail spectacularly, together.

CHAPTER 21

The mounts Ethan's grooms readied for them were very fine. Thierry steadied himself while Luc held the reins, waiting for him to swing up into the saddle. He put his foot into the stirrup easily enough, and the horse was well trained. He hoisted himself into the saddle and clutched the horse's mane so he wouldn't fall off the slippery leather and over the beast's other side.

"Steady there." Luc narrowed his eyes. "Still sore?"

"I'm fine." He was sore, but that wasn't the problem. As a farm boy, he'd ridden his family's nag, but she was so sway-backed it was nearly impossible to fall off. It wasn't as if they saddled her. His horsemanship was…limited to say the least.

He had a few seconds to learn to sit astride the healthy, finely saddled horse before Luc swung up and urged his mount forward.

Thierry could do this. He would. He wasn't going to slow his mate down over his lack of experience. Luc already wanted him to stay behind. It was likely Luc could use the excuse that Thierry wasn't exactly a good rider to make him stay.

Good thing he was strong. He found his seat, gripping with

his legs and moving with the flow of the animal while occasionally grabbing its mane to hold on for dear life.

The mare wasn't happy with him. She expected far more skill and confidence than he was betraying. She'd been giving him looks of such equine disgust, Thierry had faltered, but now she was pretty much ignoring him and taking her cues from Luc's gelding.

After a while, riding almost seemed natural. Perhaps that was because his body was already destroyed below the waist. After everything he and Luc had done during his heat, it was a wonder he didn't burst into spontaneous flames.

"You're awfully quiet," Luc said after a half hour in the noisome chaos of the capital city. "Soon we'll be through the city's gates. Then we'll be able to give the horses their heads. I'd forgotten how it feels to have a good mount beneath me."

"Really?"

Luc smirked. "I should say a good horse."

Thierry hadn't intended the double entendre, and now his face heated.

"There's my pretty blush." Luc slowed his horse. "Are you all right?"

"Of course. Why wouldn't I be?"

"You're not tender?" Luc lowered his voice. "I brought Mrs. Quinn's salve just in case."

"I'm fine." Thierry gave his mount a nudge to go around a wagon whose owner was arguing with a baker about his payment. "I'll be glad when we're out of the city."

"My sweet country boy."

"Admittedly." Thierry wrinkled his nose. "This part of city life is not for me."

"Especially here at the waterfront, I imagine."

"It's…interesting." They were passing the docks where there were so many ships' masts it looked like home if the forest were stripped bare of greenery. On their right, rows of lodgings sat, haphazardly constructed, one on top of the other. Some leaned so precariously it seemed that if one building fell, they'd all go over. The area was dotted with brothels and taverns and clogged with pedestrians and carts selling food.

It made Thierry's head hurt to take it all in.

Silence appeared. He landed on Luc's shoulder as if he hadn't been gone for days.

"There you are." Luc leaned away from the raven's sharp beak. "I wondered when you'd come back."

"Where's he been all this time?"

"Probably at the Academy. He's got friends there who spoil him. Go on, off you go. Find John. We're going home." The raven pecked Luc a couple of times before taking to the air. Thierry watched the wondrous bird catch an updraft and soar high over the city gates. Luc rubbed his head. "Ow. Not nice, Silence."

Thierry surreptitiously tried to make himself smaller as they left the city. Burly guards watched everyone coming and going. As Luc passed, one of the men gave him a nod.

The exchange made Thierry wonder how well known Luc was in the city. After all, his brother was the crown prince, and Luc had been welcomed into the family home. What would happen if Ethan got his wish and Luc became high court magus?

They'd have to move to the palace, surely.

Did he want that? Could Thierry bear it?

"Now you look positively ill." Luc stopped his horse once they'd passed the gates, leaving the city. "Are you certain you're all right?"

"I said I was fine," Thierry snapped. "You don't have to baby me."

Luc's face fell. He turned his mount and urged it into a trot. Bouncing along behind him, Thierry felt like the worst person alive. There had been no need for anger. His sudden discomfort was probably something he should admit. But for the life of him, he wasn't ready to talk about the future yet.

His mate was supposed to be an outlaw, living in a hut in the forest. Thierry should be grateful he wasn't. He should be thrilled to sit on a horse from the royal stable. He should be awed that the crown prince thought his mate worthy of a position at court, but all Thierry could think about were the long days of sunshine and fresh air and freedom afforded them in Luc's forest settlement. The long nights spent under a sky freckled with stars and the Goddess moon smiling down at him.

Once, he knew his place in the world.

Now Thierry didn't know if he would ever feel comfortable again.

When they finally passed the congestion of merchants waiting outside the city gates, Luc kicked his heels and sped his horse onward. Thierry followed, each ache compounding as his mount kept pace.

They rode in silence. Thierry had to pay careful attention. If he didn't, he'd lose his seat or betray the pain he felt. Only pride kept him in the saddle. He got better at moving with the horse instead of jouncing along like a sheep tied to its back.

Luc seemed to exult in riding at a bruising speed. Once, he let loose a shout of joy that disturbed a flock of starlings. They took to the sky in a thick array, moving in the way only starlings did, indecipherably but thrillingly into the wind.

After a while, Thierry had to admit he enjoyed riding with the sun warming his skin and the wind rushing through his hair, but his bottom had gone from numb to dull to incendiary pain.

He was determined to keep his suffering to himself, but Luc slowed abruptly and caught the reins of Thierry's mount.

"Will you please tell me what's wrong so I can do something about it? Goddess, just—" Luc pleaded with him, "Let me help you, darling."

Some of the things that had Thierry worried couldn't be changed. Whether his mate lived in the forest or city, he would follow. It wouldn't help if he talked about his feelings on the matter. It would only make Luc unhappy, and Thierry couldn't bear that. Luc probably couldn't fix his pain either, but it was his most pressing problem.

"I've never ridden a horse with a saddle before," Thierry blurted. "I've never ridden much at all."

"Are you serious?" Luc asked aghast. "Why didn't you say?"

"Because we have to get to the Temple of the Merciful Moon quickly, and how I feel about horses doesn't matter. I'm managing, aren't I?"

Luc's gaze softened. "How you feel always matters to me. You should know that."

"I do know, but it doesn't change what's necessary. We need to get there fast, and I won't slow you down."

"Oh, sweetheart." Luc dismounted and pulled their horses into the trees off the main road. "Let me help you dismount."

"Honestly, it's best you don't. I'll never get back up."

Luc held his arms up. "Come here, little fool."

"Hmph." Thierry let Luc help him off the beast, wincing with every movement.

"Stand against the tree." Luc led him to a sturdy-looking fir tree and turned him to face it.

"Luc, this isn't the time for—"

"Just do as I say." Luc laughed. "No, face the tree."

Luc's hands gripped Thierry's shoulders. His thumbs dug into the muscles of Thierry's neck. At first the pain was excruciating—Luc seemed to find all the sorest spots—but after a few seconds, the warmth of healing magic spread from Luc's fingers, soothing sore muscles, easing the tension from Thierry's upper back. Luc's magic even smelled soothing, like mint and lavender, when he used it for healing.

"Better?"

"Healing magic smells different?" asked Thierry.

"It does, depending on the practitioner. I told you I wanted to be a healer."

"Yes, but—"

"But what? My father may have cut me off from that line of study, but even he couldn't change the nature of my magic."

"Then why didn't you heal John?"

"I tried, but John was gravely ill, and the Merciful Sisters are far more learned than I am. What I didn't know was that I brought home a shady imposter."

"Thank the Goddess for Charles. I had no idea what to do."

Luc moved his hands lower along Thierry's spine. "When I think about the sheriff putting you at risk like that, I wish *I'd* killed him."

"I volunteered. I would have asked to do it even if Sheriff Lavigne had never brought it up."

"Not anymore." Luc huffed. "You're never allowed to place yourself in danger again."

"I hope you don't think you'll take away my choices." Thierry stilled.

Luc growled. "No, I don't think that."

"Good boy."

Luc bit his ear. "But I will protect you with my life, so be sure your risks are worthy."

"Same goes for you. Mmm," Thierry moaned as Luc's hands cupped his buttocks. Luc's soothing grip doused the burning agony there, but certain other sensations took its place. "Yes. Goddess, that's good."

"Don't make that sound unless you want to be fucked against this tree."

"Do we have time?" Thierry asked just to be a pest.

"No."

"Too bad." Luc spent some time on Thierry's trembling thigh

muscles, refreshing them for the next leg of the journey. "We'll need to exchange horses soon."

"We're just leaving them?" Thierry asked. He didn't love riding, but he'd grown fond of his horse. He now suspected the animal had a hand in keeping him on its back.

"It's fine. There are stables all along the route for the king's messengers. Ethan gave me a letter, ordering his stablemen to furnish us with fresh horses."

Thierry's heart sank, but he said, "All right."

If he had to learn to ride another horse, so be it.

"Feel better?"

"I do." Thierry wiggled his bottom.

"Stop that."

"What?" he asked with false innocence as he wiggled again.

"Little tease." Luc gave him a light swat. "Let's go before I take you up on your tempting offer."

Before he could turn away, Thierry caught his hand. "Thank you, Luc."

"You're welcome."

"My mate is a good man with healing hands."

Luc's cheeks held a blush when he helped Thierry into the saddle. He waited patiently until Thierry was ready to ride out.

They changed horses and made the next leg of the journey at speed before changing horses again. Thierry asked Luc for help and healing when he needed it. He did wonder what Luc got out of the arrangement. It seemed to Thierry that his mate spent most of his time rescuing, or caring for, or healing him, and he'd hardly done a thing to merit it. Even their lovemaking, wonderful as it was, was more about Luc leading and Thierry following along.

"What do you see in me?" Thierry asked suddenly. "You've been so wonderful that I can't help worrying that I'm doing nothing to earn your heart."

"I beg your pardon." Luc slowed his horse to ride beside him. "You don't have to earn my heart. You own it. You're my mate."

"But don't you think I should be doing *something*?" Thierry glanced away as they slowed to a stop. His horse shifted beneath him, impatient to be off again. "Besides being willing in bed, I mean. Which I am. Oh, I am so very willing in that area. I wish we were in bed now."

Luc's eyes sparkled.

"Or that I could be struck by lightning because now you'll get all conceited."

"Thierry." Luc reached over and laid a hand on his thigh. "You're much more than a bedmate to me. Don't you know that?"

"But you've rescued me, and fed me, and healed me, and—"

"So what?" Luc stared at him like he'd grown a second head. "You'd do the same for me, wouldn't you?"

"Of course, but—"

"I don't understand what you're trying to say."

"I'm not some fairy-tale princess." Thierry bit his lip. "I want to be your equal. Your partner. Not someone you have to look after all the time."

"I don't have to look after you. I want to. It brings me joy."

"No. Except for an accident of fate"—Thierry needed to say this—"I'd only be another one of your good deeds. How long will you ignore the inequity between us?"

"There is no inequity. Yes, I'm alpha, but you're omega and a practitioner, and when you learn to wield your magic, you'll be every bit as powerful as I am. You'll bear our children, Thierry. I can't believe I have to tell you this. You're entirely unique, as far as we know, in all of Rheilôme, possibly in all the world."

"But—"

"But nothing. If you can't see it now, all I ask is your trust. Give me that, will you? Trust that you are the very best thing that has ever happened to me."

"All right. Trust." Thierry nudged his horse forward. "I-I'll try to remember."

"No." Luc caught his reins. "It's not all right. I want you to say it. Tell me you trust me."

"I trust you, Luc." That wasn't hard. He trusted Luc with his body, his heart, his soul, his very life. "I trust you, and I *love* you."

Luc's smile was worth every ache, every doubt Thierry had ever had. "I love you too, sweetling. So much. It hurts me when you doubt me."

"I'm sorry."

"No, I am." Luc cupped his cheek and leaned over to kiss him. Mostly he missed because Thierry's horse shied away. "I'm sorry I left you to doubt. From now on, I'll remind you often."

"I wish I was more…heroic. I'd feel better if just once I'd saved the day."

"The day is young yet." Luc laughed and clicked his tongue to send his horse forward. "You still might."

Thierry clicked to his mount. His heart felt lighter. If it was only a matter of trusting Luc, trusting his judgment, perhaps Thierry could do that. If Luc thought he was worthy…perhaps he actually was.

After another hour of travel at top speed, they reached the area of the forest Luc had claimed as his unofficial empire. Here, Thierry knew, many paths had been cut—and many areas of discreet concealment created—for Luc's men to keep watch over the merchant caravans and travelers coming and going from Amivienne.

Luc veered off the road and into the trees. They rode in silence, though every so often Luc gave a birdlike whistle. Where were his men? Luc was well known for having eyes everywhere in the forest, yet no one answered his call.

Thierry glanced around nervously.

Luc halted his horse and held his hand up. Thierry immediately did the same. They sat in stillness together, Luc listening, Thierry watching his face for cues.

Luc whistled again.

Thierry heard nothing but the ordinary sounds of forest life.

"Dismount," Luc said softly. "We'll leave the horses here and make our way on foot."

"Will they be all right?" Thierry asked.

Luc nodded, but he appeared distracted.

To Thierry, nothing seemed out of place except he didn't sense any of Luc's people nearby. He ground-tied their horses as Luc had taught him, looped his satchel over his neck, and handed Luc his pack. Luc had come armed with a bow. Now he looped the strap of his quiver over one shoulder. Seeing the fierce concentration of a predator on his face, Thierry understood they were in danger. He was glad his mate was armed.

"Quiet as you can." Luc led him along one of the barely marked trails.

"Is something amiss?"

"I don't know yet," Luc whispered. "If we're approached, let me do the talking."

"All right."

Luc squeezed his hand. "Don't hesitate to use my magic for your protection."

"How?" Thierry asked. "That time with my father—"

Thierry heard a *whoosh* and then…*thud* as an arrow pierced Luc's chest.

Luc's eyes widened briefly before he stumbled backward. In a panic, Thierry caught his mate's big body and helped him gently to the ground. He didn't understand what he was seeing. Luc was pale. He was unmoving. Thierry lifted his hands to find them covered in blood.

Before Thierry could register that he should move—he should *flee*—a heavy rope wrapped around his neck, and someone hauled him backward until he hit the rock-hard body of a stinking, filthy brute of a man.

Thierry struggled to free himself but got nowhere. He couldn't turn to see who held the rope. The stench of death magic was all around them. How had he not sensed that before? Greasy magic seemed to foul the air and soil the ground beneath his feet.

Branches parted, and a second man came into view.

A horribly familiar man.

"This turned out to be surprisingly easy." The necromancer from Thierry's nightmares, the man who had used death magic to kill Charles all those years ago, stopped less than a foot away from him. He sniffed the air like a hound. "Smells rank, doesn't it? Death magic's going to change the world."

At Thierry's feet, Luc struggled to breathe.

"You spoke the truth, Peter." The mage looked exactly the same as he had five years before. Small of stature with pale skin and sullen, soulless eyes. "Your old leader's mate is indeed omega. What a wonderful surprise."

Peter. *Peter?* Luc's third in command? He'd been surly and jealous but disloyal? How had this mage won over one of Luc's best men? What could the necromancer have promised to get him to betray Luc? Thierry hated both of them with everything he had.

From the ground, Luc gave the cry of someone gravely wounded and equally betrayed.

The gurgling noises coming from Luc's throat tore Thierry's heart to shreds. Tears stung his eyes. Terror silenced him. Whatever magic he'd borrowed to use against his father, he couldn't do it now, not even to save Luc's life. And without Luc, Thierry cared nothing for his own life.

As if all the light had left the world, Thierry sagged helplessly. He had failed his mate. He would be mute again. He would give up and hopefully die quickly.

He hated himself.

"Don't just stand there gawping. Shackle the omega," the man snapped. "We have somewhere to be."

"What about the other one?"

"Leave him for the crows." The necromancer nudged Luc's ribs with his toe.

"Yes, sir."

A hood came down over Thierry's head. His hands and feet were shackled with iron. The rope around his neck pulled taut, and he was forced to move or face strangulation.

"Are you certain the outlaw's done for?" the man pulling his leash asked in low tones. "Wouldn't want to meet him again while we have his mate."

"Iron and ash," the necromancer muttered. "Arrows made from the ash tree, tipped in iron, spelled to absorb a healer's magic. Even the unlikely event someone finds him, he won't see the dawn. Pity. I'd like to keep him. He'd make for interesting experiments."

"Should I bring him, then?"

The necromancer's footsteps slowed. "You seem awfully interested in him, Peter."

By the Goddess, Thierry would murder him gladly if he got out of this mess. He would become a fairy-tale witch and boil Peter to bones for this treachery.

"Was just a question." Peter gave a shaky laugh. "Waste not, want not."

"I *hate* stupidity!" The evil mage screeched the words. They seemed to echo off the trees and bounce from the rocks. Beneath their feet, the earth shuddered. Magic burst through Thierry's body, and his leash drew up tight, choking off his air. Another thud shook the ground at his feet.

When it was quiet again, the necromancer's breaths sawed in and out. Thierry stumbled in the safest-seeming direction, toward the necromancer, who apparently now controlled the rope.

"Walk, omega. You might indeed be the prize I've been after all this time."

Thierry walked.

CHAPTER 22

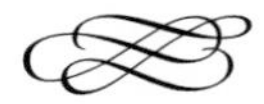

Luc's body was on fire unless he was freezing. Cool hands alternately hurt him and soothed him. They wiped sweat off his face. Tears. A woman's voice ordered him to pay attention, to keep going, to open his eyes. His mother? No…Aunt Luna.

Wherever he was, sensations came to him as if from a great distance. Anxious voices argued over him, but he didn't understand the words. People came and went from the room. Some were crying.

Slowly, slowly, he sank beyond their efforts, beyond their sorrow, beyond his senses even. He felt nothing, heard nothing, except the wind and the cry of his raven.

"Open your eyes," Silence said in his mimic's voice. "Open and see where we are, you and I."

He opened his eyes to find himself soaring—weightless—toward a vast, bruised darkness, black as pitch overhead and aubergine at the edges, filled with uncountable, eternal stars.

Was he dead?

The last thing he remembered was…Thierry. His beautiful country boy. They'd taken the fastest path to the settlement in the forest, holding hands until he'd sensed the danger. He'd knocked an arrow, hadn't he? He must have at least tried to defend his mate?

His love.

No…he hadn't gotten that far. The attack on them had been so swift, so silent, and so unexpected there in the woods that he called home that he'd barely registered it before…

Thierry.

Goddess! Where is my mate? I failed him. I failed You. Have mercy, oh Goddess...

Wings carried him away from the fading light. Beyond the moon, beyond the stars even, to a place where there was only formless light and shadow to shape the darkness.

Oh no. *Oh no.* He couldn't help but cry out, beg, and barter. He screamed and fought as the shadows took shape, shifted, and reformed as animal gods and goddesses, as monsters from his deepest fears.

Luc closed his eyes and held on to the image of his mate: Thierry's light, his hidden power. The smile that widened as soon as Thierry laid eyes on him. The soft sounds of their love-making. The taut, thin line of light that stretched between them seemed to narrow, even as he tried to grab onto it.

"I'm not ready!" he raged. "I won't leave him."

There was no reply. No tug on the bond.

Luc used every ounce of his strength to send a message of love and hope through the light. Silence cried out, a great *kraa-kraa.*

In the vast unformed place that was the shadowlands, Luc lifted his arm, "Find me, Silence. Find me and carry me home."

Despite his newfound energy, he couldn't move his corpo-real body, couldn't cry out, couldn't ask someone to find his mate and help him…if Thierry wasn't already—

No. He wouldn't believe that. He'd know if his mate had died.

Warm brown eyes. Wild, wavy locks to match. Thierry wore the sweetest smiles, the fiercest blushes.

I made you blush, sweetling. I made you mine.

I was given the perfect mate, and I failed him. I failed You, my Goddess.

Talons gripped his arm painfully. He felt the heft of his friend and companion, and then he felt Silence's magic settle all around him. They were not separate beings at all but one powerful entity trapped in the shadowlands.

They didn't want to be there.

They wanted their home.

They wanted their mate, who drew them like fish on a line toward light and love and the shared laughter of ravens and good men.

Silence caught an updraft, or Luc did, and after a dizzying time of beating wings and muscle strain and uncertainty, the waning moon came into view. It dazzled their eyes until they sopped wet with tears that streamed down their cheeks.

A fresh burst of strength made their wings beat faster. They soared up and up, arrow-straight into the heart of the moon, where they burst into a million sparkles of light.

They were nothing, formlessness and emptiness.

They were one with the sky, with the stars, with the Goddess for a second, an eternity.

Luc.

The single, despairing word radiated into the air like a vast wave of magic. They followed the sound.

Luc. Mate. Mine.

Hovering outside a window, they saw Mate. He lay in an iron cage inside a filthy room, so weak his spirit was trying to leave his body.

"Mate!" they called. "Mate, mine, mine!"

Mate didn't respond. He didn't move.

Agony burned in Luc's blood. Pain like he'd never known

before seemed to fill him. It sizzled all over his skin. It made his hair crackle. In his chest, his heart beat like a war drum. *Bang. Bang. Bang!*

His human eyes flickered open. There was bare sky above him. Dirty blankets. Aunt Luna, in her red gown and robe, now filthy with gore, gazed down at him.

"Hmm," she said with some satisfaction. "Thought so."

"Thierry." Luc tried to rise but found he couldn't move. "How long?"

"Use your power, mage." She shook her head sadly. "Your magic might work now."

Who was she—

"Thank you." Luc shifted his gaze and found Cavendish hovering nearby. His old mentor seemed blanched of all color. His hands were shaking as he picked up a small wooden spoon.

"Cavendish? How long—" Luc coughed. "What's wrong?"

"Rest, Luc." Cavendish blew some kind of powder into his face. "All will be well."

"Wait—" Immediately, oblivion claimed him. Dreamless. Timeless but not formless.

Not this time.

I'm coming, Thierry. I'm coming.

CHAPTER 23

The rope around Thierry's neck tightened if he resisted, so he stumbled along at the necromancer's side. Still hooded, he bashed into trees. He tripped over rocks. The necromancer taunted him mercilessly like a child jealous of a teacher's pet.

"You're not that powerful after all, are you?" the mage needled.

Thierry concentrated on putting one foot in front of the other. Keeping to his feet and feeling his way. The little man obviously hoped he'd fall. And the necromancer was a *little* man. He barely came up to Thierry's nose. No wonder he could drift in and out of town unseen. He was utterly unremarkable.

Thierry knew the mage schools favored alphas, and all his human senses told him the man who'd taken him—who held his *leash*—had to be alpha, but his magic knew different. This upstart villain was a beta. A deceptive, cunning beta filled with rage against a world that ignored his kind.

If Thierry slowed or tripped, the man beat his legs with the rope. Once, when he tried to gain control, the mage flew into a rage and let the rope fly anywhere and everywhere, beating

Thierry over the head and shoulders, his back and buttocks, and even the souls of his feet.

Thierry gritted his teeth and rose, determined to do nothing to earn such a punishment again. He would wait. He would bide his time. He would survive, and if the moment presented itself, he would tear the mage's throat out, as any wolf would, even omega wolves who relied on human teeth.

The mage was dead. He was already in the shadowlands where he would be seen and judged for what he was, a spineless beta weakling, grasping at straws to make himself relevant. He was dead, and he was oblivious. Thierry would kill him, even if he had to die with him to do it. But not yet. Not until he learned more because Cavendish was coming, and with or without Luc, Thierry had an obligation to see things through.

He wished he knew how a beta could pass himself off as an alpha, but the malaise that had caused his words to fail after Charles died had taken hold again, and he was unable to ask.

Perhaps that was for the best.

Words held power. They carried purpose. He didn't trust himself to make small talk with the man who'd killed his best friend and his mate.

Thierry would offer nothing to this worthless mage except a swift death when the time came. He smacked his head into a tree. Stars burst behind his eyes. The necromancer cursed. Thierry felt the ground beneath his cheek, then nothing.

Floating. A dim haze. Emptiness. Peace.

~

"Thierry, wake up." Who was bothering him? He didn't want to wake up. Sleep was better. Sleep held dreams of his mate and nature. A raven.

No. A sharp stab of pain pierced Thierry's heart. Had he dreamed the whole thing? Meeting Luc and falling in love and—

"Thierry, really, wake up now! Before"—icy water splashed over Thierry's face and chest—"that happens."

Thierry sputtered, grateful to find his head free of the odious hood. He gulped in deep draughts of air and looked around to find that he lay on the floor of an iron cage inside a room with walls made of stone. There was a window, and outside a faint blush of twilight painted the sky.

He felt Charles's magic nearby. Almost too near. It clung to him as though it was trying to become part of him. Someone—something—monstrous stood over him with a bucket. *Grotesque.* Another magic experiment gone wrong, perhaps. A man so scarred it was impossible to tell what he'd looked like.

"There you are." The necromancer stood well away from the pool of water on the floor.

Thierry tried to rise.

With a belligerent grunt, the scarred man shoved him back with a booted foot.

"I wouldn't try anything with Jacob here. He's quite loyal." The mage came forward to stand over Thierry, though he kept a careful arm's length away. Thierry averted his gaze.

"You may call me Master Beaumont."

Thierry said nothing.

"Is the old malady keeping speech at bay? That was a good ruse since it meant you could never tell what you'd seen the night we met. A clever, cowardly way to escape my notice, hmm?" He clasped his hands behind his back. Thierry still said nothing, which seemed to enrage the little man. "But you'll speak to me, won't you? You'll do as I say, when I say, or I will make things very unpleasant for you."

Thierry closed his eyes. Perhaps his inability to speak was self-preservation, but maybe it came from the omega magic inside him. Speech would return when his omega felt safe and not a moment sooner.

"A male omega." The mage clucked his tongue. "I'm fascinated by how you've been able to hide your true nature. But why? You should have embraced it. Made something of yourself. You should have fought the restraints the bastard mages placed on you as I do."

Thierry had been born on a farm. He did chores. He wasn't that smart. He'd had very little choice in the matter of how he lived.

"But instead, you chose to ally yourself to one of them. One of the worst. An alpha mage who had everything and threw it away in a fit of pique."

If that's what this man thought, he was hopeless.

"Speak, omega." The pull of greasy magic pressed against him. It pried open his mouth and pushed down his throat and made him gag. He turned his head to vomit and got a brutal kick for his trouble.

"Be strong, Thierry. I'm here," said Charles.

Charles, thank the Goddess you're here. How'd you find me.

"I always know where you are. This place is disgusting. We have to escape."

You're a mage. Help me get out of here.

"Working on it."

The scarred man tensed when his mage master squatted in front of Thierry.

The man's clammy hand took his chin.

"I can feel your magic," the necromancer crooned. "It shimmers in the air around you. It bubbles like sparkling wine. The omega witches at the Merciful Moon Temple are nowhere near as powerful as you are."

He leaned forward and licked a long, leisurely line up the side of Thierry's face. "*Mmm.* You're delicious."

Thierry jerked away with another gag and spat on the ground, wishing he could wipe his mouth.

"I'll tell you a secret, omega." The mage gripped his hair. "Everyone's got the world all wrong. Magic makes things go, so of course the alpha elite want to keep it for themselves. They ban the study of certain types of magic and say who can and can't learn because they're shit scared of losing the hold they have on our world. No betas allowed."

"I knew it," said Charles. "He was never at the Academy."

Can't he hear you?

"Guess not."

"I don't *accept* their rules." Beaumont devoured Thierry with his hungry gaze. "*I* found a way to wield more power than the academies who turned me away ever dreamed."

Charles huffed. "What a windbag."

"And you, my meek little omega, will help me destroy them once and for all."

Beaumont stood and backed out of Thierry's cage. Jacob closed the door and padlocked it.

"These grounds are warded. Any practitioner attempting to enter will be met with extreme force. If you attempt to escape, my servants have orders to destroy you in whatever way they like."

Jacob grinned and palmed his cock. Thierry shivered with acute horror.

"Think on this, omega. I plan to change the structure of our society. No more alpha aristocracy. No more omega chattel. Humans and betas will hold their heads up and take their rightful places—not in the roles of caregivers or domestics but in whatever profession they choose. The question is, do you wish to live to see it?"

Beaumont's footsteps rang against the stone. Jacob followed him out.

"The man is mad," Charles muttered.

Is he? Thierry asked.

"What do you mean? Of course he's mad. He wants to use death magic to rule the world."

Yet he sees the world clearly. If he'd been born alpha, he might have been your peer at school.

"Well, blind alpha supremacy is wrong," Charles agreed. "Obviously."

In the world Beaumont envisions, no one could bargain with omega lives. The Sisters of the Merciful Moon could openly practice magic. My sister Esme would have a brighter future.

"All right, you've made your point. Things should change, and I want that, but—"

Goddess, my head hurts. What did the laws of men matter when the Goddess ruled over the sky and the land and the seas?

Beaumont didn't want a better world. He wanted to destroy theirs.

They killed Luc. They killed my mate.

"You don't know for certain. Do you feel the bond?"

I don't know how. Thierry broke down and wept. *I don't know anything. Only that the Goddess blessed me with the most wonderful alpha mate, and...and I failed him.*

"You failed *him*? How?"

I'm the one who knows the land. I'm the one who grew up here, but I was stupid because Luc smiled at me, and the whole world fell away. I should have let Beaumont strangle me. I should have died rather than let Beaumont take me from Luc's side.

"It's not only you, though, is it? You bear Luc's claiming mark. You're carrying Luc's child."

No. Thierry argued. *Goddess, it's too soon. I can't be.*

"Your wolf will never allow you to give up now."

It wasn't possible.

Well, a pregnancy was possible, but how likely was it? Luna had said something about first heats and fertility. Oh Goddess. His deepest instincts told him to keep the babe—if there was one—a secret.

Thierry put his hand over his abdomen. Could he be with child?

Do you think Beaumont could tell if I was pregnant?

"I can. Any alpha would know. I suspect most wolves could sense it. Your magic feels different now."

That meant…

Goddess, if Beaumont knew he was carrying Luc's child…

He must find a way to escape.

How did you get past Beaumont's wards? It's your magic he senses, isn't it?

"I've stuck pretty close to you. In fact—"

What? Thierry prompted.

"You won't like it."

Has that ever stopped you?

"I…er…took you over for a bit."

"You what?"

"In my defense, you were unconscious, and Beaumont was beating you, and I—I just panicked, all right? I thought if I could move you, he'd stop. You're welcome."

What do you mean, move me?

"I…slipped inside your body for a bit."

You did what?

"Just for a bit. He had to stop beating you. I couldn't bear it."

Wait! Let me understand. You can use my body—

"I guess so. But I promise that's the only time. I mean, I'd never do anything like that without asking, but you were passed out, and…"

Oh Goddess, promise me—

Charles's magic shivered around him. "Oh, I promise. I do."

You will never, ever do that again without asking me, Charles. Give me your most solemn vow.

"I promise."

I invoke a blood sacrifice, like when we were boys.

"I would. You know I would. Unfortunately, I lack the—"

Swear it on your mother's heart.

"I swear by the Goddess's sacred magic. I will never betray your trust that way again unless it's to save your life."

That isn't—

"Take it or leave it." Charles sniffed. "You're precious to me."

Thierry closed his eyes. *All right.*

"Rest now. We have no idea what this fool has planned. Reserve your strength while I keep watch."

Can you back away? I feel like I'm wearing a damp wool blanket.

"But that's what fooled Beaumont. He thinks it's your magic. If I back away—"

Fine.

"Lift your head so I can spoon you."

No. Can you make yourself useful and generate some heat? I'm cold.

"At your service." Charles's magic settled. He generated just enough heat for Thierry's muscles to relax. "Sorry, I'm not a healer."

You healed John.

"With potions and your magic."

Thierry was too tired to ask how that could be. His thoughts were scattered. His heart hurt. His shoulder burned. Was that the mate bond? Was he feeling Luc's pain, or was Luc already past saving? He couldn't bear the uncertainty.

"Rest while you can, Thierry. Worry solves nothing."

As if Thierry's drowsy body had a mind of its own, sleep dragged him into fitful dreams.

CHAPTER 24

By the following morning, the ache in Thierry's chest had grown from bearable to agony. Each breath he took was labored. His skin burned. His mouth was dry. He could see the window from where he lay on the floor of the cage, but his vision had blurred. Colors shifted as outside night turned into day.

At some point, Jacob arrived with a tray. He even brought a skin of wine, but Thierry couldn't lift his head. His arms were too heavy. Charles's magic stayed glued to him like a second skin.

Seeing him so ill apparently frightened Jacob. The man left at a run. He returned a few minutes later with Beaumont, who took one look at Thierry and flew into a rage.

"Imbeciles! Can they do nothing right?" He barked orders, and more servants came running. All of them bore hideous scars. All of them trembled and were cowed at the sight of their master in a rage.

Jacob opened the door to Thierry's cage.

The necromancer ran his foul fingers roughly over Thierry's face and chest.

"Get him into one of the maid's rooms and put him in a real bed." Spittle flecked Beaumont's lips as he pointed at a human maid. "You. Get the healer. If the omega dies, I'll kill all of you and start over."

Jacob lifted Thierry easily. He carried him out of the room and down the hall, finally placing his chill-racked body on a small cot in a serviceable room where he covered Thierry with blankets.

"Iron and ash, iron and ash!" His master raged on outside the door. "Why in the name of the shadowlands isn't the outlaw dead? Why isn't their blasted bond *broken*?"

Beaumont's voice faded.

Thierry's lips curved into a painful grin. So much bother. Such scurrying around, and for what, Thierry wanted to know? All of this theater was so unnecessary. Thierry was meant to share Luc's pain, to bear his troubles. He could share and give Luc the time he needed to heal. Luc was too good—too beautiful—to die. Thierry wouldn't allow it.

Didn't the absurd little man know that?

But the babe, his wolf warned. *You must think of the babe.*

Thierry's eyes were too heavy. *The Goddess is good. The Goddess is merciful. The Goddess is with me.* A shape in the window drew his eye.

Kraa-kraa. Kraa-kraa.

Thierry blinked in surprise.

"Mate, mate, mate." Black wings opalescent in the brief light of dawn, Silence circled the air outside, body gliding on cold air currents. Up he winged. Up and up until he tilted and caught the air going in the opposite direction. Over and over.

Thierry's body cooled, almost as if a breeze came from Silence's beating wings.

He kept his eyes on the window.

"That's magic I've never seen before," Charles observed.

Cavendish says all the world's inhabitants carry magic.

"Right. Not just alphas."

Not just wolves.

"Do you know why you're feeling so ill?"

Luc isn't dead. Beaumont was even now in the courtyard berating his fletcher. *We're healing together. Taking turns.*

Charles chuckled. "Beaumont's plan has truly gone awry. He's lost control."

He'll think of another. We must still escape. Hard to think when his head hurt this badly. Thierry closed his eyes and tried to follow his pain to the source. Luc. *Mate. Yes, give me your pain.*

"I can nullify the wards. Pick the locks. Use a distraction spell on Jacob. Those aren't beyond my capabilities."

Thierry felt cold now. His teeth chattered. *T-to w-what end.*

"To get you away from here, of course." Charles's warmth embraced him again.

Beaumont will hunt me.

"You said the League was on its way. How long until they're here?"

Ask the bird.

"What?"

Ask Silence.

Charles's magic faded. While he was gone, Thierry watched the bird fly to the window and hover there, flapping its wings.

Thierry slept after that, not even sure anything had happened as he remembered it.

Charles added his strength into the mix. He kept Thierry calm while the fire that ravaged Luc's body burned Thierry through the mate bond.

Sometimes, he felt Charles's spirit surround him.

Sometimes, his dreams of flying were so very real that his hair rippled.

Day followed night, followed day. The necromancer's maid forced him to eat. He drank what they gave him if only for the child. The door flew open on the third morning. Jacob was no longer the servant in charge. This time, it was a slatternly human woman with no nose and half her hair burned off.

"Master says he's bored. You're to dress and dine with him tonight. And you won't be allowed to sleep until you accept, with gratitude, the honor that he's bestowed on you."

Honor?

"I think she meant the offer of er…partnership."

Beaumont tried to kill my mate. I won't appreciate anything until I've boiled the meat off his bones.

The strange woman helped Thierry dress, and another manservant—not the unfortunate Jacob—carried him to what appeared to be the dining room of a derelict inn.

Beaumont arrived and sat just as another servant opened a bottle of blood red wine.

"I thought perhaps we could start over." Beaumont sketched a comical bow. "I was wrong to use force. From now on, I promise I'll use diplomacy to win you over to my side."

A bubble of hysteria burst inside Thierry. He laughed, long and loud. His sides hurt. Despite the mottled rage on Beaumont's face, he couldn't help himself. He laughed until he cried.

Beaumont didn't lose control. This time, he spoke in a low, soothing voice.

"I understand. You don't trust me. And you think your mate will ride in with Cavendish and save the day."

At the mention of Cavendish, Thierry's mouth snapped shut.

"Oh yes. I know all about your trip to the capital to beg your mate's mentor for aid. But you see, Rheilôme is full of men who would love to loosen the League's grip on magic. They're tired of others deciding what magic they can and cannot use."

Thierry blinked at him.

"You don't have to worry about these things, Thierry. You're nothing but a container full of magic. A shiny, pretty thing, useful only to the practitioner lucky enough to realize your worth. You're a prize, boy. A treasure."

How he would have liked to hear his father say those words. His teachers. *Anyone* at his school to whom he'd been a pariah, an abomination even.

Beaumont came close without touching him. "With you by my side, we could change how the world sees magic forever. Your kind is a blessing."

Thierry had to grip the arms of his chair to stay upright. Beaumont's image wavered before him. He appeared contrite. Sincere. He even looked *handsome.*

Was he right? Was his way the only route to peace and healing?

"Beware, he's using compulsion magic," said Charles. "Don't let him confuse you."

Thierry shook his head free of the magic that had almost swept him away.

Beaumont widened his eyes. "Luc's well-being should motivate you if nothing else does. Keeping him alive only prolongs the inevitable. Right now, he's feeling one hundred times the pain you are. If you let the mate bond go, nature will take its course. If you break the bond, you can give the man you love peace."

Thierry turned away.

"Your mate is beyond even the Goddess's help by now, omega." Beaumont shook his head sadly. "Only you can stop his pain."

Thierry lowered his gaze. There was nothing the mage could promise that would make him break the bond.

"Sooner or later, your omega is going to choose between Luc and the child." Thierry's gaze flew to the mage. "You thought I didn't know? As an omega, your deepest instinct will be to protect your child. How long do you want Luc to suffer needlessly? You can relieve him. His death is inevitable."

This is not real. Again, Thierry's vision wavered. *None of this is real.*

Beaumont stared for a second and then swept his arm across the table.

Dishes of food flew everywhere, and candles fell, igniting the tablecloth. Servants scurried about, stamping out flames and avoiding their master's heavy-fisted blows.

"Idiots! Get out! Get out!" Beaumont took a deep breath. He loomed over Thierry. "I am your only hope. The future belongs to me."

Thierry closed his eyes. A hand cracked across his cheek.

"I've tried being nice," the mage hissed. "Your fate is sealed. Break the bond before the new moon, or I will break it, and then I will break you!"

"If he could do that, he'd have done it by now," said Charles. "Stay strong."

Beaumont narrowed his eyes. He leaned down and spoke directly into Thierry's ear. "You might be the most powerful omega in the history of the world, boy, but mark my words, there are other practitioner omegas. By the new moon, I must know where you stand. You and your child will be useful to me either way."

With that, Beaumont turned on his heel and swept from the room.

Exhausted, Thierry slid to the floor.

"Get up, lad," said one of the maids. She had a cut above her eye that bled freely and only one arm. "You want to make things worse?"

He shook his head and tried to rise. Clucking, she looped her good arm around his waist and lifted him. Together, they walked to his room where he sank onto his bed with gratitude.

She left, and Charles settled against him.

He drifted in and out of sleep.

Kraa-kraa. Kraa-kraa.

How long before the new moon?

"Over a week," Charles answered. "You'll have to hold on until then."

Do you know what he's planning?

"Oh yes," Charles said without inflection. "I'm afraid I know exactly what he has in mind."

Each night, the servants readied Thierry for his meal with their mad master. Sumptuous food was laid out for them, the finest beef and fish dishes, vegetables in creamy sauces, all accompanied by Rheilôme's storied wines. Beaumont began each night with his best, most solicitous behavior, trying to cajole Thierry into breaking his bond with Luc. Every night, the mage devolved into a ranting, rage-filled tyrant. As the night of the new moon approached, Beaumont's gambits became more desperate. He threatened Thierry's family and the Sisters of the Merciful Moon. One night, he went so far as to murder a human footman before Thierry's eyes.

Thierry's inability to speak helped to keep his secrets. He was healing far faster than he let on. He had Charles, occasional visits from Silence, and Luc. His pain lessened. The delirium passed.

On the new moon, Thierry would gamble everything to rid the world of Beaumont once and for all or perish trying.

As the madman's hapless servants dragged Thierry back to his spare little room, he glanced toward the tiny window.

In the heavens, the barest sliver of a moon hung amid gathering clouds.

Tomorrow, then. It would be tomorrow.

The new moon was upon them.

CHAPTER 25

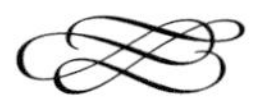

"I have orders to strip you and take you to the master." The unkempt housekeeper didn't hide her twisted delight as she lifted a large, rusty kitchen knife. "We won't be removing the shackles, so cutting your clothes off will have to do."

Thierry stood quietly, resigned. Begging was no use. She was as much a victim as he was. There was no way out for any of them.

"Right." She rid him of every stitch of clothing. Then she and three manservants dragged him through the castle to the humiliating taunts of others.

In the kitchen, Beaumont waited with an expression of grim satisfaction.

"It never had to come to this," Beaumont said as he made a long, slow perusal of Thierry's naked body. "You're a fool to decline a partnership with me."

Beaumont let his hand skim over Thierry's chest and down over his abs, his belly.

"And you've been healing faster than I realized." He pursed his lips unhappily. Thierry jerked away from his touch.

One man looped a rope around Thierry's neck and tightened it until he choked, eyes bulging. Laughing, Beaumont stepped forward and pressed his nose into the hair at Thierry's temple and sniffed.

Thierry shot his knee upward. Beaumont's grunt of pain made Thierry smile. Someone gave his *leash* a vicious yank.

"Wait," Beaumont gasped. "I need him alive."

"But, sir," one of the men argued.

"Take him to the circle."

The pressure on Thierry's neck eased, but they wasted no time dragging him from the house. There was a courtyard in back; possibly, it had once served as an outdoor dining area. A path beyond that led into the forest.

Thierry barely managed to stay upright. The moonless night made it hard to see. A thick layer of vegetation covered the ground, but beneath the leafy debris, seed pods and sharp rocks cut his feet. Branches scratched his upper body, and spiderwebs caught in his face and hair.

The delight the human servants took in taunting him and snapping his leash enraged and maddened Thierry.

"This way, doggie," one man jeered.

Thierry tripped, and they barely waited for him to scramble back to his feet.

"That's going to leave a mark," the housekeeper clucked.

"Too bad," said another. "You're a pretty doggie, eh? Isn't he a pretty dog?"

"That he is. Little-boy bitch." She did nothing to disguise her envy.

Thierry let her awful laughter fill him with determination as they made their way through the darkness.

Luc is alive. Luc is alive. They will not win. Even if they kill me, Luc is alive.

"We're going to beat this." The catch in Charles's voice

betrayed his fear. "Don't let these buffoons get to you because we'll come out of this stronger."

Thierry snorted.

"What?"

It's hopeless, isn't it? No point in keeping my spirits up now. I'm going to die in Hemlock Forest, and Luc won't even find me.

"Nothing is ever entirely hopeless."

Have you seen Silence?

"Not today."

Not for three days.

"Maybe he's with Luc?"

Maybe. Or maybe I imagined seeing him. Maybe Luc's been dead all this time, and Silence was an illusion Beaumont devised to make me lose my mind in this place.

"Silence was real. Luc is alive. You have something Beaumont needs. *We're* going to make certain he doesn't get it."

How?

They burst through the undergrowth and into a large clearing.

"Oh Goddess." Charles's magic hit Thierry's skin, sharp and jagged like falling icicles.

The awful, familiar sight caused Thierry to stumble, and for the first time he earnestly resisted the pull on the rope. He'd rather die where he stood than go any farther into this circular clearing with its green orbs casting an eerie glow from above their heads.

His worst nightmare lay before him. All his nightmares.

A clear outline made from interlocking paving stones delineated the circle's boundaries. Clay tablets etched with symbols had been embedded permanently into the ground.

"This isn't like the temporary working he did before in chalk. This is meant to be permanent."

This must be where he takes his victims. Then he puts them back on the forest path—why?

"To show he can," Charles said grimly. "To show off the power he has over life and death."

Blasted power-mad mages.

"Hey," Charles exclaimed, sounding stung. "It takes hard work and discipline to resist the allure of power. That's why we go to school. If we aren't able to practice ethically, the League strips us of our magic. I'd have learned to be a good mage."

Of course you would. I didn't mean you.

"I didn't exactly cover myself with glory the last time around."

You were new. You didn't know how.

"I knew enough," Charles admitted. "I wanted to see death magic at work. Whatever happens, I won't fail you this time, Titou."

The largest of Beaumont's human servants hoisted Thierry up to carry him the rest of the way, stepping carefully to avoid treading on the tablets.

In the center of the circle, a table with thick iron chains attached at the corners betrayed its terrible purpose. Death magic fouled the air.

Once the human had dragged Thierry inside the circle, all the familiar, friendly noises of the forest and his sense of color fell away, leaving nothing but formless shadows.

Happiness was a thing of the past.

Love, and mirth, and hope drained from his body as though someone had pulled a plug.

No life existed here. No blade of grass poked up between the symbols, no insect burrowed beneath. In Thierry's new death-magic-dampened view, he deserved to take that doomed mastiff's place. *Charles's place.* Thierry had cheated death the first time around. It seemed only right that death should return to claim him.

Beaumont's servant forced him to lie on the table. The bear of a man easily locked shackles around his wrists and ankles. He left the clearing; probably, he wanted no part of whatever came next. Thierry didn't blame him.

Now what?

Charles's magic clung to his skin, clammy and cold. "Now we wait."

Thierry didn't want Charles to relive past horrors, and he didn't want Charles to see him shame himself. Thierry would grovel if it meant getting free. He knew that now. He would beg for the life of his child. He wouldn't die like a man. He would scream and cry and die like the coward he was when they were children.

"I won't leave you." Charles's magic wavered. "Did you feel that?"

"*Maybe*?" Death magic washed over him like a sudden, cold chill.

"The necromancer's here. It will get harder to see soon. His blasted fog is creeping up from the ground. He must be using a very strong illusion to conceal himself. Or..."

Or what?

"I don't—wait. You know how you sense magic? You can feel it, but you can't see it the way that I can?"

Yes, but what does—

"Beaumont has a lot of natural talent, but he can't sense magic. You'd be dead if he'd sensed you the night we saw him, right? He'd have killed you, and whatever I am now would have died along with my body."

Maybe? What did Thierry know? He'd done nothing on purpose. It had all been instinctive.

"So *you* sense magic, but he can't." Charles's magic quivered with excitement. "That's why Beaumont created this place. It's *between* the world of the living and the shadowlands. Your magic isn't concealed here."

He'll see my magic?

"Goddess yes. Before, he was guessing how powerful you

are, but here you're positively incandescent. The bad news is that he'll perceive my magic as separate from yours in this place. He'll know there are two of us here. He'll see us, hear us—"

You should leave now, Charles. I mean it.

"No. What's he going to do, kill me again? Besides, I don't think anything can get in or out of the circle anymore."

Because of the wards?

"I wish they were only wards. These are...dimensional."

What's the difference?

"I see a barrier like the one between our world and the shadowlands. Nothing living can get through now that he's empowered the circle. Look."

Thierry tried to see a barrier but couldn't.

He did see that the area between the forest and the circle was filling up with Beaumont's horrible, mismatched beasts. They crawled and hopped and dragged themselves to stand around the circle as if to guard it from intruders. Beaumont's servants seemed to have taken up residence in the trees to watch the show.

Thierry yanked at the chains binding him, but it was clear he'd only bloody himself trying to get free. Maybe if he got bloody enough, it would facilitate slipping from the bonds. He gritted his teeth and strained against the iron.

"No," Charles whispered with awe. "In the name of the Goddess, how?"

Beaumont strode toward them from *outside* the circle.

"He should not be able to—"

"An excellent observation. I should definitely not be able"—Beaumont stepped out of and then into the circle once more—"to do that."

"How?" asked Charles.

"Proprietary secret." Beaumont gave a slow smile. "Well, now. There are two of you. Three if one were to count the babe. Suddenly, everything makes a great deal more sense."

Thierry wanted to cry. This was so much worse than he'd expected. This was no conjurer's experiment. Beaumont had gone far beyond the days when he'd practiced his craft on dogs.

"May I call you Charles, young learner?" Beaumont asked as he moved toward them, skipping between the symbols as lightly as a dancer. "Since Thierry won't speak to me, you'll have to do. Do you like what I've done with the place?"

"I'm not a student anymore, Beaumont."

"Technically, you aren't anything, but what does that have to do with—"

"The prospect of power might have been thrilling when I was a child, but now I find death magic, and you, revolting."

"Ah, well. I'm afraid you and I have already had our dance." Beaumont ran his fingers up the inside of Thierry's leg. "Thierry fills my card tonight."

Thierry's flesh burned where Beaumont's fingers skimmed over him. It felt like frostbite, like winter mornings when the bare skin of his arms froze between his jacket sleeves and his gloves.

"Look at you," Beaumont breathed the words. "Goddess, how you shine."

"Get away from us," Charles commanded.

"No, Charles, you'll find this fascinating."

Can't you do something, Charles? Didn't you say you could break locks or wards, or—

"Poor boy. Shall I tell him?" Beaumont asked. "Or do you want to?"

"I can't do it. Not here," Charles said glumly. "There's no ambient magic."

"Bravo." Beaumont clapped—a startling sound in the muted circle. "Give the boy a passing grade."

Outside the circle, Beaumont's beasts grew agitated. Their jerky movements cast frightening shadows. Movement in one of the trees caught Thierry's eye.

"You see, Thierry, he has no vessel. As he is merely *residual* here, he won't be able to help you."

None of this makes sense.

"Omegas are vessels. Did you know that? Their entire purpose is to collect and store magic. It's a bit unfair since they can't use it."

Some can use it very well.

"Outliers and unnatural women who don't know their place." The mage spat. "Is it fair that ignorant, weak omegas sit on so much power? That alphas hoard magic? Here, I've created a place of magical instability. Here, I'm both human and mage. I'm alive and dead. I'm a practitioner and a vessel, and I can *take* your magic from you and leave an empty shell behind."

Charles snarled. "Bastard."

"Yes, Thierry's mate is a bastard," Beaumont deliberately misunderstood. "What a pity. He'd make a magnificent king, wouldn't he?"

My mate would hate that.

"Maybe, but when was the last time we had a bold king? A *reckless* king? When was the last time we had a high court magus who was willing to gamble everything for knowledge? The League says, 'Play nicely,' and, 'Don't hurt anyone. We mustn't take a life, even if it means conquering death forever.'"

"They're right," Charles argued. "No one should have the power over life and death."

"Lie! Lies, you are a liar!" The necromancer flew into one of his rages. "Mages must go as far as they are able, just like the noble alpha wolves. Do you think Regnault Deathbringer asked anyone's permission before lifting Rheilôme's first crown to his head?"

"That's different," said Charles.

"How is that different? Might makes right!" Beaumont's face had turned mottled gray in the orb light. His eyes reflected their glow. "Why are mages subordinate to kings? Why are betas lower even than the lowest barren omega?"

Wings flapped high overhead. Thierry's heart quickened with joy to see Silence. If Silence was near, was Luc?

"Magic comes directly from the Goddess." Beaumont moved into position at the head of the stone table. "Because I have magic, I can make things, change things, harm, or heal. I will have power over life and death because of magic. *I* am the Goddess's direct descendant here in this world. Those without magic will kneel before me or die."

He pushed up his sleeves, revealing an ornate dagger.

"You have stolen magic," Charles shouted. "You'll pay for stealing the Goddess's gift."

Thierry kept his gaze on the black, iridescent shape plunging toward them. Beaumont muttered incantations as he gripped the dagger between his hands. Symbols etched onto Beaumont's tablets began to glow. He lifted the knife high over Thierry's head. Brought it down.

Silence was ready for his strike. He raked his talons over Beaumont's face a second before the knife could penetrate Thierry's flesh. He struck the necromancer again and again, driving the horrid mage away, each attack leaving vivid marks and dripping blood.

As if on cue, a fight began outside the circle. Through the necromancer's fog, Thierry caught glimpses of human men and women fighting bravely, armed with pikes, axes, bows, and swords. Luc's people. Tears streaked down Thierry's cheeks when he saw Mathilde stop a mangled, charging boar with an iron kettle.

Try what they might, the barrier between the inner circle and the battlefield held. The fight raged fierce and bloody. While Beaumont fought off Silence's blows, Thierry strained to escape. The necromancer managed to break free long enough to call on his magic.

Blue lightning cracked the darkness, blinding Thierry for several precious seconds. His hair snapped with energy. Huge spots blocked his vision. When he could finally see, Silence lay on the ground, still and smoldering. He looked so small, lying there. So unlike the brilliant, brave companion Thierry knew him to be. Grief swamped Thierry. He knew Luc would grieve without his friend.

Beaumont stalked toward Thierry, his face a bloody mess. He cursed with incoherent rage, but Thierry's ears rang so much he couldn't make out words. Red-flecked spittle flew from Beaumont's lips. He appeared hopelessly mad, the same way that his beasts were mad—animalistic and heedless of his own safety—only there was no one inside the circle to put Beaumont out of his misery.

Thierry frantically searched what he could see of the clearing. There weren't many swords and axes. Peter, the traitor, had died at Beaumont's hands, and men like John, who were large enough to wield a battle ax and capable of beheading Beaumont's creations, were scarce. The rest of Luc's fighters held the beasts off while John and the few who had the strength and the weapons to dispatch the creatures worked to put them down, one at a time.

Thierry felt utterly alone.

Where had Charles gone?

Where was Luc?

Where was Cavendish, who had promised to bring a cohort from the League to stop Beaumont? Thierry couldn't help anyone. Despite scraping his skin raw, he couldn't get free.

Beaumont eyed Thierry with new, maniacal rage.

Thierry lowered his gaze to Silence, and a wail of sorrow and rage and grief burst through his inhibitions to emerge as a ragged scream. It rose above the ugly miasma of death magic, above the orbs, and lifted to fill the night sky and ring off the solemn black moon.

Luc's men paused briefly in shock before leaning in to pound their foes with even greater force.

Thierry's unused, abandoned voice was so filled with anguish it caused trees to shiver and night creatures to freeze in their tracks. He wailed until he had no breath and then kept going until spots danced before his eyes and darkness closed in on him.

"Magnificent." The necromancer wiped blood from his face, stumbled to his feet, and lifted his knife once more. "Brilliant. I am well pleased with my choice."

Dizzy and sick, Thierry let his head fall on the stone table with a thud.

CHAPTER 26

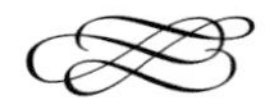

Luc heard Thierry's chilling scream, and his heart wanted to stop. Instead, he pushed harder, speeding the frightened horse he was riding between trees and over brambles to get to his lover in time. Cavendish's men rode ahead of him; they'd had to. He wasn't well enough for such a bruising pace, but he'd insisted on going with them.

Luc's people could only hold out so long against the enemy. They were out of their depth in Beaumont's territory, in his element. By themselves, they were no match for his awful beasts.

"Not much farther now," one of the men shouted.

"I see," Cavendish called. "Split up and stick to the plan. Kill the beasts. Break the circle. We have no idea what wards he's set in place, so exercise caution."

"Will do, Master."

The group broke into parties of two and three at the next turning point. Luc followed Cavendish and the Lyrienne League commander, a mage everyone called Finn.

Inside him, Thierry's scream echoed. His body resonated

like a tuning fork, and that horrible sound rang through every cell.

He couldn't think about that. Couldn't imagine what the necromancer was doing to his precious lover to cause him to cry out like that, not and stay in his seat. He had to be the leader, the soldier. He had to follow Cavendish's orders and live in the moment. Thierry might be the only truth of Luc's heart, but there were other things here that mattered.

Magic had to be used with caution. With compassion. With discretion.

Magic used for any other purpose left lunatic mages and death and despair in its wake.

Magic could make the world better or crack it wide open and allow untold misery to break free.

Listen to yourself. You're already talking like you're high court magus.

Ethan will be so pleased.

Cavendish's raiders burst through to the clearing, and the real horror began. Luc had to engage immediately despite the desperate fear of his horse, who reared and stopped and would not go further into that terrible place.

He dismounted and quickly found his people in the melee. He dared not look beyond the first engagement, or the next, or the next. Steel rang. People screamed. Blood soaked his leather jacket. His boots skidded over the gore.

He gave a cry of joy when he saw John. They arranged themselves back-to-back against all comers. John hacked at a particularly gruesome creature, some kind of large dog with the head and horns of a goat that stumbled along on three legs.

Luc had to look away when John took its head. Poor creatures. They'd never asked for this. Survival was their only goal, and with the new, well-armed combatants, most were killed within minutes.

Only then did Luc turn to the circle itself. The necromancer's acrid fog made it hard to see inside despite the mage lights overhead. He gathered his power and touched his sword to the wards around it, but they held as if they were built of stone.

He tried to pry up the pavers surrounding the circle, first with his sword, then with magic empowering his hands. They too were solid, built to outlast an assault even by mages. He glanced to Cavendish, who was having the same trouble.

"It's worse than I thought," Cavendish said grimly. "Beaumont has been very clever here. These aren't wards, they're dimensional barriers."

"Then do we mount a magical siege?" asked Luc. He'd been unable to move the stones, but surely they could dig beneath them. They could make a catapult and launch spelled ammunition over the wall. "We can use sappers to dig underneath it and destroy the stones from there."

"This is intradimensional, ancient craft. I've only ever heard about it. The barrier is powered from within the circle. Once Beaumont has charged it with death magic, nothing living gets in or out until he's done."

"No!" Luc cried in desperation. He hacked and stabbed at the barrier, but his sword rang against a magic that laced up his arms like frost. He shook the sensation free, but it took Cavendish's healing magic to stop it from freezing his flesh.

"Thank you."

"You can't go off half-cocked, Luc."

"My mate is inside that circle with a maniac." Luc stabbed his sword into the ground. "What would you suggest I do?"

"It's hard to imagine the position you're in as I have no mate, but if I did, and my mate was like Thierry, I would trust him and that friend of his to put up a defense until we figure something out."

"You heard that scream."

"What about the bond?" Cavendish placed his hand over Luc's heart. "Can you still sense your mate bond?"

Luc closed his eyes. Thierry was still there, their mate bond tenuous but keeping them connected despite this awful situation.

"He's frightened and grieving."

"He's alive." Cavendish let his hand drop to his side. "And he's not without resources. Your mate is clever and resilient. He's got every reason to want to walk out of that circle. Send him your love and trust and all the confidence you have in him."

"I will. I am, but what now?"

Cavendish toed the blood-soaked earth. "Now we look for survivors and get answers."

Inside the shrouded mystery of Beaumont's madness lay everything Luc cared about. His mate. The future they'd dreamed about.

"I believe in you," he told the bond. "Come back to me, love."

Their mate bond hummed with the magic of their connection, but no voice answered his plea. If Cavendish was right, it was up to Thierry—and Charles if he was around—to fight their way free.

The two of them were older, wiser than the first time they'd met the madman.

They better understood the nature and power of magic.

Was it enough to defeat the most powerful mage of their time?

Luc had to believe. He had to stay positive. He stood at the barrier for the longest time, seeing nothing, putting his mind in order. The rush of battle dissipated from his body, and he ached everywhere.

"How can you be calm?" John leaned on his ax, breathing hard. "If Serafina was inside that circle and I couldn't get to her, I'd go mad."

"I am going mad. I feel like I'll burst with pain and helplessness, but there's one thought that reassures me when I hold onto it."

"Tell me what that is," John whispered. "I'd like to know."

Luc swallowed, knowing he was right. "It's Thierry."

"You're right. Thierry is…Thierry." John put a hand on his shoulder.

Maybe he understood what Luc meant, or maybe he thought Luc had finally given in to madness.

They shared that quiet moment in the hope that Luc's unique, extraordinary mate could do the impossible.

Luc prayed they were right.

CHAPTER 27

One minute everything seemed to gray out, and the next, Thierry's wrists and ankles were free, and his body was rolling sideways off the table opposite Beaumont. He looked at his bloodied wrists, trying to make sense of what had happened.

Wait. I'm free! How am I free?

"Picking locks is like curse words. It's the first thing you learn at the Academy," Charles spoke from somewhere deep within him. "I told you I could do it."

Thierry felt shoved to one side, powerless and dizzy. He tried to push to his feet, but nothing happened. What in the name of the Goddess was going on?

Beaumont said you were powerless here.

"Beaumont doesn't know as much as he thinks he does. I'm so sorry. I know I promised, but I have to use your body—"

No, by all means, be my guest. Do you have a plan to get us out of here?

"Not yet." Charles dove them into the thick black mist.

"What are you doing, Charles?" Thierry could hear Beaumont stomping around to their side of the table. "You won't get away from me that easily."

Beaumont's footfalls closed in on them. Thierry's stomach swooped.

"You have no idea what to do with all that power, Charles." The mage suddenly appeared in front of them. "Don't waste your time."

"I can inconvenience you a great deal until someone better comes along." Charles leapt up and pushed both of Thierry's hands out toward Beaumont. The mage slid back several paces.

Thierry heard a low croak to his left. Where had Silence fallen? He searched the ground near the table, expecting to see the raven's body. He wasn't there.

Where's Silence?

"Is that a rhetorical question?" Beaumont sent a burst of magic their way. Charles moved them in time, but the impact on the ground sent them flying.

Charles threw a ball of pure fire in return.

Beaumont sidestepped it. "I can do this all night."

"You're old," Charles taunted. "We'll outlast you."

"You're a rank beginner." The mage's movements were quiet. He clearly learned from his mistakes. "Eventually, you'll slip up."

"I was a beginner when you started this. I've had plenty of time to learn since then."

Crack! Blue lightning arced toward them. Charles catapulted them over the table, but burning pain shot up Thierry's leg.

"Ouch. *Blast.*" Charles rolled and got Thierry to his feet somehow. They limped backward, waiting for Beaumont's next move.

"Don't you care if your friend gets hurt, Charles?" Beaumont had the most annoying, supercilious voice.

Don't worry about me. Rage built within Thierry. Charles turned on his heel and sent a powerful blast Beaumont's way.

A grunt told them that they'd winged the mage. Quick footsteps said they'd not hit him hard enough.

That was good.

"You should try it."

I don't know how.

"Here, feel it. Build the intent then visualize the—" The ground erupted at Beaumont's feet. Two of the clay tablets cracked and fell to the earth in pieces. Beaumont shuddered. His eyes narrowed.

"I'm starting to think you're too much trouble, Thierry." Beaumont screwed up his face in concentration. "There are other omegas."

"Get ready, Ti." Charles hit the dirt and rolled them as a wave of dark magic hit them hard. At the same time, he created some kind of shield. Thierry had no doubt that it would have been a killing blow had Charles not acted so quickly.

Thank you.

"He's weakening!" Charles got them back on their feet and took off into the mist. He was practically daring the mage to hit them again. "His power isn't unlimited. Not if he can't get to yours."

Can we outlast him?

"With a few more blows like that. Or…wait." Charles crouched low and aimed a ball of pure aggression at another tablet. It flew into the air and burst, showering dirt on them.

"Stop that!" Beaumont came straight at them out of the mist, claws outstretched. Magic crackled into a glowing red orb, and he hurled it. They moved, but it shattered behind them, sending what felt like shards of glass over Thierry's back and buttocks.

Charles gasped. "Are you all right?"

Keep going. Destroying the tablets must be good. Thierry would have plenty of time to heal if he got out of this alive.

Charles used Thierry's magic to keep Beaumont at bay while blowing up every clay tablet he could. With each strike, Thierry felt a physical pull as if Charles took magic from a vault in his chest, but he never felt depleted. In fact, with each small victory, Thierry grew more confident they could win.

We should break the circle! If no one can breach the circle from the outside, we need to demolish it from inside.

"That's brilliant." Charles took off running. The distance to the edge of the circle stretched out before them. It seemed like miles as Beaumont hurled every single curse in his arsenal at them. His noxious fog grew thicker as they neared their goal. Thierry could barely see a foot in front of him.

His outstretched hands hit the barrier hard. Thierry winced. Momentum carried the rest of him into it, and he bounced back, slightly stunned.

Find the pavers. I bet we don't have to take out too many to break the circle.

Another crack of blue lightning missed them by several feet, leaving the fragrance of petrichor and disturbed soil.

Charles tried moving the pavers with Thierry's hands, but they held fast. He gathered magic and intention and tried again.

Nothing. The pavers seemed impervious.

"It won't work!" he cried.

Try again.

"I'm not strong enough."

Doubt crept over the two of them, paralyzing and painful.

Thierry remembered holding his hand out, trying to hoist Charles to safety. The worst moment of his life. He'd been a child then. He hadn't known then what he knew now. He had more strength inside him than he'd ever believed back then.

We can do it together.

Charles made Thierry's head nod. "All right. On three. Ready, steady. Go!"

Thierry willed the pavers to move. They remained interlocked. Beaumont came up from behind them, searching for a way to end this.

Again! Don't give up now. We'll beat him this time. Show him!

Charles counted silently. Thierry put all his will behind his magic.

Charles had once told him that every spell brought the will of a mage to life through magic. What did Thierry want? To move the pavers, obviously. But what was deeper than that? What was truer than that?

He wanted his mate.

He wanted to protect his child.

He wanted a future.

He wanted to *live...*

Boom!

The ground beneath the pavers exploded, sending chunks of stone flying. A piece the size of a coin cut Thierry's cheek. He barely felt it.

Before the debris even had a chance to settle, mages and humans and shifted wolves rushed past them. Thierry barely had a chance to realize they'd won their way free when a pair of muscled arms wrapped around him.

Mate. Mate! Mine. Thierry sagged with relief.

Wings flapped next to his head. "Mate."

Somehow, Thierry found his voice.

"Silence!" he gasped. "I thought you were dead."

"He looked pretty gruesome when he crawled out of the circle. He seemed to know where you'd come out."

"How?" Thierry asked. "For that matter, how did he get inside in the first place?"

"Hush," said the bird.

Luc tilted his head. "Silence has *secrets*."

The bird gave a happy *kraa-kraa*. If it wasn't for the battling mages behind them, it would be too easy to smile at them.

"Come with me, darling. Let me see to your wounds." Thierry tried, but without Charles to keep him upright, he found he didn't have the strength. "I don't think so."

Luc caught Thierry and lifted him easily into his arms. They left the circle. Luc avoided the worst of the slippery gore.

"Is this what you did while you waited for us to get free?" Thierry asked.

"For a bit. Then it got dead boring. It took you long enough."

Thierry heard the teasing lilt in Luc's luxurious voice.

"Next time"—Thierry poked Luc's chest—"*you* get kidnapped by the evil necromancer."

Mathilde, who was with John giving aid to those injured, pointed at a spot on the ground. "Set him down there, Luc."

"I see you have your voice back," said Charles. His magic glittered triumphantly.

I see you took on the most powerful necromancer in our time and won the day. How does it feel?

"Better than I imagined." Thierry wished he could see his friend. He was sure that if he could, he'd see Charles's happy-go-lucky smile again, the one that said how confident and certain he was of his place in the world.

Maybe you can teach me more. When we return to the Temple of the Merciful Moon—

"Titou." Charles's glittering magic took on the chill of frost. "I don't think I'll be going back with you."

What? Of course, you will. We're a team, aren't we? We beat Beaumont together.

"It's not that I don't want to go. I don't think I'll be able to."

You—oh...

"I guess now that Beaumont is gone, my time here is over."

Does it have to be? You said I hid your magic. I kept you with me.

"I used up my magic tonight, Ti. I did what I was meant to do with it, and now I have to go."

"No." Thierry must have said that aloud because Luc glanced his way.

"Are you all right?"

No, Charles. What will I do without you? You kept me alive, kept me sane. You even helped me through the guilt and grief I felt over losing you. Over failing you.

"You never failed me. We won. Together, we won. That's how we'll remember this night, isn't it?"

Already, Charles's voice was growing faint. His magic was softer.

Already, the place in Thierry's heart that would always belong to Charles shriveled, becoming an empty, dried-out husk without Charles's magic to fill it.

Don't. Thierry's tears fell. *Don't leave me.*

"Sweetheart. What can I do?" Luc caught both his hands and rested his forehead against them. "Tell me what you need."

Charles called from a great distance. "I think you're in good hands, don't you?"

No, no, no. Thierry wanted his friend to stay, but what could he do? No one could give Charles his life back. Not if the Goddess had other plans for him.

Thierry hoped She did. He hoped She cherished Charles.

"Was that—" Luc broke off with a frown. "Did—"

"Charles is gone. He moved on, I guess."

"He's finished with what he set out to do."

"I guess so."

"Thierry." Luc stared at him. "We've never talked about what Charles means to you. Our bond—"

"You are the love of my life." Thierry caught Luc's face between his hands. "You are my soulmate. I will miss Charles every day, but you're my mate, the father of my child."

"Goddess. Our child. I like the sound of that." Luc's gaze heated. "I love you, Thierry. I hope you never doubted that. Even though I couldn't—"

"Not once. I never doubted." Thierry laid his head on Luc's shoulder. "Can we go home?"

Luc nodded against his cheek. "What's home to you? The settlement or the Temple or Ethan's townhouse?"

"*You* are home to me, though I'd like to go to the Temple for a while if that's all right. I want to talk to Mother Luna."

"Of course. We'll go anywhere you want."

"Guh." Thierry leaned against his mate. "Getting there is going to be a nightmare. I don't think I can walk or ride."

"You'll be fine. I'll take you up with me, and you can sleep in my arms the whole way."

"That sounds suspiciously unlikely."

"Because I'm lying to you. But I'll use what healing magic I have to help as much as I can. Will that do?"

"Thank you." Thierry breathed his lover in. *Petrichor, leather, and vetiver. So good.* "Thank you for rescuing me."

Luc kissed his forehead. "It's sweet of you to say so, but you rescued yourself."

"Mmm." If he could only close his eyes for a few minutes. "It's the thought that counts."

Despite the din and clamor of Cavendish's small but successful army, sleep claimed Thierry a few breaths later.

In his dream, Charles's smiling, fourteen-year-old face reappeared, full of light, and mischief, and love.

"Bye for now," Charles called, turning at the crossroads where they always parted ways after school.

Thierry lifted his hand and waved. "Bye, Charles."

EPILOGUE

Bright moonlight spilled over the wide balcony of their rooms in the palace. Thierry sat on one of the wide wicker chairs, fanning sweat from his face. Luc had stayed in bed, exhausted from satisfying the demands of Thierry's heat.

Somewhere, an owl called.

When it had become clear that the king had lost his grip on reality, Ethan became Prince Regent, and once he had power, he systematically removed Luc's every objection to moving to Avimasse. Luc had honored his promise and become high court magus.

Luc had been right. Thierry didn't hate the palace. He guessed that the rich liked to leave just enough nature intact to remind them where they came from. The palace gardens were truly lovely this time of year, full of flowering cherry and almond trees, herbal garden walkways, woods, ponds, and mazes. It took nearly an entire day to stroll through the opulent palace grounds.

Wildlife thrived there. Everything was perfect. Maybe too perfect for a flawed farm boy from the middle of Hemlock Forest to appreciate, but he was learning. Trying to learn.

Give me a little chaos, please. No one likes perfection.

He'd learned not to expect a reply from Charles, but he'd held on to the slightest hope. Now his thoughts seemed to echo in an empty place inside his heart.

"Couldn't you sleep, sweetheart?" asked Luc from the double glass doors that led inside.

"It's too beautiful a night for sleep." Thierry turned to see his handsome husband pad onto the balcony, naked.

Lust stirred in his belly. "*Mmm*. Hi."

"Hello." Luc sank to his knees in front of him. "Having fun?"

Thierry let his legs fall apart. "I am now."

Luc crept between them. "Looks like you need me."

"Looks like." Thierry hid his smile. He would never not need this man, this warrior, this alpha mage who held his heart.

Gently, Luc took his cock and balls in hand. "Do you need the salve first?"

"You took such good care of me earlier. I'm fine."

"That was my pleasure." Luc lowered his head and licked up the length of Thierry's leaking cock. He flicked his tongue over the head and gathered the sweet nectar there before lifting his face for a kiss.

Thierry bent over and took his mouth.

This man, this alpha, owns me.

"Please fuck me." He cupped Luc's jaw. "Out here, on the balcony, under the sky. Give me your cock, alpha."

Luc wrapped his arms around Thierry's waist and stood. He carried Thierry to the balustrade. Thierry leaned on the ornately carved stone and spread his legs wide.

Luc's fingers entered him first. There was little pain, only the sweetest of burns, of anticipation, and yearning, and need.

Thierry wriggled, and Luc slapped his buttock. "Stop that."

"Just do it."

"I'm not going to hurt you."

"I need you, husband. I don't wish to wait."

"You will wait, and you'll like it," Luc teased, giving the other buttock a matching handprint. His cock breached the entrance of Thierry's body, huge and hot. The feel of it entering him satisfied every primal need.

Mate, mine, claim me, want me, need me, take me.

Make me yours.

"Shh. Little wolf…I've got you."

Thierry arched his back and pushed, greedily trying to swallow his mate's cock. Luc grunted and caught his hips.

"Naughty," he warned. "I'll take what I want. How I want."

"Yes. Yes." Thierry wasn't above begging. Not when he knew it spurred Luc on. "Please, alpha. Please take me. I'm yours. Yours, alpha."

Luc buried himself to his balls and jerked out just as quickly. As Thierry had hoped he would, he set an almost punishing pace, striking the secret sweet spot inside Thierry over and over as Thierry's hands flexed and gripped the wide railing that kept him from falling three floors to his death.

His body melted and grew pliant. Luc took and took, used him like a beast, and Thierry loved every brutal second of it.

"Touch yourself. Make yourself come," Luc commanded.

"Yes, alpha." Thierry took hold of his cock and gave it a merciless tug. It took a lot to bring him off when he was in heat like this. He needed to be fucked hard, and fast, and roughly when the moon rode him like this.

With a snarl, Luc pounded into him. "Who's your mate?"

"You are, alpha." Fingers tangled painfully in his hair.

"Who do you belong to?"

Thierry groaned. "I'm yours, alpha. Only yours."

"What do you want?"

"Your knot. Give me your knot, Luc. I need—"

Ahh. There it was, he was coming, spattering onto the balustrade and the slate beneath his feet. Luc's teeth clamped so hard on his shoulder that he felt the warmth of his blood seeping from the wound. Luc licked him clean.

"You're mine."

"Yours, alpha."

"I'll do whatever I want with you."

"Yours, alpha." Tears stung Thierry's eyes when Luc's hips stuttered. His release, hot and slick, filled Thierry's body with warmth and magic, and his knot stretched his hole impossibly. "Goddess, Luc. Oh, love. *Oh.*"

Luc kissed his nape, his back, his shoulders. He ran his hand down Thierry's arm and laced their fingers together.

"All right?"

"How"—Thierry panted—"can you even ask? That was brilliant. Oh my Goddess."

"I fear we'll be here for a bit."

"No surprise there." Thierry lifted his gaze to the stars. "It's beautiful. I don't mind."

"It is beautiful," Luc agreed. "You're beautiful, and you're all I see."

"*Mmnh.*" Thierry purred for him. "Did you like that?"

"Yes."

"Better than when I dress up in my red cloak?"

"Ooh. That's a tough one. You bring me goodies, little red cloak."

Thierry chuckled. "You've got to keep up your strength, wolf."

"That I do, given you're an insatiable, greedy omega."

"Don't say that like it's a bad thing."

"Never."

Together, they watched the moon sail across the sky. When Luc's cock softened, Thierry turned in his arms, and they kissed like sweethearts.

"I love you." Thierry pressed his cheek to Luc's beard-roughened face. "You give me everything I need, even when it scares you."

"Sometimes I'm too rough, love. You wind up with bruises, and I'm appalled by what I've done."

"I give you blanket permission," Thierry reminded him. "Mark me. I'm proud to wear you on my skin."

"You have no idea what that does to me."

Thierry bit his lip. "I have an inkling."

A soft cry floated on the breeze, then another. A wail followed.

Thierry pushed Luc back. "It seems our son is awake."

Luc followed him into the luxurious suite of rooms that was their home. Luc lit the lamps until soft light fell over their son's unhappy face. Silence gave them a stern *kraa-kraa* and flew off to a quieter place to return to his dreams.

"Hush, Lucien. Papa's here." Thierry picked the baby up out of his crib and held him eye to eye.

He looked like Luc: dark hair, pale eyes. He was going to be as stunning an alpha wolf as any omega could want when the time came. He had his father's temperament too. At almost a year, Lucien dominated the palace. The servants were besotted with him, and his uncle adored him. His parents—well, they were little more than the men who fetched him things, but they couldn't have loved him more.

Lucien was Thierry's miracle. Together, they'd survived all the attacks on Thierry's body and nearly been pulled into the shadowlands.

Lucien got what he wanted.

To a point.

Luc wrinkled his nose. "Someone soiled his diaper."

Thierry held him out. "It's for you."

Muttering, Luc took the boy from him. He made short work of cleaning him up while Thierry sat in the amazing rocking chair that Luc had made for him and waited to nurse.

"Here you go." He handed Lucien over to Thierry, who put the baby to his breast and hummed while he took his fill.

"You look so happy." Luc sat back to watch. "This is a sight I'll miss when you wean him."

"It's almost time too." Thierry said wistfully. "It will break my heart."

"You might be required to nurse our next baby."

"Oh Goddess." This was his first full moon heat since Lucien's birth. Could he be with child even now? "You're right. I didn't even think of that."

"You were a little preoccupied." Anxiety shadowed Luc's features. "I would have given you more time. I hate seeing you in pain."

"I didn't like it much either, but it passed, and look." His singsong voice made Lucien smile and clap his hands. "We got a baby!"

"Oh yes, we did." Luc squatted next to his chair at the baby's eye level. "We got this baby. The best baby. We got Lucien."

"Dada." Delighted, Lucien slapped his hands over his father's cheeks.

"Say Papa," Thierry tried.

"Dada," Lucien squealed.

"You'll pay for this." Thierry glared at his husband, who smirked.

"I pay for everything." A self-satisfied grin accompanied his words. "Now that I'm high court magus, and you're—"

"Don't you say it."

"What is it you do again?" Luc teased.

"I plot murder." Thierry leaned over to whisper in his ear. "Court intrigue is fascinating. One learns so quickly here."

"You are the light of my life, darling."

"I love you too." Thierry rocked his son until exhaustion made his eyelids droop.

"Here. I'll take him. You go to bed."

"Fine." Thierry let his mate take their boy. "I'm too exciting for him. You try boring him to sleep."

Luc walked him to the bed and kissed his forehead. He covered Thierry with a light blanket.

Thierry didn't remember going to sleep. He didn't dream.

When he woke, all he knew was that every bell in the palace was ringing as were others, farther away.

"What's happening?"

"I don't know." Luc was beside him, so obviously he'd gotten their son back to sleep. Except now, Lucien was screaming in fright. Blast those bells.

"I'll get him." Luc hoisted himself out of bed. "See if you can find out what's going on."

"I'm going." Thierry pulled a robe over his naked body and went to the door. There were no servants in the corridor. That wasn't unusual for this time of night. Luc came up from behind with the baby in his arms just as pounding footsteps came up the stairs toward them.

"I have news." Ethan pushed them back into their rooms and closed the door behind them.

Luc tensed. "What's going on?"

Instinct made Thierry take Lucien from Luc and wrap him protectively in his blanket. The bells hadn't stopped ringing. What did it mean?

"Father's dead. He died in his sleep. His attendants found him half an hour ago. The court physician says he died of natural causes. Old age."

Luc dropped to his knees. "Long live the king."

Thierry joined him and bowed his head. "Your Majesty."

"I'm having a hard time believing it," Ethan whispered.

"You'll be a great king, brother."

"And you'll be by my side, my recalcitrant magus."

The baby reached for his uncle, who picked him out of Thierry's arms.

"Can you say, 'Uncle King'?"

Thierry scoffed. The baby said, "Dada."

"Aw, sh—oot," Ethan complained. Then he froze. Gave the air a discreet sniff. "I'm…not interrupting anything, am I?"

"Not right now," Luc said dryly. The air must reek of sex, though. They'd been at it for over twenty-four hours.

Ethan flushed. "I should probably go be…majestic or something."

Luc sighed. "Could you start with those bells? Thierry hasn't had a wink of sleep."

"Whose fault is that, I wonder?" Ethan gave them both a fond smile. "As soon as you're back to…you know. Come see me. There's much to plan."

"Yes, Majesty." Luc bowed his head.

Ethan grinned. "That cost you, didn't it?"

"No, Majesty." Luc smirked.

"Enough." He handed the baby to Luc. "I'm leaving. I'll see you soon, Magus. Goodnight."

Ethan turned on his heel and strode away. Luc closed the door behind him.

"This will change things." Thierry stroked the baby's fine, soft hair.

"Nothing that matters." Luc kissed his temple. "Not us, not what we have. Our future is going to be brilliant."

"And full of love."

Luc nodded. "And full of love."

"I can't wait." Thierry sighed against his mate's strong chest.

And they lived happily ever after.

~

If you loved this new twist on a favorite old fairy tale, be sure to check out **Ember's Moon**: Cinderella like you've always wanted it to be!

A cash-strapped earl risks everything to take his sisters to the prince's ball, only to be tempted by his fated mate!

Get yours!

As you know, reviews are the lifeblood of the independent author. Please leave your review of Red Cloak Moon at Amazon, Goodreads, and anywhere you review books today! (Thanks in advance, <3 Fiona)

ALSO BY FIONA LAWLESS

Ember's Moon

Red Cloak Moon

COPYRIGHT

Cover art: SelfPubBookCovers.com/ DesignzbyDanielle
Edited by: Lisa Lakeland

Published in the United States of America.

Manufactured by Amazon.ca
Acheson, AB